FRANK RICHARDS

Billy Bunter
The Bold

COVER ILLUSTRATION BY
MARY GERNATT

TEXT ILLUSTRATIONS BY
R. J. MacDONALD

Armada

CONTENTS

CHAPTER 1

SO NEAR YET SO FAR

"Oh!" gasped Billy Bunter.

His eyes popped.

In fact, they almost popped through his spectacles, as he blinked in at the doorway of No. 1 Study, in the Greyfriars Remove.

That study had quite an unusual aspect.

In the first place, it was spotlessly tidy, which was rather uncommon in the Remove. No books, no unfinished exercises, not even an odd football boot lay about. In the second place, the table was laid for tea : but evidently not for an ordinary, every-day tea—it was laid for a spread of unaccustomed magnificence.

There was a table-cloth, and it was absolutely clean. There were plates and cups and saucers, of which not a single one was cracked. Clearly, Harry Wharton and Co. must have been borrowing crocks up and down the passage, from many studies, to put up that imposing array.

But these details, impressive as they were, did not impress Billy Bunter so much as the foodstuffs.

Bunter was always interested in food. It was a subject seldom, if ever, far from his thoughts. And such an imposing supply of comestibles was seldom seen in a junior study.

There was a cake—quite a large and handsome cake. There were three kinds of jam. There were scones and éclairs and even meringues. There was ham on a dish—quite a lot of ham. There were hard-boiled eggs. There were nuts—a jam-jar full of them. There was cheese—nice little triangular French cheeses in their silver foil. There were other appetising and delightful things. It was no wonder that Billy Bunter's little round eyes almost popped through his big round spectacles. It was a feast of the gods that was toward, in No. 1 Study.

Five fellows were in the study : surveying the tea-table with satisfied, indeed, complacent looks. It was not often

5

that the Famous Five were able to put up a show like this
—or had occasion to do so. This, evidently, was a very, very
special occasion: equally evident, such magnificent preparations must have exhausted their financial resources.

"Looks all right, I think," remarked Harry Wharton.

"Topping!" said Frank Nugent.

"The topfulness is terrific!" declared Hurree Jamset
Ram Singh.

"Well, we don't have old Wingate to tea very often,"
said Bob Cherry, "it's worth a bit of an effort."

"What-ho!" agreed Johnny Bull.

"I say, you fellows," gasped Billy Bunter. "I say, that
looks a topping spread. Lot of fellows coming?"

Harry Wharton glanced round at the fat figure in the
doorway.

"Only one!" he answered. "Wingate of the Sixth! It's
rather a special occasion, having the captain of the school
to tea."

"Well, I think you might ask a pal, to a spread like
that!" said Bunter, reproachfully. "I've had a measly tea
in my study, and nothing else at all since class, except tea
in hall. Like me to come?"

"No!"

"Beast! I mean, look here, old chap, it's just rot to
waste all that on a Sixth-form man. Who's Wingate, anyway? I say——."

"Roll away, barrel."

"Oh, really, Wharton——!"

"Hook it!" said Johnny Bull.

"But I say——."

"Scat!" exclaimed the Famous Five, all together.

Billy Bunter did not roll away. He did not hook it. He
did not scat. His eyes and spectacles lingered lovingly
on the tea-table. He seemed unable to tear himself away
from that beatific vision of almost unlimited tuck.

There was enough on the table for six fellows—the
Famous Five, and their distinguished guest from the Sixth
Form. There was, therefore, enough for Billy Bunter. Even
the hungry Owl of the Remove would have had to exert
himself a little, to pack it away at a single sitting. Indeed
even Bunter would probably have had to leave a nut or
two.

Life, to Billy Bunter, would have been one grand sweet

6

song, if he could have had the run of that well-spread table. But alas! the fat Owl could only gaze upon it, like a podgy Peri at the gate of Paradise.

Harry Wharton glanced at his watch.

"Just five!" he said. "Wingate's due at half-past! Everything's ready, I think?"

"Every jolly old thing!" said Bob Cherry. "Now let's get out."

"Let's!" agreed Nugent.

Billy Bunter's eyes gleamed behind his spectacles, as he heard that.

The Famous Five, having completed their preparations for the honoured guest, were going out, having half-an-hour to kill before tea-time. If that gorgeous spread was left at Billy Bunter's mercy for half-an-hour, they were likely to find it in a very depleted state when they came in.

"I say, you fellows——!" squeaked Bunter.

"Hallo, hallo, hallo! You still there, fatty? Waiting to be rolled away like a barrel?" asked Bob Cherry.

"Oh, really Cherry! I say, if you like, I—I'll stay in the study while you're out, and—and see that nobody snoops any of that tuck——."

"Ha, ha, ha!"

"Blessed if I see anything to cackle at!" hooted Billy Bunter. "I mean it! I'd do more than that for fellows I really like!"

"And you wouldn't scoff the tuck while we're gone?" inquired Johnny Bull, sarcastically.

"Yes—I mean, no! Nothing of the kind! You fellows cut out," said Bunter. "Smithy and Squiff and some other fellows are punting a ball in the quad. You chaps would like to join them——."

"We're going to," grinned Bob, "and we'd leave you in charge of the spread, Bunter——."

"Oh, good!"

"——only we should have to borrow a microscope to see what was left when we came back with Wingate——."

"Beast! I mean, look here, old chap——."

"In fact, we're going to boot you as far as the end of the passage before we go down," said Bob. "Turn round, Bunter! Now then, you men, all together!"

"Beast!" roared Bunter.

He turned round—to take a hurried departure, without

waiting for assistance from the chums of the Remove. A chuckle from No. 1 Study followed him, as he rolled down the passage to the landing.

There he sat down on the settee by the banisters. Two or three minutes later, Harry Wharton and Co. passed him. They glanced at the fat Owl, in passing, with grinning faces. They were all laughing, as they crossed the landing to the stairs, and went down: though why, was rather a mystery to Bunter. He could see nothing to laugh at. They were not likely to laugh, at all events, when they came back to the study—after Bunter had been there.

Almost breathlessly, the fat Owl watched them disappear down the stairs. Then he heaved up his weight from the settee. He almost shot into the Remove passage, to the door of No. 1 Study.

That door was shut. Grinning, Billy Bunter turned the door-handle. To his surprise, the door did not open. He wrenched at the door-handle, and shoved. Still the door remained fast.

"Oh!" gasped Bunter.

The terrible truth dawned on him! That was why they had been laughing when they went downstairs They knew, just as well as Bunter did, what was scheduled to happen to that spread while they were gone. And they had locked the study door on the outside, and taken away the key.

"Beasts!" hissed Bunter.

He glared at that door. It was really a wonder that the glare he bestowed upon it did not crack his spectacles. But the door was locked: the spread was inside the study, and Bunter was outside: only a few feet away, but solid oak intervened—so near, and yet so far!

CHAPTER 2

AT LAST!

BILLY BUNTER breathed hard, and he breathed deep.

His feelings were really too deep for words.

Bunter was hungry. Generally, he was hungry. Sharp weather gave an edge to his appetite, always vigorous. In matters of tuck, Bunter seemed absolutely unconscious of the distinction between "meum" and "tuum". No fellow's tuck was safe from Bunter. How often he had been booted for snooping tuck in the studies, he could never have computed. But bootings produced no effect whatever in bringing up Bunter in the way in which he should go. He did not like bootings; but the lure of tuck was irresistible. But a locked door baffled even the unscrupulous grub-raider of the Remove. There was no way of getting through a locked door.

But was there not?

Suppose a fellow could get another key——!

And a fellow could, perhaps! Fisher T. Fish, the business-man of the Remove, had an immense bunch of keys in his study, which any fellow in want of a key could borrow—for a consideration. One of those keys might fit the door of No. 1 Study——!

True, Fisher T. Fish, who could not wait till he was grown up before entering on a commercial career, "traded" those keys. They were at any fellow's disposal for the moderate sum of twopence.

This presented a difficulty, as Bunter was not in possession of that sum, moderate as it was. On the other hand, Fishy might be out as most of the Remove fellows were that bright afternoon after class, and Bunter knew that he kept that bunch of keys in his table drawer. Hope springs eternal in the human breast. Billy Bunter revolved on his axis, and rolled up the Remove passage to No. 14 Study: hoping that Fisher T. Fish was out, or alternatively, as the lawyers say, that he might lend that bunch of keys on "tick".

The hope that Fishy was out, faded away as he blinked into No. 14 Study. There sat Fisher T. Fish, at his study table. But the other hope remained—a very faint one, no doubt.

"I say, Fishy!" squeaked Bunter.

"Yup?"

Fisher T. Fish was busy. He was almost the only Remove fellow up in the studies that sunny afternoon. A crowd of Remove men were punting a footer in the quad till tea-time: but Fishy had no desire to join in urging the flying ball. He was engaged in much more congenial occupation: counting his money. He was threepence out in his accounts: and with a wrinkled and worried brow, he was striving to trace that elusive threepence, when Billy Bunter happened.

However, he paused for a moment to snap out an interrogative "Yup?" If Bunter wanted to sell something at half its value, or buy something at twice its value, the business-man of the Remove was prepared to deal.

"I say, Fishy, I want you to lend me——."

"Forget it!" said Fisher T. Fish, briefly: and he turned back to his accounts.

"—your bunch of keys——."

"Oh! Tuppence!" said Fisher T. Fish, looking up again.

"I'll settle later, Fishy——."

"Say, whadyer know!" ejaculated Fisher T. Fish, in disgust. "Travel, you fat clam! Shut that door after you."

"I'm expecting a postal-order, old chap——."

"I sure said travel."

"Look here, you beast——!" hooted Bunter.

"Git!" said Fisher T. Fish. He picked up a cushion.

Without waiting for the cushion, Billy Bunter banged the door. Outside that door, once more he breathed hard, and once more he breathed deep. Then he rolled down the passage to his own study, No. 7. He rememebered that Peter Todd, his study-mate, had lines on hand for Mr. Quelch: so Toddy would be in, and surely good for so moderate a loan as twopence for a pal in distress! Minutes were passing: and there really was no time to lose.

"I say, Toddy, old chap!" Bunter blinked in at the door of No. 7. There sat Peter Todd, at the table, with

Virgil propped against the inkstand, just beginning Latin lines.

He seemed to have no time for Bunter. Possibly he was in a hurry to get through, and join the other fellows in the quad. At all events, he did not look up as the fat junior squeaked in at the door.

Billy Bunter gave him an exasperated blink.

"Deaf?" he hooted. "I say Toddy——."

"Conticuere omnes——!" murmured Toddy.

"What?"

"——intentique ora tenebant——."

"I'm speaking to you, Toddy!" hooted Bunter.

"——inde toro pater——."

"For goodness sake, Peter, shut up that rot for a minute——."

"——Æneas sic orsus ab alto——."

Peter murmured Virgil aloud as he wrote, in self-defence against the persistent squeak at the door. What Bunter wanted, Peter did not know. Neither did he want to know. What Peter wanted was to get through his lines. With the selfishnes of which Bunter was sorrowfully accustomed, he was concerned about his own affairs, not Bunter's.

"Look here, Peter, I'm in a hurry!" howled Bunter.

"——Infandum, regina, jubes renovare dolorem——."

"Will you lend me something till my postal order comes——?"

"——Troianos ut opes et lamentabile regnum——."

"Only twopence!" shrieked Bunter.

Peter looked up at that. Billy Bunter was a borrower of deadly skill. He extracted numerous half-crowns, more numerous shillings, and innumerable sixpences from other fellows in the Lower School. Peter was not surprised that Bunter wanted to borrow. But he was surprised by the moderation of the sum. Bunter was not accustomed to deal in coppers.

"Did you say twopence?" he ejaculated.

"Yes, old chap! If you've got some coppers you don't want——."

"I haven't!" said Peter, shaking his head.

"Oh, lor'. I say, old chap——."

"I've got some I do want!" explained Peter.

"You silly ass!" gasped Bunter. This was no time for

11

Peter's little jokes. "Look here, will you lend me two-pence——?"

"Yes, if you'll shut that door, and keep your face on the other side of it. It worries me. Catch!"

Peter Todd extracted a couple of pennies from his trousers' pocket, and tossed them over to the fat Owl at the door. He told Bunter to catch: and Bunter caught them—one with his fat little nose, and the other with a plump chin. There was a loud howl, as two pennies clinked on the floor, and the fat Owl clasped a fat nose with one hand, and a fat chin with the other.

"Beast!" hissed Bunter, no doubt by way of thanks for the loan. He grabbed up the two pennies, banged the door, and rolled away up the passage again, leaving Peter to the delight of P. Vergilius Maro.

Fisher T. Fish turned a frown on a fat face that looked into No. 14, and reached for his cushion.

"Aw, you agin, you pecky piecan!" he exclaimed. "I guess——."

"Here you are!" yapped Bunter. "Now hand over those keys, and quick!"

Fisher T. Fish picked up the two coppers Bunter laid on the table—just in time before the cushion whizzed. He nodded his Transatlantic head, slipped the coins into his pocket, and pulled open the table-drawer. From that drawer he extracted an enormous bunch of keys. How many keys there were on that bunch Fishy himself probably did not know: he was always collecting old keys to add to it, and it had grown and grown. Certainly it looked as if Billy Bunter had a sporting chance of finding what he wanted in that big bunch.

"Mind you don't lose any of them keys, bo," admonished Fisher T. Fish. "If you find one to suit, and want to buy it, it's sixpence. And——."

Billy Bunter did not wait for Fishy to finish. He grabbed the keys and departed in haste from No. 14.

There was a cheery clinking of old metal, as he rolled once more down the passage, and arrived at the door of Harry Wharton's study.

He cast a cautious blink around before he commenced operations. But the coast was clear. Only two Remove men were up in the studies: Peter Todd and Fisher T. Fish and both were busily occupied. Having ascertained

12

that no eyes were upon him, the fat Owl began trying key after key on the lock of No. 1 Study. Key after key he tested, with growing irritation and impatience. Some were too large. Some were too small. Some were the wrong shape. The quarter-past five chimed from the clock-tower as Bunter jammed key after key into the lock, and jerked it out again. A whole quarter of an hour had been lost—and in another fifteen minutes, the Famous Five would be back—accompanied by their honoured and distinguished guest! Billy Bunter breathed hard through his fat little nose as he continued to jam in keys that would not turn. Minutes were precious—moments were invaluable—and still he could not find a key that would fit.

But even the weariest river winds somewhere safe to sea! At last, at long last, there was a click, which was music to Bunter's fat ears. The fifteenth key on the bunch turned the lock.

The door opened.

"He, he, he!"

Billy Bunter chuckled, as he rolled into No. 1 Study.

He blinked at the well-spread table through his big spectacles. For one moment he feasted his eyes. But it was for only one moment The next, he was feasting the inner Bunter.

Bunter was a quick worker in this line of business. In a few minutes the ham and the hard-boiled eggs had disappeared. Meringues and éclairs followed, going down like oysters.

Then Bunter paused. He was reluctant to pause: but there was danger in the air! The proprietors of that spread would be back at half-past five: they might even come in a little earlier. What would happen to Bunter, if they found him in the study travelling at express speed through the feast that had been prepared in honour of the captain of Greyfriars, did not bear thinking of. With his mouth full and his plump jaws working busily. Bunter proceeded to cram his pockets. In a few minutes, he was bulging at every pocket. Then, cramming a last meringue into his capacious mouth, and taking the big cake under a fat arm, he rolled out of the study, and shut the door after him.

He did not linger in the passage. The coast was still clear: the Remove fellows were not coming in to tea yet. Billy Bunter rolled up the passage, and following the example of Iser in the poem, he rolled rapidly. He puffed and blew as he clambered up the box-room stairs at the end of the passage—but he did those stairs swiftly. He did not stop at the box-room: they might look for him there. A narrow winding stair led further up to disused attics at the top of the building. Up that winding stair went the fat Owl, gurgling for breath. Bunter did not like stairs. But "safety-first" was his motto.

Half-past five was chiming, as he reached the top attic. Bunter did not heed the chime. In the top attic, he sat shown on an old box, and gasped for breath. Having got his second wind, he took the big cake on his fat knees, and opened his pocket-knife. A beaming smile irradiated his fat face as he commenced operations on the cake. It was a scrumptious cake. There was enough of it even for Bunter. Secure in that secluded retreat, with a supply of tuck he often dreamed of but seldom possessed, the Owl of the Remove proceeded to enjoy life to the very full.

CHAPTER 3

NOT A TEA-PARTY

"Oh! Ah! Yes!" said Wingate.

Wingate of the Sixth, captain of Greyfriars, was standing at the door of Gwynne's study in the Sixth, talking to Gwynne in that study. They were discussing no less a matter than a first eleven match with Carcroft School: so it was not surprising, perhaps, that the chime of half-past five had passed them by unheeded.

The fact that so great a man, so tremendous a "Blood", as Wingate, was to "tea" in a junior study that afternoon, was of tremendous importance to the juniors concerned. Such an event seldom happened: and the honour and glory had fallen to Harry Wharton and Co. They had played up to mark the great occasion: every resource had been called upon to make the tea in No. 1 Study worthy of it. Even if Wingate did not care quite so much for sticky things as Lower boys did, at least he could not fail to be pleased,

14

indeed impressed, by the splendid preparations in No. 1 Study.

But while to the juniors this was an almost historic occasion, a day worthy to be marked with a white stone, as Hurree Jamset Ram Singh happily expressed it, in Wingate's eyes it did not loom so large. Sad to relate, in discussing the Carcroft match, the captain of Greyfriars had momentarily forgotten that he was due to tea in a Remove study.

He was reminded of it by five juniors coming along to the Sixth-form studies. It was several minutes past five-thirty, and they were calling for him.

So seldom was so great a man entertained in a junior study, that the juniors were not quite sure of the etiquette suitable for such an occasion. Whether to wait the distinguished guest's arrival in the study, with friendly, hospitable, yet respectful smiles turned on, or whether to escort him there in a body, was a rather moot point. They decided on the latter for two reasons—first, because they had no objection to all Greyfriars beholding them in such distinguished company: second, because at half-past five Wingate had not yet emerged from the Sixth-form quarters.

So there they were: and Wingate, seeing them come, remembered. He gave them a nod and a smile. But as Gwynne, in the study, was speaking, he gave them only "Oh! ah! yes!" to go on with, as it were, and waited for Gwynne to finish.

It was a full minute before Gwynne's remarks came to a close. Harry Wharton and Co. waited with patience and politeness.

Then Wingate turned to them again, before answering Gwynne.

"Half-past five?" he asked.

"Turned," said Bob Cherry.

"Oh, all right! Cut along, and I'll be up in a minute or two!" said the captain of Greyfriars.

The idea of escorting the great man, in a body, to No. 1 Study in the Remove, had to be dropped. It was rather a blow, for there were crowds of fellows about to see the procession, had it taken place. However, it could not be helped, as Wingate evidently had something more to say to Gwynne before he came: so the five juniors departed, leaving him to follow at leisure.

15

The Famous Five went up to the Remove studies. Other fellows were coming in to tea now, some heading for hall, others for their studies: but one fat figure, generally rather conspicuous at tea-time, was not to be seen among them. If anybody had thought of Billy Bunter, it might have been remembered that he had tea'd early in hall, and Peter Todd might have remembered that he had tea'd early in No. 7 Study: but as a matter of fact, nobody thought of Billy Bunter—though Harry Wharton and Co. remembered him, when they reached the door of No. 1 Study, and they smiled. They were quite aware that Bunter had had nefarious designs on the spread in No. 1: hence the locked door when they left. They found the study door shut, just as they had left it, and had no doubt that all was well within.

Harry Wharton drew a key from his pocket, and inserted it in the lock. He turned it back—or rather, tried to do so, but the key failed to turn. As the door had been left locked, the captain of the Remove naturally supposed that it was still locked, and he tried to unlock it. A door already unlocked couldn't be unlocked again: the key did not turn.

"Bother!" said Harry, and he added pressure to the key.

"Anything the matter?" asked Nugent.

"The dashed thing won't unlock."

"Oh, my hat!" ejaculated Bob Cherry. "Is something wrong with the lock? For goodness sake get it open before old Wingate blows in."

"Sure you locked it?" asked Johnny Bull.

Harry Wharton paused, for a moment, in the pressure on the key, to bestow an expressive glance on Johnny.

"Think I should forget to turn the key, with that fat cormorant Bunter waiting for a chance to wolf the spread we've got ready for Wingate?" he asked.

"Well, fellows do forget things——."

"Fathead!"

"Try turning the handle, anyway," suggested Johnny.

Harry Wharton breathed hard.

"It's no good turning the handle, when the door's locked," he said. "It won't open till it's unlocked."

"Well, try——."

"Don't be an ass, old chap!"

16

Harry Wharton made another effort to turn back the key. But it was of no avail. The key refused to stir.

"Dash it all, this won't do," said Bob, uneasily. "Wingate will be up—we don't want him to find us fumbling at that door."

"It seems to be jammed somehow," said Harry. "Nothing wrong with it before, that I know of. But it's jammed somehow now."

"All that fat tick Bunter's fault," growled Bob. "I'll jolly well kick him for this."

"The kickfulness of the esteemed and idiotic Bunter is the proper caper," agreed Hurree Jamset Ram Singh, "but the openfulness of the door is a sine qua non."

"Blow the thing!" said Harry.

"Look here——!" said Johnny Bull.

"Well?"

"Let me try turning the handle. If you forgot to lock it——."

"Oh, talk sense."

"If you're going to get shirty——."

"Who's shirty?"

"My esteemed chums," murmured the Nabob of Bhanipur, "speechfulness is silvery, but a still tongue makes Jack a dull boy, as the English proverb remarks. The arguefulness will get us nowhere."

"Oh, all right," said Harry, resignedly, "as Johnny's so sure that I forgot to turn the key, let him try the door-handle. Go it, fathead."

He stepped aside, and Johnny Bull grasped the door-handle, turned it, and shoved. The door flew open.

"Oh!" ejaculated Harry Wharton.

He stared blankly at the open doorway. He was absolutely certain that he had turned the key in the lock on leaving. On that point there was no doubt in his mind—not a possible shadow of doubt, no possible doubt whatever. He had been so assured of it that he had disdained to try the simple expedient of turning the door-handle. He could scarcely believe his eyes as the door flew open.

"Looks as if you locked it!" remarked Johnny.

"I did lock it!"

"My dear chap——!" said Bob.

"I tell you I did lock it," exclaimed Wharton, his voice

17

rising. "Think I'm a fool? I locked that door when we left."

"The lockfulness does not seem to have been terrific," remarked Hurree Jamset Ram Singh.

"I tell you——." Wharton was getting a little heated.

"Well, the jolly old door's open now, in time for Wingate," said Bob, soothingly. "Never mind whether you locked it or not—it's open now. Come on."

Bob Cherry tramped into the study. The other fellows followed him in. The next moment there was a roar.

"What——!"

"Look!"

"Oh, crumbs!"

"Oh, holy smoke!"

"Somebody's been here——."

"Oh, crikey!"

"That fat villain Bunter——!"

"Scoffed the lot!"

"If you'd locked that door——."

"I did lock the door."

"Well, look!"

The Famous Five gazed at the tea-table. They had left it well-spread and spotlessly tidy. It was neither well-spread nor tidy now. Crumbs and fragments were scattered over it. Those crumbs and fragments were all that remained of the magnificent spread prepared for the honoured guest. The provender had vanished. Even the milk was gone from the jug. Whoever had disposed of the spread had apparently washed it down with the milk. It was a scene of absolute desolation. The Famous Five gazed at it, as Marius doubtless gazed at the ruins of Carthage, but with deeper feelings.

"Must have been Bunter!" said Bob Cherry, breathing hard.

"Who else?"

"That's why we were going to lock the door," said Johnny Bull. "We knew that fat tick had an eye on it. If Wharton——."

"I did lock the door."

"Oh, don't be an ass, old chap!" Think Bunter crawled in through the keyhole?"

"I did lock the door."

"You couldn't have——."

18

"I did,"

"We'll scrag him!" breathed Bob, "we'll spiflicate him. We'll burst him all over Greyfriars——."

Bob broke off, as there was a step outside in the passage. The distinguished guest was arriving. The juniors looked at one another in utter dismay.

Splendid preparations had been made for that distinguished guest. Resources had been exhausted for a man whom the Removites delighted to honour. A spread of unusual magnificence was to have greeted his eyes when he came. Instead of which he was to behold—this! There was no time to repair the damage, even had any financial resources remained at the disposal of the Famous Five. Wingate was coming in to tea; and there was hardly a crumb in the study. As they gazed at one another in speechless dismay, the stalwart form of the captain of Greyfriars appeared in the doorway, and he looked in with a cheery smile on his good-natured rugged face.

"Not late, I hope," he said genially.

"Oh!" Harry Wharton gasped. "Yes—no—but—oh, crumbs!"

Wingate stepped cheerily in.

He started a little, as his glance fell on the tea-table. Probably it had not occurred to Wingate that the juniors would be making tremendous preparations for his visit. But certainly he had not expected to behold a tea-table looking like that!

"Oh! I'm afraid I'm a bit late," he said, "you've started all right!"

"Oh! No! But——."

"You—you see——."

"Oh, crikey! "

The unhappy juniors really hardly knew what to say. Wingate glanced from distressed face to distressed face.

"Anything up?" he asked.

"Oh! No! Yes! No! That is—well, yes," Harry Wharton stammered. "We—we're awfully sorry, Wingate——."

"Awfully! " gasped Bob Cherry.

"The awfulness is terrific," mumbled Hurree Jamset Ram Singh.

"You—you see——!" stammered Nugent.

"Better get it out," said Harry Wharton, desperately. "we—we—we had a jolly good tea ready, Wingate, but—

19

but some fellow must—must have nipped into the study and—and scoffed it, while we were out—and—and—and there's nothing left——."

"Oh, gad!" said Wingate.

"We—we're awfully sorry——."

"The sorrowfulness is terrific."

"We—we—we——."

"Oh, crikey!"

"We—we——!" You—you see——!"

"I see!" said Wingate. "Look here, if some young rascal is pilfering tuck in the studies, that's a matter for me to deal with as a prefect. Perhaps I'd better look into it——."

"Oh! No!"

"Not at all!"

"You—you see——!"

The Famous Five were feeling almost homicidal towards the raider of the feast. They were feeling like boiling him in oil. But they did not want the hand of authority to intervene in the matter. Wingate of the Sixth was as popular as a Greyfriars man could be: but nobody wanted a "pre" butting into the affairs of the Remove. The Co. were quite unanimous on that point.

"Well, I came here as a guest, not as a prefect!" said Wingate. "Just as you like. Sorry it's such a frost—cheerio!" He turned in the doorway.

"Another time, perhaps," ventured Bob.

"Eh? Oh! Yes! Perhaps!"

Wingate walked away to the stairs. Considerately, he did not smile till his back was turned to his dismayed hosts.

The Famous Five were left in the study, with the denuded tea-table. There was no tea for them, any more than for Wingate: but that was really a trifling matter in the awful, overwhelming circumstances. The great occasion had come—and gone—and this was how it had turned out!

"That fat villain Bunter!" breathed Bob.

"This is the limit!" said Frank Nugent. "Bunter's got to learn to behave."

"Yes, rather."

"Must have been Bunter——!"

"Of course it was," grunted Johnny Bull. "Didn't we

know he was after it? Wasn't that why Wharton was going to lock the door?"

"I did lock it."

"Looks like it!"

"I tell you——"

"Hallo, hallo, hallo, what's this?" exclaimed Bob Cherry. He picked an enormous bunch of keys out of the study armchair. He held it up, clinking, and all the juniors stared at it. Billy Bunter had been too busy packing foodstuffs, when he left, to remember Fishy's bunch of keys. He had left them behind.

"Oh!" exclaimed Harry Wharton. "So that's it! The fat villain got a bunch of keys from somewhere, and found one that would fit the lock——."

"That's it!" said Nugent, with a nod.

"Oh!" said Johnny Bull.

"Perhaps Johnny believes now that I did lock the door!" added Wharton, sarcastically.

"Let's go and look for Bunter!" said Bob, "or—or perhaps we'd better push into hall while there's something left——."

"Come on!"

There was no tea in No. 1 Study: and the chums of the Remove remembered that they were hungry. They cut down from the studies and "pushed" into hall, where, as might have been expected, there was little left for such late comers. After which, they looked for Bunter. But they did not find him. The fat ornament of the Remove was not seen again till the bell rang for prep.

CHAPTER 4

FORM TRIAL

"A FORM trial!" said Harry Wharton.

"Hear, hear!"

There was a crowd of Remove fellows in the Rag, after tea. One member of the form—the fattest—generally to be seen frowsting in an armchair before the fire at that hour, was conspicuous by his absence.

21

Five fellows had looked for Bunter quite assiduously. Other fellows had helped look for him. But he had not been found. By that time, the unscrupulous pilferer of tuck had no doubt disposed of the feast. But no doubt he was reluctant to reapper in the public eye till the latest possible moment. Billy Bunter was not bright: but he was bright enough to realise that something would be coming to him for his exploit in No. 1 Study. He was putting off the evil hour. For the present, at least, he was under-studying the shy violet. In what remote corner he had found cover, nobody knew: Fisher T. Fish guessed that he had sure got into a hole and pulled it in after him, and really it looked like it. But if the fat Owl hoped that wrath would diminish with the passage of time, that hope was quite delusive. It did not diminish. Rather it improved, like wine, with keeping.

Often and often had Bunter sinned. Now it was agreed on all hands that he had gone over the limit. Something had to be done about Bunter. The meeting in the Rag was to determine what was to be done; and a "Form trial" was passed unanimously.

A Form trial was a time-honoured institution in the Lower School at Greyfriars. There were fellows present who had been through one: Bolsover major on the charge of bullying: Fisher T. Fish for money-lending among the fags: Skinner for being a footer funk. Then sentence varied, from six on the bags from a fives bat, to a term in "Coventry", or perhaps both. Now it was Bunter's turn.

"This is the limit!" went on the captain of the Remove. "There's hardly a fellow here who hasn't had his tuck scrounged by that fat villain, at one time or another——."

"Hear, hear!"

"Now he's cleared us out, and he's jolly well going to have a lesson he's wanted for a long time——."

"Your tuck more important than anybody else's?" inquired Skinner.

"Shut up, Skinner!" roared Bob Cherry.

"Only asking a question," said Skinner, meekly "Some-body snooped chocs from my study yesterday, but I didn't hear Wharton proposing a Form trial about it."

"Kick him," said Johnny Bull.

"Hold on," said Harry Wharton, "the question is in order! It's more important this time, Skinner, because the

22

captain of the school was coming to tea in our study, and he had to go away without any——."

"And so the poor dog had none!" sighed Skinner.

"Ha, ha, ha!"

"Wingate would have taken the matter up as a prefect," went on Wharton, "and that would have meant a pre's whopping for Bunter. But we don't want pre's butting in in the Remove, not even old Wingate——."

"Hear, hear!"

"We can handle it ourselves, and make that fat scrounger understand that he's got to learn to behave——."

"If he did it!" said Peter Todd.

"We all jolly well know that he did!" hooted Johnny Bull.

"Who else?" said Vernon-Smith.

"Aut Bunter aut nullus!" said Nugent.

"Oh, keep that for Quelch!" said Skinner.

"I said 'if'!" Peter Todd was firm. Peter was a solicitor's son, and knew—or fancied he knew—all about law. "It's not proved till Bunter's had his trial. What you jolly well know, Bull, isn't evidence. An accused person is innocent till he's found guilty by a jury of his peers. That's law."

"Blow law!" said Johnny Bull. "We're going to scrag the fat scrounger."

"Not unless he's found guilty," said Peter.

"We'll find him guilty fast enough," growled Johnny. "Bunter did it, as we all jolly well know. Didn't he get a bunch of keys from Fishy——."

"He sure did!" said Fisher T. Fish.

"And didn't we find them in Wharton's study, where he jolly well left them?" demanded Johnny. "And isn't he keeping out of the way now, because he jolly well knows what's coming to him?"

"It's clear enough——!" said Harry Wharton.

"The clearfulness is terrific."

"All the same, Bunter's going to have a fair trial, by all the form," went on the captain of the Remove. "First of all we've got to appoint a judge. Who's going to be judge?"

"Mauly!" suggested Bob Cherry.

"Hear, hear!"

"Wake up, Mauly!" chuckled the Bounder. "You're wanted."

"Eh?" Lord Mauleverer sat up in his armchair, and yawned. "I wasn't asleep—I heard all you fellows were saying——."

"You're going to be judge, Mauly!"

"Eh? Judge of what?" asked Mauly. Apparently he had not heard quite all that the fellows were saying!

"Bunter's up for a Form trial, you yawning ass, and you're going to sit as judge!"

"Oh, all right! I'll find him guilty. What's the charge?"

"Ha, ha, ha!"

"The charge will be made when he comes before the court," said the captain of the Remove, "and that will be as soon as he crawls out of his hide-out. Who's going to be prosecuting counsel?"

"Leave that to me!" said Johnny Bull, with a snort. "I'll prosecute him all right."

"Bunter's entitled to a defending counsel, if anybody feels like sticking up for him. Does anybody?"

"Me!" said Peter Todd, promptly.

"Why you tick!" roared Johnny Bull. "You jolly well know that he did it, just as much as we all do."

"What I know isn't evidence, any more than what you know!" explained Peter. "I shall do my best for my client——."

"Your whatter?"

"My client!" said Peter, firmly. "I shall do my best for my client, as a lawyer is bound to do. It is for the jury to decide whether he's innocent or guilty, as you'd know if you knew anything about law. I hope to be able to prove that he is spotlessly innocent——."

"When you jolly well know he's guilty?" yelled Johnny.

"Certainly! That's what a lawyer's for."

"Oh, my hat! Seems to me that the lawyers ought to go to chokey along with the prisoners at the bar," said Johnny.

"Your ignorance, my dear chap," said Peter, condescendingly. "As a member of the Remove, I agree that Bunter ought to be ragged, and scragged, and lynched, and then boiled in oil. But as a lawyer for the defence, I shall get my client off if I can. I hope to see him discharged by the court without a stain on his character."

"Oh, my hat!"

"Well, I fancy the jury will see to that," said Vernon-Smith. "We're all on the jury—I'm going to be foreman of the jury, and I can jolly well tell you that we're going to find him guilty. Why, he had a pineapple from my study the other day."

Peter shook his head. A Form trial was a chance for Peter to display his knowledge of the abstruse subject of the law, which he was always keen to do. Peter was quite in his element now.

"I shall object to that member of the jury," he said. "Vernon-Smith is prejudiced against my client, and not qualified to sit on the jury. As a point of law——."

"You can object till you're black in the face, old bean, but I'm on the jury all the same," said Smithy, belligerently.

"Look here——."

"Well, you look here——."

"Hold on," said Bob Cherry. "The judge can over-rule counsel's objection. Isn't that law, Toddy?"

"Oh! I—I think so——."

"Good! Mauly, will you over-rule Toddy's objection?"

"Eh? Oh! Yaas! Certainly! What does he object to?"

"Ha, ha, ha!"

"That's settled," said Harry Wharton. "Now we're all ready, and the court is in session—except——."

"Except for the jolly old prisoner!" grinned Bob Cherry.

"The fat villain! We shall have to wait for him to turn up."

Which was all the court could do, in the circumstances. Only, as it happened, Billy Bunter did not turn up: and the court had to be adjourned when the bell called the Remove to prep in the studies.

CHAPTER 5

AFTER THE FEAST

"I—I—I say, you fellows!"

Billy Bunter stammered a little.

He was feeling uneasy.

At the time of his raid on No. 1 Study, the fat Owl of
the Remove had been thinking only of foodstuffs: of annexing the same, and devouring them. He had done so,
and, having had time for reflection since, he realised that
he had, perhaps, done so not wisely but too well.

Snooping tuck was no new performance on Billy
Bunter's part. He was a very old offender. But even Bunter
had seldom "snooped" on such a scale: and never on so
important an occasion. His business as a grub-raider had
been, as it were, retail: now he had gone in for it wholesale. Somewhat too late for it to be of any use to him,
he remembered that after the feast came the reckoning.
His only hope of escaping condign punishment was that
the fellows wouldn't know who had done it.

They might guess. Bunter was aware that when tuck
was missing, fellows thought of him, automatically as it
were. But guessing wasn't proving. He had not been seen.
He had not left a clue. If taxed with it, he was prepared,
like Mr. Jaggers' celebrated witness, to swear "in a general
way, anything". Telling the truth had never been one of
Bunter's weaknesses. He was not likely to think of it now.

He hoped for the best: but he had a very uneasy and
uncomfortable feeling that the worst might happen!
Judiciously he kept out of sight till the bell rang for prep.
Then he had to show up: and it was a very uneasy Owl
that reappeared in the public eye.

On the Remove landing, he came on the Famous Five,
coming up for prep. To his surprise, and relief, they did
not rush upon him, booting him right and left. He had
dreaded it: but it did not happen. They glanced at him,
but that was all—merely that, and nothing more.

Bunter's hopes rose. This looked as if they did not even

26

suspect him, after all, of that wholesale grub-raid. Nevertheless, there was a stammer in his fat voice as he squeaked:

"I say, you fellows."

"Hallo, hallo, hallo! So you've turned up again, like a bad penny?" said Bob Cherry.

"Oh, really, Cherry——."

"Look here, I'll jolly well give him one jolly good kick, to go on with!" growled Johnny Bull.

"Order!" said Harry Wharton. "Kicking the fat villian won't meet the case. If it was Bunter——."

"Don't we jolly well know it was?" hooted Johnny.

"We do—but——."

"A man's innocent till he's found guilty," said Bob. "That's good law—you can ask Toddy! Bunter's entitled to the benefit of the doubt—if any!"

"If!" snorted Johnny. However, he did not kick Bunter. That, again, was a relief to the fat Owl. But it was not an unmixed relief. He could not help feeling that there was something behind this unexpected forbearance. He could not guess what it was: but he was sure there was something. It was a very uneasy and apprehensive Owl.

"I—I say, you fellows, it wasn't me, you know!" gasped Bunter.

"What wasn't?" asked Nugent.

"Oh! Anything—I—I mean, nothing! If—if you've missed anything from your study. I—I don't know anything about it. I'm not the chap to bag another fellow's tuck, I hope."

"Hopeful chap, Bunter," remarked Bob.

"I haven't been in the study at all," continued Bunter. "and I never touched a thing while I was there, either."

"Oh, my hat!"

"I say, you fellows——."

"You needn't say anything, you fat fraud," said the captain of the Remove, "you'll have a chance later to say it, if you've got anything to say. Come on, you men—prep."

The Famous Five went up to the Remove passage, to scatter to their various studies. Billy Bunter blinked after them with an uneasy blink through his big spectacles. Something was in the wind, he could see that—something that was going to happen to him—later! Really, he almost

27

wished that the Co. had booted him, and left it at that. Bunter did not like being booted: often as it had happened, he had never acquired a taste for it. But a booting, at least, would have been over and done with. Now he dismally realised that the affair was very far from over, and very far from done with. His latest exploit as a snooper was being taken with unusual seriousness.

Herbert Vernon-Smith and Tom Redwing came across the landing from the stairs, and Bunter gave them an anxious blink. The Bounder grinned.

"Here's the shy violet," he said. "Where have you been parking yourself all this while, Bunter?"

"I—I—I say, you fellows—is anything on?" asked Bunter. "Is—is—is there going to be a row, or—or something?"

"Bet your life!" answered Smithy.

"But I—I—I say, what's up?" asked Bunter anxiously.

"Your number!" answered Vernon-Smith, and he went on his way with Redwing, laughing.

"Oh, crikey!" breathed Bunter. He was growing more and more uneasy. It was borne in on his fat mind that something was going to happen—apparently after prep, as it was not happening now. Almost he wished that he had restrained his fat hands from picking and stealing: almost he wished that he had left that spread in No. 1 Study alone. Yet, remembering that delightful scrumptious cake, he could hardly wish that!

Ogilvy, Wibley, Tom Brown, Squiff, Hazeldene, and Bolsover major came across the landing in a bunch. They all grinned, at the sight of Billy Bunter. Whatever it was that was "on", it seemed that all the Remove fellows were in it, and that they found the prospect entertaining.

"I say, you fellows," squeaked the alarmed Owl. "I—I say, has—has anything happened?"

"Something happened to a spread in Wharton's study," answered Squiff. "You wouldn't know anything about it, of course." And the other fellows chuckled.

"Of—of course not," gasped Bunter. "I haven't been in Wharton's study. You see, the door was locked, and I never thought of borrowing Fishy's bunch of keys——."

"Ha, ha, ha!"

"You fat cormorant," said Tom Brown. "Wingate had
28

to go away without any tea, after being asked to tea in the Remove! It's the limit, you fat tick—you're going to have a lesson this time."

"I—I say, Wharton ain't going to Quelch, is he?" exclaimed Bunter, in great alarm. The bare idea of an interview with Mr. Quelch, his form-master, on the subject, was quite horrifying. "Why, Quelch would call it pilfering—you know what Quelch is——."

"What do you call it?" asked Hazeldene.

"Oh, really, Hazel——."

The juniors went on to their studies, leaving the Owl of the Remove more alarmed than ever. Skinner and Snoop and Stott came up, and like the other fellows, they grinned at Billy Bunter.

"Here he is!" said Skinner. "The fat frog has crawled out of his hole. Look out after prep, Bunter."

"What—what—what for?" gasped Bunter.

"Toco!" said Skinner, and the three walked on, laughing.

"Oh, lor'!" breathed Bunter. By this time, he quite wished that he had left that spread in No. 1 Study alone. Something was going to happen after prep. What was it? The suspense was really awful.

The fat Owl rolled away to his own study at last. He found one of his study mates, Tom Dutton, in No. 7 Study: Peter Todd had not yet come up. Dutton gave him a stare.

"Oh! You!" he said. "You fat sweep! You're for it."

"I—I say, what's up?" gasped Bunter. "I—I haven't done anything, and—and I wish I hadn't too! What are the fellows up to after prep?"

"Eh?"

"Oh, you deaf ass!" Bunter, in his agitation, had forgotten for a moment that Tom Dutton was deaf. He put on steam. "I say, Dutton, what's up?"

Tom Dutton frowned.

"Who's a pup?" he demanded, warmly. "If you're calling me names, Bunter——."

"Oh, crikey! I didn't say pup," yelled Bunter, "I said what's up? After prep, I mean—what are the fellows going to do?"

"Might be going to the Zoo in the hols," answered Dutton. "The hols are a long way off yet, though. You

29

needn't worry about going to the Zoo—you'll have something else to think about after prep."

"No Zoo—do!" shrieked Bunter. "Is it a rag?"

"You seem to be jolly interested in the Zoo, all of a sudden," said Dutton, staring at him. "Yes, I've seen a stag there, if you want to know. And you needn't yell at me, either—I'm not deaf."

"Will you tell me what's on, when we're through prep?" raved Bunter.

"I know we've got to do prep. That's what we've come up to the study for, ain't it? It's the second book of Virgil, if you've forgotten——."

"Oh, crumbs!"

"I hear that you've been snooping tuck again in the Remove, and that Wingate had to go away without any tea," said Dutton. "I can tell you that the fellows are fed up with you, Bunter! Nobody's tuck is safe from you, and I can jolly well tell you that you've got it coming."

"I—I never went into Wharton's study——."

"I never noticed that Wharton was muddy. What do you mean?"

"Not muddy—study!" howled Bunter.

"Eh? Was his study muddy? What about it?" asked Dutton. "Did you make it muddy, when you were there snooping his tuck?"

"Oh, you deaf dummy——."

"Well, it would be rummy, if his study was muddy when he was expecting Wingate to tea. They'd clean it up a bit, I should think."

"I never went there at all!" shrieked Bunter. It wasn't me at all."

"I know you had it all—every scrap—cleaned out the study as clean as a whistle. I'm glad you own up, at any rate! It would be more like you to tell whoppers about it."

There was a chuckle at the door, and Peter Todd came in. Billy Bunter's spectacles turned on Peter. He was getting tired of conversation with Tom Dutton.

"I—I say, Peter, old fellow, is—is—is something up?" asked the fat Owl. "Do—do the fellows think I—I had anything to do with—with—with——."

"They know you had, if that's what you mean," answered Peter. "Where have you been all this time? You've missed the meeting in the Rag. You've gone over the jolly old limit this time, you fat scrounger, and the whole form are going to deal with you. Look out after prep."

"But I—I never—I—I didn't—I—I wasn't!" gasped Bunter, "I—I was up in the attics when I was in Wharton's study—I—I mean, when I wasn't."

"Not guilty?" asked Peter.

"Nunno, old chap!"

"Well, if you're not guilty, you're all right! You're going to have a Form trial in the Rag after prep——."

"Oh, crikey!"

"You'll get justice!" said Peter, encouragingly. "I'm for the defence."

"Oh, crikey!" repeated Bunter, in dismay. Apparently the prospect of getting justice did not reassure him. "I—I say, Peter——."

"Shut up now—prep!" said Peter.

"But I say, old chap——!"

"Pack it up—prep!"

"Beast!"

Two fellows in No. 7 Study sat down to prep: Billy Bunter had much more urgent matters than prep to think of. While Peter and Dutton dealt with the section of the *Æneid* assigned by Mr. Quelch for preparation that evening, Billy Bunter sat in the study armchair, blinking at them dismally and dolorously. After the feast came the reckoning. He had enjoyed the feast—but the reckoning was an absolutely joyless prospect.

CHAPTER 6

THE ARTFUL DODGER

"HALLO, hallo, hallo!" roared Bob Cherry.

Prep was over. Billy Bunter, for the first time in his fat life, wished that it had lasted longer. On that particular evening, he would have been quite pleased had prep continued till the bell rang for dorm.

But it was over now; and there was a tramp of feet, and a buzz of voices, in the Remove passage. The Lower

31

Fourth were going down: but they were not in a hurry to go: quite an army of the Remove gathered in the passage outside No. 7 Study. The door of that study was hurled open as if a battering-ram had hit it, and a ruddy face and a mop of flaxen hair appeared in the doorway as Bob Cherry's cheery roar woke the echoes.

Harry Wharton and Frank Nugent, Johnny Bull, and Hurree Jamset Ram Singh, Herbert Vernon-Smith and Lord Mauleverer, and six or seven other fellows, looked into the study, bunched round Bob. Billy Bunter blinked at them with a lack-lustre eye. He realised that he was called for.

"Ready!" said Peter Todd. "Come on, Bunter."

"Get a move on, podgers," said Bob. "You're wanted, old fat man. You're featured in the programme."

"I—I say, you fellows, I—I can't come," stammered the fat Owl, "I—I haven't finished my prep——!"

"Nor started it," remarked Peter.

"Oh, really, Toddy——."

"Too late!" said Bob, shaking his head. "No more prep for you, Bunter! Of course we know how you just yearn for it, and can't bear to be parted from it——."

"Ha, ha, ha!"

"But you'll have to give it a miss now: you're wanted in the Rag. It's a Form trial, old fat pippin: come on."

"I—I'd come with pleasure, old chap, but—but I've got to go to Quelch—I—I want to ask him something about something in the something—I—I—I mean, there's something I—I don't understand in Virgil, and——."

"Quite a lot, I fancy," agreed Bob. "But this thirst for knowledge is a bit too sudden, old fat bean. Come on."

"I—I'll come along to the Rag after I've seen Quelch——."

"You wouldn't forget to come?"

"Oh! Nunno——!"

"The forgetfulness would probably be terrific," chuckled Hurree Jamset Ram Singh, "and a bird in hand is worth two cracked pitchers that make Jack a dull boy, as the English proverb remarks."

"Look here, hook the fat rotter out!" growled Johnny Bull.

"Beast!" groaned Bunter.

"Come on, you fat brigand," said Harry Wharton.

"Shan't!" roared Bunter. "I'm staying here. I suppose a fellow can stay in his own study if he likes! I ain't coming, so yah!"

Bob Cherry stepped in No. 7. Three or four fellows followed him in. The hapless fat Owl eyed them apprehensively through his big spectacles.

"Getting out of that armchair?" asked Bob.

"I—I can!t I—I've got a pain!" gasped Bunter. "I—I've got a fearful pain in my leg—like burning daggers—I—I think it's pneumonia——,"

"Oh, my hat!"

"I—I—I can't move—I—I just can't get up——."

"We'll help!" said Bob. He grasped the back of the armchair and heaved. The armchair tilted, and a yelling fat Owl rolled out of it.

"Ow! ow! wow!" Billy Bunter scrambled up. He cast a longing blink at the doorway. But the passage outside was crammed with grinning Removites: there was no escape for Bunter. "I—I say, you fellows—I—I never touched that spread, and—and I'm going to pay for it—I'm expecting a postal order to-morrow——."

"Roll out," said Bob. "Waiting for you, old fat man! I'm going to boot you till you get going—like that!"

"Yaroooh!"

Billy Bunter got going. He rolled out of the study: and an army of Removites gathered round him in the passage, and marched him along to the landing. As they marched across to the stairs, Bunter blinked right and left, rather like a scared fat rabbit. Billy Bunter did not want to arrive in the Rag. Bunter had assisted at "Form trial" as a spectator in his time, but he did not want to assist in them as prisoner at the bar. Very much indeed he didn't. And suddenly, as the mob of juniors poured across the landing, Bunter made a rush, dodged three or four outstretched hands, and darted into the Fifth-form passage.

"Stop him!"

"Collar him!"

"After him!"

Billy Bunter flew. The Fifth-form passage was dangerous territory for a mob of juniors: pursuit was hardly practicable among the senior studies.

Unfortunately for Bunter, Horace Coker, of the Fifth Form, was just coming down the passage to the landing.

Bunter charged into the passage like a runaway lorry,
and Coker met him in full career

It was unfortunate for Coker also. Bunter charged into the passage like a runaway lorry, and Coker met him in full career.

Crash!

"Why—what—who—oooogh!" spluttered Coker, as he reeled from the shock. A charge with Billy Bunter's uncommon weight behind it was too much for even the hefty Horace to withstand. He went over backwards, and the back of his head tapped on hard, unsympathetic oak.

Bunter, winded, staggered. Before he could recover, five or six pairs of hands were upon him. He was whirled back to the landing.

"Wrong turning, old fat man," said Bob Cherry, cheerily. "This way to the stairs. I'll keep hold of your ear, in case you take another wrong turning."

"Yow—ow—ow—ow!"

"Ha, ha, ha!"

With a finger and thumb on a fat ear, Billy Bunter marched down the stairs. He went reluctantly, but he went. His fat ear had to go: and the rest of him had no choice but to accompany it.

But at the foot of the staircase, there was another glimmer of hope! Mr. Quelch, the master of the Remove, was standing at a little distance in conversation with Mr. Prout, the master of the Fifth. It was not on record that Billy Bunter had ever been pleased to see Quelch before. But in the present circumstances the lean figure, the severe face and the gimlet-eyes, were as welcome as the flowers in May. Bunter uttered a loud squeak.

"If you please, sir——!"

"'Ware beaks!" murmured Frank Nugent. Bob's finger and thumb relaxed: the fat ear was liberated. A fellow couldn't be marched along by the ear, under the eyes of a beak: especially the gimlet-eyes of Quelch.

The Remove master looked round.

"Did you speak to me, Bunter?" There were more than a dozen Remove men round Bunter: and they all gave him expressive looks. But in the Presence, they could give him nothing but looks.

"Oh! Yes, sir!" gasped Bunter. "May—may I—I—may I ask you something about a pi—pip—pip——."

"What?"

"A pip—pip—passage in the *Æneid,* sir—I—I'm a little

35

puzzled, and—and if you'd give me a minute or two when —when you go to your study, sir——."

"Certainly!" said Mr. Quelch. His severe face took on a benign expression. It was uncommon—very uncommon indeed—for that member of his form to seek enlightenment like this. Undoubtedly there were many passages in the *Æneid* that puzzled Bunter: probably all of them, in fact. But Bunter's view of the classics was that ignorance was bliss: and assuredly he had never sought out his formmaster's aid, of his own accord, before. For once, Mr. Quelch was pleased with Bunter! He almost smiled. "You may go to my study, Bunter—I shall be coming in a few minutes——."

"Oh! Thank you, sir!" gasped Bunter.

He blinked round at expressive faces—and grinned. Then he rolled away for the masters' studies: and not a finger was raised to stop him. Under Quelch's eye, it couldn't be done! With deep feelings, Harry Wharton and Co. watched the fat Owl disappear, and with deep feelings, they went on to the Rag without him!

"The artful dodger!" breathed Bob.

"The fat spoofer!"

"Trial postponed!" grinned the Bounder.

Every man in the Remove, with the exception of William George Bunter, was gathered in the Rag. All was ready for the Form trial—except the prisoner at the bar! But lacking that indispensable individual, evidently the proceedings could not proceed. The trial of W. G. Bunter, for his many and manifold misdemeanours, was unavoidably postponed.

CHAPTER 7

ANY PORT IN A STORM

BILLY BUNTER sat in Mr. Quelch's armchair, in Mr. Quelch's study, with a wary eye on the door. A fellow told to wait in his form-master's study was not supposed, or expected, to sit in his form-master's armchair. But William George Bunter had more weight to support than most fellows: and he never stood if there was a chance to sit. He was ready to jump up when Quelch's step was heard in the corridor, keeping a wary eye and ear open.

Mr. Quelch had said that he would be coming to the study in a few minutes. But getting away from Prout in a conversational mood was seldom a matter of minutes, and there was delay. Bunter was quite content to wait. All he wanted was to keep clear, for the present, of the other members of his form—Quelch's study was a haven of refuge: and the fat Owl would have been quite satisfied had Quelch's talk with Prout gone on till the bell rang for dormitory.

That, however, was too much to hope for: even Prout could not keep his victims so long as that. Only ten minutes had elapsed when Quelch's step was heard: and Bunter heaved himself out of the armchair in time to meet the gimlet-eye standing, as Quelch came in.

Mr. Quelch gave him quite a kindly glance. Bunter's new and unaccustomed thirst for knowledge on the subject of Virgil's works naturally pleased him. Quelch had almost given up that particular member of his form as a hopeless proposition: so any sign of amendment was gratifying. His leisure was scanty, but he was prepared to sacrifice some of it to help a backward pupil who was eager to improve.

"Ah! You are here, Bunter," said Mr. Quelch. "I shall be very glad to give you some assistance, my boy. The passage you referred to in the *Æneid*."

"Oh! Yes, sir!" mumbled Bunter. "I—I hope you don't mind me taking up your time, sir——."

"Not at all, Bunter! I am very pleased!" assured Mr. Quelch. "The passage you referred to, I conclude, is in the section set for this evening's preparation?"

"Oh! Yes, sir!" gasped Bunter.

"What is the passage, Bunter?"

Billy Bunter could have groaned. He had not even looked at the section of the second book of the *Æneid* set for that evening's prep. What might or might not be in it, he just didn't know. His fat mind was blank on the subject.

It was very awkward, for Quelch naturally wanted to know which passage it was that Bunter required his aid in elucidating.

In requesting Quelch's aid, Billy Bunter had thought of

37

nothing but getting out of the hands of the Amalekites, as it were. He had succeeded in that. But there was no rest for the wicked! The Removites were at a safe distance: but Quelch was dangerously near at hand: and if he discovered that Bunter had been pulling his leg——!"

"Well, Bunter?" said Mr. Quelch, still kindly.

"I—I—I——!" stammered Bunter?"

"You remember the passage, Bunter?"

"Oh! Yes! Of—of course, sir. I—I——."

Brrrrring! Brrrring!

It was the telephone bell.

The ring of a telephone bell is not, in itself, a grateful or comforting sound. It is distinctly unmusical. But no sound could have been more welcome to Billy Bunter's fat ears at that moment than the sound of his form-master's telephone. The music of the spheres would not have been so welcome. It was a blessed interruption!

"Oh! You must wait a few moments, Bunter!" said Mr. Quelch, and he crossed over to the telephone, and picked up the receiver.

"Oh, yes, sir!" gasped Bunter. He would have been glad to wait more than a few moments! Indeed he hoped that the unknown person on the telephone might prove as long-winded as Prout.

"Mr. Quelch speaking!" said the Remove master in reply to something from the other end. "Oh! That is you, Pawson! Mr. dear Professor, how are you!"

Quelch's face was very genial. Evidently he was pleased to hear the voice of Professor Pawson, whomsoever Professor Pawson might be. Bunter concluded that it was some old crony of Quelch's—very likely another schoolmaster. He hoped that Professor Pawson had plenty to say. Every minute that he was able to stay in Quelch's study was a minute to the good—with the Remove fellows on watch for him!

"My dear Quelch." A rather high-pitched, squeaky voice came through on the telephone, and it was audible to Bunter as well as to Quelch. Sad to relate, the fat Owl edged a little near, in order to hear. That was one of Billy Bunter's little ways. He always had a fat ear ready for anything that did not concern him. "I trust you are at leisure——."

"Oh, quite, quite."

"If next week would suit you, Quelch—one day next week——."

"Perfectly! If you could make it Wednesday, that is a half-holiday here, and I shall be wholly at leisure."

From which Billy Bunter deduced that Professor Pawson was coming to Greyfriars to see his form-master. Really, a schoolmaster friend visiting Quelch was a matter of absolutely no interest to any fellow in Quelch's form. But the fat Owl went on listening: habit is strong.

"Wednesday next week, then!" came the squeaky voice. "I shall be very glad to see you, Quelch—very glad indeed to consult you on certain points in my translation of the Odes."

"I trust that the translation is progressing, Pawson." It was a matter of sheer wonder, to Bunter, to hear the note of deep interest in Quelch's usually crusty voice. Schoolmasters, he reflected, were queer fish. Quelch was actually and keenly interested in Horace's Odes: which would have made Billy Bunter's fat head ache merely to look at them!

"Somewhat, somewhat," came back the squeaky voice. "As you know, Quelch, my endeavour is to observe, and preserve, the original metres—the true Horatian metres——."

"A difficult matter in English," said Mr. Quelch. "A gallant enterprise, my dear Pawson, but presenting many difficulties." Quelch had forgotten that Bunter was in the study, by this time.

"Many, many, Quelch! The spondee is, of course, the snag. One is continually tempted to throw it over, and fall back upon a trochee—but that would not be Horace: it would be Alcæus, doubtless, but not Horace."

"Precisely!" agreed Mr. Quelch: while Billy Bunter wondered who Alcæus might have been, and what might be the difference, if any, between a spondee and a trochee.

"At the moment, Quelch, I am engaged upon the alcaics, and I am determined that they shall be truly Horatian, and nothing else. Otherwise one might as well translate into iambic verse, as so many others have done."

"Quite!" agreed Mr. Quelch, "but——."

"I have recently come upon an Italian translation of the Odes, Quelch, which claims to conform to the original

39

metres. I do not admit the claim. Take for example the thirty-seventh in the first book—you recall it——?"

"Naturally," replied Mr. Quelch. "Nunc est bibendum——."

"Quite, quite—nunc est bibendum, nunc pede libero. Our Italian friend translates this—'Or s'ha da bere, con il pié libero'. Where is the spondee in the second foot? I ask you, Quelch, where?"

Mr. Quelch reflected for a moment.

"Certainly I should term 'bere' a trochee! " he said.

"Exactly! Now, as in Horace the second foot is invariably a spondee——."

Billy Bunter moved further off, and lost the rest. Inquisitiveness was Bunter's besetting sin: but inquisitiveness failed him now: Bunter had had enough of this! Indeed the fat Owl wondered how two old donkeys—which disrespectful description he applied to his form-master and his form-master's friend!—could talk this tosh and find any glimmer of interest in it. Bunter, at any rate, found no such glimmer. He was more than content to let Quelch have the rest to himself.

Quelch had the rest to himself for a good ten minutes. But Quelch, if not the Professor at the other end, was a practical man, and remembered that there were such things as telephone bills! Trunk calls that went on and on and on were likely to tot up to a sum far exceeding any imaginable receipts for the masterly translation of Q. Horatius Flaccus, even in the original Horatian metres! He interrupted.

"My dear Pawson, we will discuss this at length next week. You must remember the telephone charges on trunk calls——."

"Bless my soul! I had quite forgotten that! The subject is so absorbing——."

"Oh, quite! But——."

"——so extremely absorbing—so fascinating——."

"Undoubtedly! On Wednesday, Pawson, you will take your train for Courtfield, and change there for the local train for Friardale. If you do not get out at Courtfield the train will take you on to Pegg, which would mean a long walk to the school."

"I shall remember, Quelch! You say I get out at Pegg——."

"No: at Courtfield."

"Oh, quite! Quite! Then I walk to Pegg——."

"No, no: you take the local train for Friardale."

"Oh! Yes! Exactly! Dear me, there go the pips again. I think I have heard them several times already! Good-bye, my dear Quelch, till next week."

Mr. Quelch put up the receiver. His friend at the other end certainly was a little absent-minded: with much more knowledge of alcaics, sapphics, and asclepiads, than of more mundane matters. Quelch could only hope that he would arrive at Greyfriars, the following week, some time and somehow. He turned from the telephone, and became once more aware of the existence of William George Bunter.

CHAPTER 8

OUT OF THE FRYING PAN——!

"Oh! Bunter!" ejaculated Mr. Quelch.

"Yes, sir!" mumbled Bunter.

"Dear me! I had quite forgotten—I regret that you have had to wait so long, Bunter! However, we will now proceed."

Mr. Quelch sat down at the table, and opened an *Æneid* at Book Two, and placed a lean forefinger on line 268.

"This is the section, Bunter! Tempus erat—is it the first passage that you have found so difficult?"

"Oh! Yes, sir! No, sir! I—I mean, yes, sir!" gasped Bunter.

"Then you may sit at the table, and we will go into it together, Bunter," said the Remove master, benignly.

Billy Bunter suppressed a groan.

It had been a case of any port in a storm: and Quelch's study, so far, had proved a secure haven. But even a secure haven had its drawbacks, in the circumstances. The deathless verse of Virgil did not attract Bunter. It had in fact a reverse effect on him. For a dismal moment, the fat Owl wondered whether what was coming to him in the

Rag could be worse than doing Virgil with Quelch! But he was "for it" now! What the passage beginning "tempus erat" might or might not mean, Bunter did not know, and couldn't have cared less. But he had to go through with it now.

And through it he went, under Quelch's kind guidance. From "Tempus erat" to "jaculatus puppibus ignis" Bunter was not spared a word, not even a syllable: for a good half-hour he suffered under the pious Æneas and the stout Hector, and loathed them both with a deep loathing. The ordeal, indeed, might have continued longer, so kind and dutiful was Quelch: but luckily for Bunter he was now due in Common-Room, and he rose from the table.

"I think you have fairly mastered the passage now, Bunter," said Mr. Quelch, genially.

"Oh! Yes, sir! "

"I regret that I cannot give you a little more time——."

"Oh! Thank you, sir, you—you've been very kind! " mumbled Bunter; shuddering at the thought of Quelch giving him a little more time.

"You may go now, Bunter."

"If you pip—pip—pip——! "

"Eh?"

"If—if you pip—please, sir, may I—I stay and go over it again once or twice, sir, while you're gone——."

Mr. Quelch fairly beamed!

"Certainly, Bunter! I am pleased—indeed, I may say that I am delighted with this keenness on your part. I shall return here before dormitory, and shall then be very pleased to go through the passage with you again, if there is any point on which you have any doubts."

"Oh! Thank you, sir."

Mr. Quelch left the study.

When the door closed on him, Billy Bunter wiped the perspiration from his fat forehead. He had escaped the Remove in the Rag—by falling into the clutches of Quelch: rather like the ancient mariners who dodged Scylla and came to grief on Charybdis, or the fish that hopped out of the frying pan into the fire. Still, it was all right now.

He did not go over that passage once or twice again! Nothing would have induced him even to blink at it, now Quelch was gone. He shifted to Quelch's armchair, and sprawled there for a much-needed rest. It was still some considerable time to dorm: and he was safe for that period: at least until Quelch came back and turned him out. He hoped that the tide of chinwag in Common-Room would keep Quelch till the dormitory bell rang. After that he would be all right: the beasts could not hold their beastly Form trial in the dormitory; noise in that quarter would bring up the prefects.

Bunter's intention was to remain on the alert, and jump out of that armchair as soon as Quelch came to the door, as he had done before. But that happy half-hour with Virgil had tired him out: his fat chin drooped, and his little round eyes closed behind his big round spectacles.

Then there was an unaccustomed sound in Quelch's study: a sound as of the rumble of distant thunder. Bunter slept and snored. He did not dream of the pious Æneas. He dreamed of that gorgeous feast in the attic that afternoon, and a smile illuminated his fat face as he slumbered and snored. He did not dream of Quelch—Quelch came back undreamt-of, and started a little, at his door, as he heard the rumble within. When he came in, he stood and looked at Billy Bunter, quite expressively. But his frown relaxed. After all, Bunter had been displaying uncommon keenness—he had been working hard, if for the first time in his life!

Mr. Quelch bent, and shook a fat shoulder.

"Urrrrggh! " gurgled Bunter.

"Bunter! "

"Beast!"

"Wha—a—t?"

"Let a fellow alone! 'Tain't rising-bell! Leggo, you beast."

"Upon my word!" ejaculated Mr. Quelch. Bunter, half-awake, apparently had the impression that he was in bed in the Remove dormitory, and that some Remove man was shaking him! "Bunter——."

"Beast!"

"You absurd boy, wake up at once!" rapped Mr. Quelch, and he administered a vigorous shake that brought Bunter, with a jump, out of the land of dreams.

"Oh!" gasped Bunter. He sat up and blinked at Mr. Quelch. "Oh! I—I—I wasn't asleep, sir—I—I—I was thinking over that—that——."

43

"You may leave my study, Bunter."

"Oh! Yes, sir."

A bell began to ring: a glad sound to Bunter's fat ears. It was dorm! He rolled out of Mr. Quelch's study.

That study had proved a secure haven. But the fat Owl felt a tremor as he joined the Remove crowd on the dormitory staircase. All of them gave him expressive looks: the Famous Five, indeed, looked almost as if they could have eaten him!

"Hallo, hallo, hallo, here's the fat burglar!" exclaimed Bob Cherry.

"I—I say, you fellows——."

"Kick him!" said Johnny Bull.

"Oh, really Bull——."

"You've got it coming, you fat villain!" said Harry Wharton.

"I—I say, if you kick up a shindy in the dorm, you'll have the pre's up!" gasped Bunter. "I say, it's Loder to-night: and if he catches you kicking up a row after lights out——."

"You'll keep till to-morrow."

"Beast!"

It was a relief to Bunter to "keep" till the morrow: a respite, at least. The Form trial, twice postponed, had to be postponed again—and perhaps the fat Owl nourished a hope that there might be further postponements! Justice was on the track of the offender: but as the ancient poet has remarked, "Justice follows with a lagging foot!"

CHAPTER 9

ALAS FOR BUNTER!

BILLY BUNTER paused in the passage outside the doorway of the Rag after dinner the following day, and blinked round him cautiously through his big spectacles.

Bunter was on his guard.

He was very wary.

So far, that day, the fat Owl had been keeping ahead, as it were, of the lagging foot of Justice.

In morning break, which lasted only fifteen minutes, a Form trial could scarcely be held: Bunter had felt safe in break. After third school, he had disappeared till dinner time, emerging into view again only when the bell rang for tiffin. After dinner, he had loitered by the big window at the end of Masters' Studies, eyed from a distance by a good many Remove fellows: but safe, in such a spot, from being collared and walked off. Now, an hour later, he was feeling that the coast was clear. That day was Wednesday, a half-holiday, and the Remove were booked to play the Shell at soccer. And certainly they were not likely to cut a football match on account of Bunter, or a thousand Bunters for that matter. Kick-off was at three: and from three till at least half-past four, all was, so to speak, calm and bright. Or seemed so!

But Bunter was wary—very wary. He was prepared, if needful, to disappear up among the disused attics: or even to seek Quelch's assistance with a spot of Latin: even, as a last desperate resource, to go to Lascelles and ask him something about maths. But he did not want to spend un-necessary time in a cold attic: he did not want spots of Latin with Quelch, and still less maths with Lascelles. What he wanted was an armchair before the fire in the Rag, where he could frowst at his lazy ease. And for the next hour and a half it seemed to Bunter that he could venture to take his ease without alarm.

Nevertheless, he was very wary. The fellows were making quite an unexpected fuss about his latest exploit as a grub-raider, which had indeed been on rather an un-usual scale: but given time, no doubt it would fade out: at least Bunter hoped so. But for the present, he could not be too careful. In the passage outside the door of the Rag, he looked this way and that way, like Moses of old: and like Moses again, he saw no man. All the footballing fellows would be in the changing-room, he had no doubt: and the others were scattered about their various avoca-tions. A Form trial required the presence of all the Form, and at least half the Form would be on Little Side, the rest anywhere. For a happy hour and a half, Bunter was going to enjoy a frowst in the Rag—after which he would have to consider the various resources of dodging up to the

45

attics, a spot of Latin with Quelch, or a spot of maths with Lascelles—or any other dodge that might occur to his fat brain.

He blinked in at the doorway of the Rag. Lord Maul-everer was seated in one of the armchairs, with one elegant leg crossed over the other, meditatively gazing at the sky through the window. Near the window Skinner, Snoop and Stott stood in a group, discussing some matter of interest in low tones—probably the chances of Nobbled Nick in the two-thirty. Fisher T. Fish sat on a corner of the long table, his bony legs swinging, his sharp eyes scanning a column of figures in a little account-book: probably a record of his financial transactions amongst the fags. Nobody else was in the Rag, and Bunter rolled in quite confidently. Mauly did not even look at him: Fisher T. Fish did not look up from his account-book: Skinner and Co. glanced at him, and grinned, but took no further heed. All was safe. There was a cheery fire burning, and it was very warm and comfortable in the Rag, so the fat Owl wheeled an armchair in front of the fire, deposited his unusual weight in it, and relaxed.

He groped in his pockets, drew out a handful of nuts, and proceeded to crack them and devour them. The nuts were left over from his raid on No. 1 Study the previous day: all that remained of that gargantuan spread.

Frowsting before the blazing fire, cracking and eating nuts, Billy Bunter naturally did not think of turning his eyes and spectacles on the window. He was not interested in the view: neither was he interested in the weather. But the weather was, if he had thought of it, a matter of interest to him. Lord Mauleverer, gazing dreamily at the sky, noticed the black clouds that rolled in from the sea, and the rain-drops that began to spatter. Billy Bunter did not. Lord Mauleverer reflected that it did not look much like football for the Remove and the Shell: but no such reflection occurred to Bunter. He went on happily frowsting and cracking nuts, while the rain came down, increasing in volume, and everyone out of doors scuttled for shelter. He did not realise that anything was going wrong with his plans for the next hour and a half, till there was a tramp of feet and a buzz of voices in the passage, and a crowd of Remove men poured into the Rag.

"Rotten!" came Bob Cherry's voice.

46

"The rottenfulness is terrific."

"It would rain!" sighed Frank Nugent.

"Filthy weather!" growled the Bounder. "Can't try it on in this."

"Hardly," said Harry Wharton.

"Blow the rain!"

"Bother the rain!"

"Bless the rain!"

Billy Bunter sat up and took notice. His fat face registered alarm and despondency! A whole crowd of them had come in without noticing, for the moment, that Bunter was there; the high back of the armchair screened him from view. But that was not likely to last long.

"Oh, crikey!" breathed Bunter.

He ceased to chew nuts.

Bunter had not foreseen this—never dreamed of it! A shower would not have deterred the footballers: but it was not a shower: it was a heavy downpour. The footballers had waited some time in the changing-room, hoping that it might be possible to get out: but as the weather grew worse instead of better, they had had to give it up—and here they were! Instead of changing for soccer, and keeping at a safe distance from the fat Owl for a happy hour and a half, here they were! The unexpected, as so often it does, had happened!

It was a blow! The weather had done it! The most disgruntled among the footballers was not so dissatisfied with the vagaries of the British climate as was the unhappy Owl in the armchair.

"It's a wash-out," said Harry Wharton. "Can't be helped —it's just one of those things!"

"Well, we can't get out, unless in a swim-suit," said Bob Cherry. "What about the jolly old Form trial?"

"Oh, lor'!" breathed Bunter.

"Good egg! Anybody know where Bunter is?" asked Johnny Bull.

"Hallo, hallo, hallo!" roared Bob Cherry. "Anybody seen a porpoise about?"

Skinner chuckled.

"He's here," he answered.

"Oh, good!" Bob looked round the Rag. "Show up, Bunter! Roll out! Show a leg, old fat frump! You're just where we want you."

"Oh, scissors!" groaned Bunter. He detached himself from the armchair, and blinked at the crowd of Removites. "I—I say, you fellows, I—I've got to go to Quelch—I—I say, don't shut that door, Smithy—I say——."

Herbert Vernon-Smith banged the door shut.

"I—I say, I—I've got to go to Mascelles for laths," gasped Bunter. "I mean to Lascelles for maths. I—I say, let a fellow pass, you know. I can't keep Quelch waiting—I mean Lascelles—I—I mean the Head! Dr. Locke told me to go to his study—I—I can't keep the Head waiting——!"

"They'll all have to wait!" said Bob Cherry, shaking his head. "Quelch and Lascelles and the Head—the whole jolly lot. You're wanted, Bunter."

"Oh, really, Cherry——."

"Nice of you to be on the spot, just when we want you!" said Bob. "Now then, gentlemen, chaps, and fatheads, the court is going into session—here's the prisoner at the bar—get ready, Bunter! Now then, wake up, Mauly! Gather round, my infants——. Where are you going, Bunter?"

"Ha, ha, ha!"

Billy Bunter did not delay to state where he was going. He made a frantic rush for the door.

Smithy put his back to it, and stood there grinning. That door was not going to open again till the trial was over.

"Gerrout of the way, Smithy!" yelled Bunter.

"I don't think!" grinned the Bounder.

"Collar him!" called Harry Wharton.

"Bag him!"

"You're for it, Bunter."

Billy Bunter was desperate. Only in a quite desperate state would he have attempted to shift the Bounder from the door. Now he did. A fat fist landed unexpectedly in Vernon-Smith's ribs, and he staggered. The fat Owl grabbed at the door-handle. But at the same moment, the Bounder grabbed at the back of a fat neck. Bunter was whirled away from the door.

"Ow! Leggo!" yelled Bunter. "I—I say, you fellows—yaroooh! I say—whoop! Leave off kicking me, Smithy, or I'll—yow—ow—ow—ow!"

"Ha, ha, ha!"

There was no escape for Bunter. The lagging foot of Justice had overtaken him at last: and he was "for it".

CHAPTER 10

TRIAL BY JURY

"Mauly!"

"Yaas?"

"Up with you! You're judge."

Bob Cherry had placed a chair on the long table. That elevated seat was the judge's bench. Lord Mauleverer, from his armchair, eyed it doubtfully.

"I'm all right here!" he suggested.

"Tired?" asked Bob, sympathetically.

"Yaas."

"Then I'll help you out of that chair."

"Oh, gad! It's all right!" said Mauly, hastily, and he jumped out of the armchair without waiting for Bob's strenuous assistance. He clambered on the table, and sat on the judicial bench.

"The court is now open!" said Bob. "I mean, the court is now sitting——."

"Most of us standing!" remarked Skinner.

"Shut up, Skinner! Mr. Bull will open the proceedings with a speech for the prosecution——."

"You ass, what are you calling me Mr. Bull for?" inquired Johnny.

"This is a court of law now," said Bob. "Your learned friend, Mr. Todd, will speak for the defence. The public are requested to keep order in this court," added Bob, with a glance round over a crowd of grinning faces. "Stop barging, Bolsover. The member of the public who is whistling will be ejected if he doesn't pack it up at once. Now then, get going—I mean, the proceedings will now proceed."

The gravity of a court of law was not very conspicuous —except in the fat face of the prisoner at the bar. Billy Bunter was very serious. But there was undoubtedly an element of hilarity in the "public", as if they regarded the trial of W. G. Bunter rather as a happy resource on a rainy afternoon, than as a solemn judicial proceeding.

"On the ball, Johnny!" called out several voices.

"Well, look here——!" began Johnny Bull.

"I rise on a point of order!" said Peter Todd. "First of all——."

"Shut up, Toddy! Your turn comes next, if you've got anything to say for that fat, foozling scrounger."

"First of all——!" repeated Peter, firmly.

"Order! Sit down, Toddy!"

"First of all," roared Peter, "you have to ask the prisoner whether he pleads guilty or not guilty."

"Oh, by gum, so you do!" said Bob. "I forgot that bit! Prisoner at the bar——."

"Oh, really, Cherry——!"

"Do you plead guilty or not guilty?"

"Beast!"

"Ha, ha, ha!"

"Silence in court! The prisoner at the bar will answer, or he will be booted! Are you guilty or not guilty?"

"Yes—I mean no!" gasped Bunter. "I—I ain't guilty of anything! I never went into the study at all, and never touched a thing while I was there——."

"My client pleads not guilty!" said Peter Todd. "Speak up, you fat owl—I mean, answer the question, Mr. Bunter."

"Not guilty!" gasped Bunter. "I never——."

"That will do, you fat villain!" said Bob Cherry. "We all know you're jolly well guilty, but you're going to have a fair trial. Go it, Johnny—I mean Mr. Bull."

"That fat tuck-hunting twerp——!" began Johnny Bull. Up jumped Peter again.

"Your lordship——!"

"Eh?" ejaculated Lord Mauleverer. "What are you calling me your lordship for, you fathead?"

"Because you're the judge, you silly ass! I mean your lordship! I object to such an expression as 'tuck-hunting twerp' applied to my client by my learned friend opposite, as liable to prejudice the minds of the jury. I trust that your lordship will uphold my objection!" added the counsel for the defence, with dignity.

"Oh! Yaas! Draw it mild, Johnny."

"Look here, doesn't every man here know that Bunter is a tuck-hunting twerp?" demanded Johnny Bull.

"I submit that what everybody knows is not evidence,

50

your lordship," said Peter. "My learned friend opposite will kindly allude to my client as Mr. Bunter."

"Oh, all right!" said Johnny. "Mr. Bunter sneaked a spread from No. 1 Study yesterday afternoon—and old Wingate, who was coming to tea, had to go away without any——."

"And so the poor dog——! " began Skinner.

"Kick Skinner, somebody."

"Yaroooh!"

"The accused," went on Johnny, "is known all over Greyfriars as a pincher of other fellows' tuck. There's hardly a man in the room who hasn't kicked him for it. But has it done him any good? It hasn't. I've walloped him with a fives bat myself, and the very next day he had a bag of tarts from my study——."

"I didn't!" yelled Bunter.

"Don't interrupt counsel, prisoner at the bar," rapped Bob Cherry.

"I tell you I didn't!" howled Bunter. "I never touched that bag of tarts, and there was only four tarts in it, too——."

"Ha, ha, ha!"

"Silence in court! Prisoner at the bar, shut up."

"Beast!"

"He had my tarts, and he's had something from every study in the Remove," went on Johnny. "What he wants is a jolly heavy sentence, to teach him how to behave. He cleared out our spread that we'd specially got up for old Wingate, to the last monkey nut——."

"Not a crumb or a plum left," said Nugent. "It was a clean sweep."

"The cleanfulness of the sweep was terrific."

"That's my case," concluded Johnny, "and I demand the heaviest sentence that it is in the power of this court to pass!"

"O.K.," said Lord Mauleverer, "I sentence him——."

"Hold on, Mauly," interrupted Harry Wharton, "you haven't heard the defence yet, you ass: and the jury haven't found him guilty yet."

"Oh! My mistake! " said the judge, gracefully. "Carry on. I'm ready to sentence him as soon as you fellows are ready."

"Ha, ha, ha!"

"Oh, really, Mauly——." squeaked the prisoner at the bar.

"Shut up, Bunter."

"Yah! "

"Go it, Toddy! "

Counsel for the defence rose. What Peter had to say in defence of his "client" was really rather a mystery, as every fellow in the Rag, including Peter, knew that Bunter had raided the spread in No. 1 Study. But Peter rather fancied himself as a lawyer: and he was going to say something, whether he had anything to say or not.

"Your lordship, and gentlemen of the jury," said Peter, "my client stands accused of abstracting comestibles——."

"Snooping tuck! " said Bob Cherry.

"——of abstracting comestibles," repeated Peter. calmly, "and I trust to be able to clear him of this absurd, this frivolous charge, to the complete satisfaction of your lordship and the gentlemen of the jury——."

"You jolly well know he did!" bawled Johnny Bull.

"I appeal to your lordship to rule that my learned friend opposite is not entitled to interrupt counsel's speech! " said Peter.

"Oh! Yaas! " agreed his lordship. "Pack it up, Johnny."

"I thank your lordship! " said Peter, with dignity. "I will now proceed. My client pleads not guilty, and it is for the prosecution to prove this case. I submit that there is no evidence to satisfy an intelligent jury. No one saw Mr. Bunter snooping the tuck—I mean, abstracting the comestibles——."

"He took jolly good care of that," said Nugent.

"The seefulness was not great, but the knowfulness is terrific," declare Hurree Jamset Ram Singh.

"Tuck was missing," continued Peter, "but none of the missing tuck was found upon my client——."

"Couldn't have spotted it without an X-ray outfit!" remarked the Bounder.

"Ha, ha, ha! "

"My client, according to his statement, never went near the study from which the comestibles were abstracted! It is admitted that in such matters his reputation is far from good——."

"Oh, really, Toddy——."

"But the jury must banish from their minds all consideration of previous convictions, which carry no weight in the present proceedings. My client must be judged on the evidence, and I submit that there is no evidence that he ever entered No. 1 Study yesterday at all. If the prosecution can produce any such evidence," added Peter, in the same dignified manner, "I shall be glad to hear it. Otherwise, I demand the discharge of my client by this court, without a stain on his character."

"Oh, my hat!"

"Rats!"

"Draw it mild!"

"Is that the lot?" asked Lord Mauleverer.

"That, your lordship, is the lot!"

"All right! I will now sentence the prisoner at the bar——."

" Ha, ha, ha!"

"Hold on, Mauly, you ass!" roared Bob Cherry. "Can't you wait for the jury to find him guilty?"

"Oh, gad! Yaas, go ahead and find him guilty, then."

"The jury will now consult on their verdict," said Bob Cherry.

"I say, you fellows——."

"The prisoner at the bar will shut up! "

"Beast! "

Billy Bunter had had a glimmer of hope when his "counsel" concluded his speech. But it faded out as he blinked anxiously at the faces of the jury. Almost all the Remove were now in the Rag, and every fellow was a member of the jury: and it was quite clear that every fellow had made up his mind on the subject. If there was a lack of evidence, as counsel for the defence had pointed out, it did not seem to worry the Removites. As everyone knew that Bunter had snooped the tuck, or as his counsel preferred to put it, abstracted the comestibles, there was unanimous agreement on the verdict. Vernon-Smith, as foreman of the jury, announced the result.

"My lord, we find the prisoner at the bar guilty on this charge! The verdict is unanimous!" announced the Bounder.

"Oh, crikey!" gasped Bunter.

"Oh, good! I suppose I can sentence him now?" asked Lord Mauleverer.

"Lemme see! I think you have to ask him first whether he has anything to say before sentence is passed on him," said Bob, thoughtfully.

"Oh, all right! Bunter—I mean prisoner at the bar—have you anything to say before sentence is passed on you?" inquired Lord Mauleverer.

"Oh! Yes!" gasped Bunter. "Lots! I—I say, I—I never did it! I never went into the study at all. I—I couldn't, you know, because the door was locked, and I never even thought of borrowing Fishy's bunch of keys—I never knew he had a bunch of keys. I—I never borrowed tuppence from Toddy—I mean, I—I borrowed that tuppence to give to a blind beggar—a pi—pip—pip—poor old blind man, and—and if I did borrow Fishy's keys, it wasn't to go into a study, it was because I'd lost the key of my box in the dorm. I—I never touched the tuck while I was in the study, and I certainly never took the cake up to the attic to eat it—I—I don't like cake! I—I never had a single one of the nuts, and I never ate any of them, and I ain't got the rest in my pockets now. And——."

"Ha, ha, ha!"

"Oh, gad!" said Lord Mauleverer. "I think that will do! You can now pack it up, prisoner at the bar, while I pass sentence on you."

"Oh, really, Mauly——."

"Shut up, Bunter."

"Silence in court!"

"Go it, Mauly!"

"Prisoner at the bar, you have been found guilty by a jury of your peers, and a jolly good verdict too——."

"Hear, hear!"

"It is now my duty to pass sentence upon you——."

"Look here, you beast——."

"I sentence you to be sent to Coventry by the whole form, and barred by every man in the Remove, till you learn to behave like a decent Greyfriars man——."

"Beast!"

"And in addition," continued Lord Mauleverer, "to be kicked out of the Rag, every fellow here putting in at least one kick."

"Oh, crikey! I say, you fellows——."

"Hear, hear!"

"Ha, ha, ha!"

"Go it, you men!" roared Johnny Bull.

54

Lord Mauleverer, his functions as judge at an end, hopped off the table, and returned to his armchair. Every other fellow crowded round the prisoner at the bar. Billy Bunter flew for the door. How many kicks he collected, before he escaped from the Rag, he could hardly have computed. Every fellow put in at least one: some two or three: lucky ones three or four. There was ample room on Bunter's plump form for feet to land: and they landed with a very high frequency. It was a wildly-yelling Owl that escaped at last, and fled for his fat life. Not for the first time in his podgy career, William George Bunter was finding that the way of the transgressor was hard.

CHAPTER 11

BILLY BUNTER IN COVENTRY

"I SAY, you fellows!"

No reply.

"I say!" hooted Billy Bunter.

Silence!

"Look here, you beasts——!"

Stony silence!

Billy Bunter breathed hard through his fat little nose.

It was morning break the following day. Bunter rolled up to the Famous Five in the sunny quad, and addressed them: only to discover that they seemed to be deaf, or at least dumb.

Bunter was in "Coventry".

He was finding "Coventry" a cold, cheerless and solitary abode. Not a fellow had spoken a word to him since the "trial by jury" in the Rag the previous day. The sentence passed on the fat Owl for his many sins was being carried out by every man in the Remove. Even in No. 7 Study, Peter Todd had been as dumb as the rest of the form. As a lawyer, Peter had done his best to get his "client" off: but as a Remove man, he heartily concurred in the sentence passed on his fat study-mate. Every fellow in the Remove agreed that it was time—high time—that

55

the unscrupulous Owl had a lesson—and he was getting it.

Bunter was finding it quite a hard lesson.

It was a loquacious Owl. Bunter liked the sound of his own voice—musical to his ears if to no others. In his list of the joys of life, eating certainly came first: but wagging his fat chin was a good second. Now he was, no doubt, at liberty to wag his fat chin as much as he liked, but his voice was like unto the voice of one crying in the wilderness: it evoked no response.

And Bunter was a gregarious animal. His own company, fascinating as he had no doubt that it was, palled upon him. Sages are said to have seen charms in the face of Solitude: Bunter, even with the aid of his big spectacles, could see none at all. He did not like solitude. He did not like silence. Now he had both in abundant measure.

Harry Wharton and Co. in a group in the quad, were talking football, discussing a coming match with Rookwood School, when Bunter blew along. They ceased to dis--ss soccer and Rookwood, and remained quite silent: gazing Bunter, but with an unseeing gaze, as if they did not reall see him there at all. With one accord, they remained elaborately unconscious of his fat existence.

"I say, Harry, old chap——!" recommenced Bunter.

Harry old chap continued unconscious of his existence.

"Bob, old fellow——."

Bob old fellow remained as unconscious as Harry old chap.

"I say, Franky—look here, you ain't jolly well deaf, you can jolly well hear me," hooted Bunter. "Frankly, old pal——."

There was no more sign from Franky old pal than from Harry old chap or Bob old fellow. Bunter breathed harder.

"You deaf and dumb too, Bull?" he snorted.

Johnny Bull seemed, at least, to be both deaf and dumb.

"Inky! I say, Inky!" Bunter turned an almost despairing blink on the dusky face of the Nabob of Bhanipur, "I say, Inky, I've always been a pal, haven't I?—I've never called you a nigger, or if I did it was only my little joke. I say, Inky old boy."

Not a sign from Inky old boy! Hurree Jamset Ram Singh's dusky face did not indicate that he heard a word.

"Beasts!" roared Bunter at five unconscious faces,

gazing at him as if he were not there. "Rotters! You jolly well can't keep this up! Think you can?"

That query received no answer.

"Think I want to talk to you?" went on Bunter. "I jolly well don't, as I can jolly well tell you. Yah!"

The Famous Five got into motion. Still absolutely unconscious of Bunter, they walked away. Billy Bunter was left breathing wrath.

"Oh, lor'!" he murmured.

Only a short time had elapsed since Bunter had been sentenced to Coventry. But already he was feeling the strain severely. Already there were immense amounts of conversation stored up, as it were, in the fat Owl. He was beginning to feel that he must either talk or burst. Never had his plump chin had so long a rest.

Lord Mauleverer was strolling under the elms, with his hands in the pockets of his elegant trousers. Bunter rolled to intercept him. Mauly was so good-natured—"soft", in Bunter's opinion—that the fat Owl hoped to find him more amenable than other fellows.

"I say, Mauly——!" squeaked Bunter.

Lord Mauleverer gave him a glance, changed his direction, and walked away.

"Deaf?" howled Bunter.

Mauly walked on.

Bunter rolled in pursuit. His next remarks were addressed to the back of Mauly's head, as Mauly accelerated.

"I say, Mauly, old chap, stop a minute. I say, don't race! I'm out of breath. I say, Mauly——."

Mauleverer's easy saunter was changed into a quick walk. Billy Bunter put on a spurt, and grabbed an elegant sleeve.

"Look here, Mauly, old chap——!" he gasped. "I say, can't you speak, you ass? I'm speaking to you, Mauly."

Lord Mauleverer, without replying, shook off the fat hand. Then, still without speaking, he took out his handkerchief, and wiped the sleeve where Bunter's fat sticky fingers had clutched. Then, as silent as a stone image, he walked away again—Bunter's eyes and spectacles gleaming wrath after him.

"Beast!" groaned Bunter. There was no hope in Mauly.

A chuckle caught Bunter's fat ear, and he blinked round

57

at Skinner, Snoop, and Stott. They were grinning, apparently amused by the little scene they had just witnessed. Bunter gave them an anxious blink.

"I say, you fellows, you ain't in this, are you?" he asked. "I say, I'm going to ask you to a feed in my study when—when my postal order comes. I say, you fellows, don't walk away while a fellow's talking to you."

But Skinner and Co. did walk away, laughing.

"Oh, crikey! " mumbled Bunter.

He blinked round the quad through his big spectacles. He simply had to speak to somebody. It was a case of "a victim must be found". Catching sight of his minor, Sammy of the Second, he rolled over to him. Bunter minor, of the Second Form, was with Gatty and Myers of that form, and he did not look particularly pleased as his major bore down on him. Bunter, in fact, was not an exemplary elder brother. Sometimes he forgot for whole weeks that he had a minor at Greyfriars at all. It was quite unusual for him to seek Sammy's society. But he was seeking it now. Anything was better than nothing!

"Hallo, Sammy," he said, quite affectionately, "I haven't seen you for days——."

"You could if you'd wanted to," answered Sammy, staring.

"Oh! Ah! Yes! But—but a chap is so busy, you know —a chap with so many friends in his own form, you know——."

"I don't think! " said Sammy.

"Well, I've been looking for you now——! " said Bunter.

"Not much good," said Sammy, "I haven't a bean."

"I don't want to borrow anything of you, you young ass."

"Don't you?" asked Sammy, in surprise.

"No! " roared Bunter.

"Then what have you been looking for me for?"

Billy Bunter breathed hard. Brotherly affection was not highly developed in the Bunter clan. A spot of it would have been welcome to Bunter now. But no such spot was visible anywhere about Sammy Bunter.

"Here, young Bunter," said Gatty, "are you coming, or are you going to stop and jaw with that Remove tick?"

"Coming! " answered Sammy.

And he went.

"Sammy, old chap——!" squeaked Bunter. But his squeak fell on deaf ears. He was not in Coventry so far as the Second Form were concerned: but evidently Bunter minor had no use for his company.

Billy Bunter was still surrounded by silence, and still utterly failing to discern any of the charms that sages have seen in the face of Solitude, when the bell rang for third school. He rolled away dismally to the House. He went in with a crowd of the Remove: not one of whom had a word to say. Skinner grinned, with that malicious grin of his, and Snoop giggled an unmusical giggle: but nobody else seemed aware that Bunter was there at all. Unseeing eyes met his dolorous blinks.

"I say, Harry, old fellow——!" Bunter's fat squeak was almost beseeching. The captain of the Remove, like Pharaoh of old, hardened his heart, and remained insensible to the beseeching squeak.

"Can't you speak, you dummy?" hissed Bunter.

Apparently Wharton couldn't. At all events, he didn't.

"Beast!" hissed Bunter.

No reply.

"I'll jolly well tell you what I think of you!" hooted Bunter. "You're a stuck-up fathead! You can't play football for toffee! You're a rotter, and a tick, and a smudge! Yah!"

Bunter expected a reply to that! He received one, but it was not verbal. Harry Wharton reached out, grasped a fat neck, and banged a fat head against the wall. Then he walked on, still silent.

"Yarooooooh!" roared Bunter.

"Ha, ha, ha!"

The Removites went on to the form-room. Billy Bunter rolled after them, rubbing a fat head.

CHAPTER 12

THE ONLY WAY

PETER TODD came into No. 7 Study, and grinned at a fat figure sprawling in the armchair in that apartment. Billy Bunter did not grin. He blinked at Peter with a lack-lustre eye. His fat face registered despondency. Never, indeed, had the fattest member of the Greyfriars Remove been seen to look so pessimistic. A smear of jam round an extensive mouth seemed to indicate that he had found a little sticky consolation somewhere. But his look was gloomy. ʺ ʺ the troubles of a troubled universe, and a few over, had piled on Bunter's plump shoulders, he could hardly have looked gloomier.

All through that day, right up to tea time, Billy Bunter had lived, and moved, and had his being, in a world of silence. He was beginning to feel like Robinson Crusoe on his island. If he spoke to any Remove man, that Remove man turned his back—in silence. He was an outcast—a pariah—an Ishmael—barred by the form: to be barked at by Quelch in the form-room. And the worst of it was, that it was going on. One day in Coventry made Bunter feel like Cain of old that his punishment was greater than he could bear. And there were more days to come—days and days and days! It was an unnerving prospect.

"I say, Peter, old chap!" Bunter almost moaned.

Peter proceeded to clear books and papers off the study table, no doubt in preparation for tea. Bunter eyed him morosely.

"I say, Peter, I think you might stand by a pal!" he said. "You spoke up for me in the Rag yesterday, didn't you? You didn't believe that I snooped that tuck in Wharton's study, did you?"

Peter opened his lips: but closed them again. He nodded.

"Can't you speak?" hooted Bunter.

Peter shook his head.

"Look here, Peter, you ain't going to be down on a fellow like the other fellows, are you?" pleaded Bunter.

Nod!

"Can't you speak, even in the study?"

Shake!

"It's all right in the study!" urged Bunter. "Nobody will hear us, and if the fellows ask you, you can say you haven't spoken a word, see?"

"You fat villain!" ejaculated Peter, inadvertently finding his voice.

"Oh, really, Toddy——."

Peter opened his lips to say "Shut up!" but again closed them with the words unuttered.

" 'Tain't fair!" mumbled Bunter. "I never had that tuck in Wharton's study, Peter. Never touched a thing. I say, like some nuts, old chap? I've got some of the nuts left in my pocket."

Peter chuckled.

"Oh, snigger!" yapped Bunter. "This is what you call pally, I suppose, after all I've done for you. Talk about a serpent's gratitude being sharper than a toothless child——.'

"Ha, ha, ha!" roared Peter.

"Well, what are you cackling at now?" hooted Bunter, "that's how Shakespeare puts it: we've had it in English literature with Quelch."

"Didn't he say that it was sharper than a serpent's tooth to have a thankless child?" asked Peter, again inadvertently finding his voice.

"No, he didn't! You can't teach me Shakespeare, Peter Todd. Or—or—perhaps you're right, old chap," added Bunter, hastily. "You're an awfully clever chap, Peter—I—I've always admired your intellect, old fellow."

This tribute, however, elicited no further response from Peter.

" 'Tain't fair, I tell you!" resumed Bunter. "I wouldn't have touched a thing in Wharton's study, if I'd known there was going to be all this fuss. I—I say, Peter, I—I—I don't like being in Coventry. I say, old chap, you might stand by a pal when he's in a jam like this!" The dolorous fat Owl blinked reproachfully at Peter. "It—it's too jolly thick, you know."

Peter looked at him. He hesitated. But Peter had a

61

kind heart: and Bunter did undoubtedly look dismal and doleful.

"Now, look here, you fat ass," said Peter. "You've been sent to Coventry, and you jolly well asked for it: begged and prayed for it. Nobody's tuck is safe from your paws. You've always got off too jolly easily. But there's a limit—and you've stepped over it. It's the last drop in the cup, see? Every man in the Remove is fed up with you. You're in Coventry, and you're going to stay there till you learn to behave. There's one way out——."

"What's that?" asked Bunter, eagerly.

"The jolly old straight and narrow path," said Peter. "You've got to reform, see? You've got to leave other fellows' tuck alone——."

"I never touched——."

"And you've got to stop telling whoppers about it," went on Peter. "Fellows are fed up with your snooping and your fibbing. Cut it out, see? When you haven't snooped any tuck, or told any crammers, for a week or two, the fellows will come round. Not till then."

"Oh, crikey!" said Bunter.

His look, if possible, was more dolorous than before. No doubt Peter was right—the path of reform was the only way out of the cheerless solitude of Coventry. But the path of reform was an uphill trail that Billy Bunter's feet were very reluctant to tread.

"That's that!" said Peter, "and now shut up! Have you been snooping any tuck to-day?" he added.

"Oh, really, Toddy! As if I'm a fellow to snoop tuck? I never——."

"You look pretty sticky," said Peter, surveying him.

"I—I haven't had any jam, Toddy! I—I haven't tasted jam since—since yesterday!"

"Well, that may be true if you haven't washed since yesterday," admitted Peter, "and I daresay you haven't. You look it!"

"Beast! I—I mean, look here, old fellow—I—I haven't had any jam, and—and if any's gone from the cupboard——."

"What?"

"If—if it's gone, I don't know anything about it, Peter. I—I haven't looked into the cupboard, and—and I didn't

62

see any jam there, either, and I certainly never ate it with a tablespoon——."

Peter Todd gave him a look: and almost bounded to the study cupboard. Billy Bunter rose rather hastily from the armchair. He had a feeling that there was going to be trouble.

Peter stared into the cupboard. There was jam for tea in No. 7 Study—or had been! One glance was sufficient to reveal that it was a case of "had been". An empty jam-jar and a sticky tablespoon met Peter's gaze. He whirled round from the cupboard, with quite an alarming expression on his face.

Bunter backed hurriedly to the door.

"I—I—I say, Peter, I never—I—I—Yaroooh! Leave off kicking me, you beast! I say—oh, crikey! Wow!"

Peter's foot landed thrice before the fat Owl dodged out of the study.

He did not come back to No. 7 for tea. A dolorous Owl tea'd in hall, and as he disposed of what the juniors called "doorsteps and dish-water", perhaps he meditated upon Peter's sage advice. The path of reform was the way out of Coventry: unattractive as it was, it was the only way!

CHAPTER 13

A ONE-SIDED CONVERSATION

"Harry, old chap——!"

Harry Wharton glanced at a fat figure in the doorway of No. 1 Study, and opened his lips to say "Prep". He closed them again without saying "Prep", remembering that Billy Bunter was in Coventry.

"Franky, old fellow——!"

Frank Nugent grinned, but did not speak.

In No. 1 Study, they were sorting out their books for preparation. Bunter, certainly, ought to have been doing the same in No. 7. But he was not, apparently, thinking of prep. Much weightier matters were on his fat mind.

Bunter had been thinking!

This was rather unusual on Bunter's part. But circumstances had fairly driven him to that unaccustomed mental exertion. "Coventry" was getting on his fat nerves. Any way out of that cheerless solitude was welcome: even the toilsome and uphill path of reform. Not that Bunter realised that he deserved his sad fate. He was quite satisfied with himself. But he did realise that nobody else was satisfied: and that his manners and customs made for unpopularity. On that point Bunter was left in no doubt.

And he had come to a resolution: which, considering that he was Bunter, was really heroic. He was sentenced to Coventry till he learned to behave! He was going to behave! Somehow or other—he did not yet know how— he was going to resist the lure of other fellows' tuck! Henceforth it would be safe for any fellow to leave the door of his study cupboard wide open: even to leave a plate of jam tarts on his study table, or a bag of bull's-eyes on his mantelpiece. Such was the resolve to which the Owl of the Remove had been driven by a single day in Coventry.

"I've got something to say to you fellows," went on the fat Owl, blinking at the occupants of No. 1 Study. "I—I—I own up that I did snoop that spread yesterday."

"Oh, my hat!" ejaculated Harry Wharton, involuntarily, while Frank Nugent stared. Really, it was hardly necessary for Bunter to own up to what everybody knew. Still, it was a new departure on his part.

"And I'll jolly well square you fellows for it, too!" continued Bunter, "as soon as my postal order comes——."

"Ha, ha, ha!"

"Blessed if I can see anything to cackle at. I'm expecting a postal order—I've told you fellows so," yapped Bunter. "I've mentioned it more than once."

"Ha, ha, ha!"

"Well, I mean it, and you can cackle if you like," snapped Bunter, "a fellow can't say fairer than that. Now what have you got to say?"

Harry Wharton opened the table-drawer, groped in it, and picked out a stick of chalk. Bunter blinked at it, wondering what he wanted chalk for. He learned what it was for, as the captain of the Remove stepped to the glass over the fireplace, and chalked thereon:

"You silly ass!" howled Bunter. "Can't you speak?"
No reply.

"I say, you fellows, do be pals!" urged the distressed
Owl. "If you come round, Harry, old chap, the other fellows will follow your lead—they always do, blessed if I
know why. You're nobody in particular that I know of."

Harry Wharton took a duster in his left hand, and
wiped the glass. Then he chalked on it again:

THANKS

"Beast!" hooted Bunter. "I mean, look here, dear old
chap, can't you speak a word to a fellow?"
Harry Wharton chalked again:

NO

"I'm fed up with being in Coventry!" wailed Bunter—
a quite unnecessary statement. His woebegone aspect revealed only too clearly that he was fed up to his fat chin.
"I—I say, you fellows, I—I—I want you to let me off."
Silence.

"Not that I've done anything," added Bunter; the old
Bunter again for a moment. "If you fellows were up to
my mark, you'd be a jolly good deal better than you jolly
well ain't, so yah."
Wharton chalked again:

HOOK IT

"Oh, really, Wharton! Look here, I'll do anything you
jolly well like," gasped the dolorous Owl. "Not that I care,
you know! I jolly well don't care."
The chalk came into use again:

YOU LOOK IT

"Well, look here, what do you want me to do?" pleaded
Bunter. "I—I'll do anything you like, there!"
Wharton chalked once more:

C

"I—I—I'm going to," groaned Bunter. "If you mean about the tuck—is that what you mean?"

Chalk once more:

THAT'S IT

"I—I—I'll never snoop tuck again, honest Injun. Not that I ever did, you know—I—I mean, I—I won't do it any more! There!"

Chalk again:

STICK TO THAT

"I—I—I mean it!" mumbled Bunter. "You—you fellows could leave tons of tuck in your study, and I—I wouldn't touch it. If that's all, it's all right. Now you can jolly well chuck that rot about Coventry, see?"

Wharton wielded the chalk:

NOT YET

"Beast! I mean, how long are you going to keep it up?" hooted Bunter. "I tell you I ain't going to snoop tuck any more. Ain't that what you want? When are you going to call it off, then?"

The reply was chalked on the glass:

NEXT WEEK—PERHAPS!

"Oh, lor'!" groaned Bunter.

The chalk continued:

IF YOU KEEP IT UP

Billy Bunter blinked sadly at that reply. He had made up his fat mind that honesty was the best policy. Somehow or other he was going to keep his fat fingers from picking and stealing: not, sad to relate, because his fat conscience was at work, but because he was fed up with the cold shades of Coventry. But whether he would be able to keep it up was, he could not help realising, dubious. The lure of tuck was strong: and though the spirit perhaps was willing, the flesh was decidedly weak. Certainly a Bunter who refrained from helping himself to other fellows' tuck would be a new Bunter, hardly recognisable as William George Bunter of the Greyfriars Remove.

Wharton added two more words with the chalk:

NOW TRAVEL

"I—I say, you fellows, I—I'm going to keep it up!" mumbled Bunter. "If—if there's any tuck missing in any fellow's study, it—it won't be me. What are you grinning at, you beasts?"

The beasts did not explain what they were grinning at. But Wharton chalked on the glass again:

GET OUT!

"Beast!" roared Bunter. "Can't you speak, you silly ass, instead of chalking on that glass, you blithering idiot?" Wharton chalked once more:

PREP

"Blow prep!" hooted Bunter. "Bother prep! I ain't worrying about prep. Now, look here, you fellows——."

Harry Wharton laid down the chalk. Apparently that one-sided conversation was at an end. He picked up a cushion. Prep had to be done, whether Bunter was worrying about it or not.

"Look here, you beast, if you chuck that cushion at me——."

Whiz!

"Yoo-hoop!"

Billy Bunter disappeared from the doorway, accompanied by the cushion. A yell floated back as he disappeared. After which, Harry Wharton and Frank Nugent were able to settle down to prep, untroubled further by a dismal and doleful fat Owl.

CHAPTER 14

PUT TO THE TEST

"POOR old Bunter!" said Bob Cherry.

"Bow-wow!" grunted Johnny Bull.

Bob's look was commiserating. His tender heart was touched, as he glanced at a fat dolorous face in the quad, in the Friday morning break. Johnny, it seemed, was made of sterner stuff.

"He doesn't look as if he's enjoying life!" remarked Bob.

"Why should he?" grunted Johnny.

"The joyfulness of the esteemed Bunter is not great," remarked Hurree Jamset Ram Singh, "but the learnfulness to behave is a necessary evil and a sine qua non, my absurd Bob."

Harry Wharton laughed.

"I fancy Bunter's learning already," he said. "He told us in the study last night that he's turning over a new leaf —and there hasn't been any tuck missing in the studies, that I've heard of."

"Well, if he means that——!" said Bob.

"If!" grinned Nugent.

"The fat tick would say anything, to crawl out of Coventry," said Johnny Bull. "He couldn't tell the truth, if he tried. Has any fellow ever heard him try?"

"Well, he's a born idiot, you know," said Bob, in extenuation. "Blessed if I like to see any chap looking down in the mouth. Hallo, hallo, hallo, here he comes."

Billy Bunter rolled over to the Famous Five.

"I say, you fellows——!" he began.

Bob Cherry opened his lips: but Johnny gave him a glare, and he closed them again. Billy Bunter's blink was really quite pathetic: but Bunter was in Coventry for his many sins, and there he was staying.

"I say, you fellows ain't keeping it up, are you, with an old pal?" asked the dismal Owl.

No reply.

68

"I say, I've been disappointed about a postal order," went on Bunter. "I was expecting it to-day—it's from one of my titled relations, you know—but—but it hasn't come. If you fellows could lend me——."

Five fellows walked away.

The hapless Owl was left blinking after them, with a doleful and pessimistic blink. Out of hearing, Bob remarked once more:

"Poor old Bunter!"

"Rot!" grunted Johnny Bull.

"Well, look here, we've sent him to Coventry to teach him a lesson," said Bob. "If he's learned it already——."

"Try him!" said Johnny, sarcastically. "Leave a jam tart where he can see it, and see what will happen."

"By gum!" said Bob. "So I will! Put him to the jolly old test, what? If he comes through all right, we'll let him off, what?"

"If!" snorted Johnny.

"The if-fulness is terrific."

"Well, we'll jolly well see!" said Bob. "Every chap's entitled to be given a chance. Come into the tuck-shop."

"But what——?" asked Nugent.

"Oh, come on! Break doesn't last for ever."

"Oh, all right."

The Famous Five walked into the school shop, where a good many fellows were gathered, in break. Billy Bunter's eyes and spectacles followed them mournfully. The tuck-shop had a magnetic attraction for Bunter, but it was of no use for him to join the crowd there: once more he had been disappointed about a postal order, and he was in his usual stony state: and in present circumstances no Remove man was likely to accede, or even reply, to a request for a small loan to tide him till that postal order came. Bunter could only blink at the little diamond-paned window and feast his eyes, as that was the only feast available.

Two or three minutes later, Bob Cherry came out of the tuck-shop, leaving his friends within. He had a paper-bag in his hand, and Bunter's eyes and spectacles lingered on it: he could guess what it contained—jam-tarts, or doughnuts, or something equally attractive in the sticky line.

Bob did not seem to observe the fat Owl blinking at him in the offing. He crossed over to the big tree that stood opposite the tuck-shop, round the trunk of which was an old oaken bench. On that bench he sat down, laying the bag down beside him. Apparently he was going to dispose of those sticky things in the open air.

But some sudden thought seemed to occur to him, for he rose from the bench, and went back into the tuck-shop. The bag remained where he had laid it.

Bunter blinked after him—and then blinked at the paper-bag on the bench. Apparently Bob had forgotten it.

The fat Owl expected him to emerge again. But he did not emerge. That paper-bag, with the delightful things it contained, lay deserted, on the bench under the shady old elm.

"Oh!" breathed Bunter.

In a casual sort of way, he moved nearer to the tree. If Harry Wharton and Co, came out, he was prepared to roll on his way, as if he hadn't noticed the bag on the bench at all. But if they did not come out——.

They did not come out! That they were gathered just inside the door of the tuck-shop, watching him through the upper half of that door, which was of glass, Bunter was not aware. Bunter's thoughts were concentrated on that deserted paper-bag.

He reached it. A fat hand stretched out to it.

Inside the tuck-shop, Johnny Bull gave a snort, Harry Wharton laughed, Frank Nugent and Hurree Jamset Ram Singh grinned, and Bob Cherry looked worried. He was putting the fat Owl of the Remove to the test, and hoped that he would pass the test successfully. It did not look like it, however!

"Well?" inquired Johnny Bull, sarcastically.

"Oh! Look!" breathed Bob.

To the surprise of the Famous Five, the fat hand did not immediately clutch up the paper-bag. It was stretched out towards it—but it stopped, and was slowly withdrawn. Bunter was hesitating. Never in his fat career had Billy Bunter, in such circumstances, hesitated before. But he was hesitating now. Whether it was the effect of Coventry, and the desire to emerge from that cheerless abode, or whether Bunter's fat conscience had really been awakened on the subject of "mine" and "thine", it was an undoubted fact that the fat Owl was hesitating to clutch up that bag of sticky delight.

The chums of the Remove watched, quite curious to know what was going to happen. If Bunter resisted that lure, it was an indubitable sign that reform had set in, and that a sojourn in Coventry had produced the desired effect.

"He's going! " breathed Bob.

Bunter took a step onward—a single step—leaving the bag on the bench. He was resisting the temptation.

But it was, alas, only a single step that was taken by the fat Owl. The next moment, he retraced it.

Again the fat hand was stretched out to the bag. This time contact was established.

"Oh! " murmured Bob.

Grunt from Johnny Bull.

Bunter clutched the bag on the bench. But there was yet another pause. He released it again, and blinked round him cautiously through his big spectacles. Then he blinked at the bag. Apparently a last struggle was going on within his podgy breast. Then he made a sudden clutch at the paper-bag, whipped it up from the bench, tucked it under a fat arm and rolled rapidly away.

The die was cast! It was a still unreformed Bunter that rolled off with the paper-bag, and disappeared to the distance.

"Well?" asked Johnny Bull, in the same sarcastic tone.

"That fat villain! " said Bob.

"Looks like turning over a new leaf! " grinned Nugent.

"The lookfulness is not terrific," chuckled Hurree Jamset Ram Singh.

"Did you really think he would leave that bag alone, Bob?" asked Harry Wharton, laughing.

"Well, I hoped he would," said Bob. "Give every fellow a chance, you know. But as it's turned out, it's lucky I only put an old cabbage in that bag, isn't it?"

"Ha, ha, ha! "

The chums of the Remove laughed loud and long. But Billy Bunter, when in a secluded corner, safe from all eyes, he opened that bag, prepared to devour jam-tarts, or doughnuts, or éclairs, or whatsoever it contained in the way of tuck, did not feel like laughing. No jam-tarts, no doughnuts, no éclairs, met his startled gaze. What met it was a very ancient cabbage, at which the fat Owl blinked with his eyes almost bulging through his spectacles. Billy Bunter could eat almost anything: but even Billy Bunter

71

could not eat that venerable and disused cabbage. He gave it a devastating blink, hurled it to the earth, and rolled away with feelings too deep for words.

CHAPTER 15

DOGGO!

"OH!" breathed Billy Bunter.

It was quite an interesting little scene, on the tow-path by the flowing waters of the Sark. Billy Bunter was interested in that scene. But he preferred to remain an unseen spectator. He backed promptly behind a tree in the wood that bordered the tow-path.

After class, Bunter was taking a walk abroad.

Exercise did not appeal very much to Bunter. Frowsing was more in his line. He did not feel, like Bob Cherry, the insistent call of the open spaces. A walk by the shining Sark in the autumn sunshine, in the keen fresh air from the sea, was really better for him, and really more enjoyable, than wedging his fat person into an armchair before the fire in the Rag. Bunter would have preferred the armchair before the fire. Nevertheless, there he was, taking a walk abroad. In the Rag he was also in "Coventry"; and he was quite tired of deaf ears and unseeing eyes. It was a relief to get away from Coventry for a while, if only by taking a walk on his solitary own.

But a short walk was enough for Bunter. At quite a brief distance he had come to a stop, and was leaning his fat shoulders on a tree-trunk, to rest his fat limbs, when Skinner passed him, going up the tow-path.

Skinner grinned as he passed, and Bunter gave him an angry blink in exchange for his grin. But Skinner only grinned, and did not speak. Bob Cherry might feel compassion for the disconsolate Owl, in spite of all his sins of omission and commission: but Harold Skinner had no sympathy to waste on a lame duck. He passed Bunter by, and walked on up the river, the fat Owl's eyes and spectacles following him as he went.

And then it happened.

72

Two fellows came in sight from the opposite direction: Ponsonby and Gadsby, of the Fourth Form at Highcliffe. The tow-path was rather winding, and they did not come in sight till they were quite near. They almost ran into Skinner, who came to a sudden stop. And it was then that Billy Bunter cautiously backed behind the tree against which he had been leaning.

There were fellows at Highcliffe who were good friends with Greyfriars fellows: but Pon and Co. were not among them. When Pon and his pals came across Greyfriars fellows, a "rag" was very likely to ensue. Billy Bunter was deeply thankful that he had not walked on further, and fallen in with the Highcliffians. He would have fallen an easy victim: and at the very least, Pon would have stuffed his cap down his back, or pitched it into a high tree, and perhaps dipped his fat face into the Sark. Pon was always out for mischief.

But though he was thankful personally that he had not fallen in with the Highcliffians, he was rather glad that Skinner had. Skinner was more than welcome to the attentions of Pon and Co.

Having backed behind the tree, Bunter watched, and grinned. He was ready to dodge away through the wood if the enemy spotted him. But they had not seen him, and all their attention was given to Skinner.

"Greyfriars cad!" remarked Ponsonby, by way of a pleasant beginning. He stopped directly in Skinner's path, and Skinner backed away a pace or two. Ponsonby and Gadsby, grinning, followed him up.

"Look here——!" muttered Skinner. "Let me pass." He backed further away: and again the Highcliffians followed up.

"In a hurry?" smiled Gadsby.

"Yes, I—I'm rather in a hurry," mumbled Skinner, uneasily: and he made an attempt to walk round the two Highcliffe juniors. They side-stepped at once to intercept him, and he had to stop again.

Billy Bunter's grin widened, as he watched from behind the tree at a little distance. Something was coming to Skinner, that was evident. Only a few minutes ago, he had passed Bunter, grinning. Now it was Bunter's turn to grin.

Gadsby made a snatch at Skinner's cap. Skinner jumped away and eluded the snatch: but the next moment it was jerked from his head by Ponsonby. Pon waved it in the air, laughing.

"Look here, give me my cap!" howled Skinner.

"Come and take it!" invited Ponsonby.

Skinner cast a glance back along the tow-path. Little as he liked the Famous Five, he would have been happy to see some member of that cheery company coming up the river. In which case, Ponsonby would probably have become quite lamb-like in a moment. He had no use for hard punching.

But there was no one on the tow-path to be seen. And Skinner was not the man for hard punches. He eyed Ponsonby rather like a cat, but he made no attempt to recapture his cap. Pon waved it in his left, his right ready for a punch if Skinner came on. But Skinner did not come on.

"You cheeky rotter!" muttered Skinner. Gladly he would have rushed on the two Highcliffians, hitting out right and left. Instead of which, he backed a little further away, as they came nearer.

"They never wash at Greyfriars," went on the cheery Pon. "What about giving him a wash, Gaddy?"

"Good egg!" said Gaddy, heartily. "Duck his head!"

Skinner jumped back. His obvious funk encouraged the two young rascals, and they closed in on him, and grasped him. Even Skinner put up a struggle as they hustled him to the river's margin, with the intention of ducking his head in the Sark.

Billy Bunter watched breathlessly.

What almost any other Remove man would have done in his place, the fat Owl was aware. Harry Wharton, or Squiff, or Tom Brown, or Bob Cherry, or almost any Removite, would have rushed to Skinner's aid. But William George Bunter was no fighting-man. Had he rushed boldly into the fray, no doubt he would have captured a tremendous punching from Pon and Gaddy: but so plucky an exploit might very probably have set him right with the Remove. Fellows would hardly have kept him in "Coventry" had he returned to the school covered with the glorious signs of heroic combat against the enemy. Really, it was a chance for the ostracised Owl if he had taken advantage of it.

But he didn't! Glory, certainly, he would have liked:

74

but he did not want the punches. Bunter's cue was to remain "doggo".

He remained in cover behind the tree, and allowed that opportunity like the sunbeams to pass him by.

Skinner was struggling desperately as the grinning Highcliffians hustled and dragged him down to the water, to duck his head. Even Billy Bunter felt a qualm. As a Greyfriars man, it was up to him to take a hand in the unequal struggle. He even thought of doing so. But second thoughts, not always the best, prevailed: and he remained where he was, a breathless and interested spectator.

Splash!

Skinner's head went in.

"Oooooooogh!" spluttered Skinner.

"Ha, ha, ha!" roared Pon and Gaddy.

Skinner's head came up drenched and dripping. Before it could be ducked again, he gave a frantic wrench, and tore himself loose. The next moment Pon and Gaddy were grabbing at him: but a moment was enough for Skinner, and he flew. Like a hare he tore back along the tow-path. In two seconds he passed Bunter's tree, and went racing on, leaving the two young rascals of Highcliffe yelling with laughter.

"Don't you want your cap?" shouted Ponsonby, waving it in the air.

Skinner did not answer. He was not bothering about his cap. He tore on and vanished.

Ponsonby, laughing, tossed the Greyfriars cap carelessly away in the grass. Then he walked on with Gaddy, both of them laughing: evidently highly entertained by Skinner's ducking, and his frantic flight.

Billy Bunter hugged cover very closely as they walked past his tree. He did not want to go through Skinner's experience at their hands.

But the thick trunk hid him: and they passed on without a suspicion that a fat Greyfriars junior was lurking there.

Anxiously he peered round the trunk through his big spectacles, watching their backs till they disappeared down the river.

"Oh, crikey!" murmured Bunter.

He was relieved to see the last of the Highcliffe pair. Neither had he any sympathy to waste on Skinner, who, in Bunter's opinion at least, deserved all that he had received, for grinning at a fellow in Coventry. But he was not feeling quite at ease in his fat mind.

Billy Bunter's self-esteem was very considerable. If there was one person whom he deeply and sincerely admired, that person was William George Bunter of the Greyfriars Remove. Nevertheless, he could not feel, at the moment, quite so self-satisfied as was his wont.

Even Billy Bunter couldn't feel proud of the fact that he had hugged cover behind a tree, while a Greyfriars man was ragged, two to one, by the Highcliffe enemy. If the Remove fellows knew, they would call him a funk: and his popularity, already at a low ebb, would be right down to zero. There would be less chance than ever of emerging from Coventry.

Bunter, certainly, had no idea of relating that somewhat inglorious episode. But what about Skinner? Skinner had passed him, only a minute or two before he ran into the Highcliffians: Skinner knew that he had been at hand. No doubt he had forgotten him, in the excitement of the shindy with Pon and Gaddy: but he would remember. It would be just like Skinner, Bunter reflected bitterly, to make out that a fellow was a funk—Skinner was a fellow to give another fellow a kick when he was down!

"Oh, lor'!" mumbled the fat Owl.

He emerged dismally from cover, as soon as he was quite, quite sure that the coast was clear. That episode was going to make matters worse for him, when he rolled back to Greyfriars. It was a pessimistic prospect, and Bunter's fat face registered despondency as he rolled on his way.

As he passed Skinner's cap, lying in the grass where Pon had thrown it, he paused, to kick it into the thicket bordering the tow-path. But he paused again, as he was about to deliver the kick.

A glimmer came into the little round eyes behind the big round spectacles. A sudden thought had flashed into his fat brain.

"Oh, gum!" ejaculated Bunter: and then he chuckled, "He, he, he!"

Instead of kicking the cap into the thicket, he cast a cautious blink up and down the tow-path, and then picked it up and tucked it under his jacket. He grinned, an exten-

76

sive grin that extended almost from one fat ear to the other.

Like many obtuse persons, Bunter had a vein of artfulness in him. And the idea that had germinated in his fat brain was undoubtedly remarkably artful. It was, in Bunter's own estimation, a bright idea—indeed a brilliant one.

Skinner had fled, leaving that trophy in the hands of the enemy. Bunter had recaptured it! Certainly, the recapture had been quite a simple matter—he had only had to stoop and pick it up. But who was going to know that, unless Bunter chose to tell?

"He, he, he!" chuckled Bunter.

He rolled on his way, with Skinner's cap under his jacket. His bright idea expanded and amplified in his fat brain as he rolled. He thought it out in all its details, and was satisfied with it. Billy Bunter was in Coventry, and it had seemed that only the unattractive path of reform could lead him out of it. Now he fancied that he had found an easier way. Skinner could tell the fellows, if he liked, that Bunter had been skulking and funking: Bunter had a very different story to tell. This, he hoped, was going to set him right with the Remove!

It remained to be seen whether that hope was well-founded.

CHAPTER 16

BILLY BUNTER'S BLACK EYE

"Hallo, hallo, hallo!"

"Bunter——!"

"What——?"

"Where did you pick up that eye?"

It was quite a buzz in the Rag, as Billy Bunter rolled into that apartment. Every fellow there stared at him.

They quite forgot that Bunter was in Coventry.

It was close on lock-ups when the fat Owl rolled in. Skinner had long been in, and all the fellows knew that he had been collared and ducked by the Highcliffe enemy,

77

two to one: while that fat funk, Bunter, quite near the spot, had not chosen to lend a hand. Bunter was, in fact, the topic in the Rag, when he put in his belated appearance.

Kind-hearted fellows like Bob Cherry had already begun to relent towards the fat Owl. But this, so to speak, put the lid on! Even the kind-hearted Bob was feeling more disposed now to boot him than to let him out of Coventry. Nobody expected Bunter to be of the stuff of which heroes are made: but to hunt cover while a Greyfriars man was ragged by the enemy, two to one, was the limit. Bunter could not possibly have been more unpopular. And then——!

Every eye was on him, as he rolled into the Rag! His aspect struck every fellow there! It was, indeed, striking! One of Bunter's eyes was as black as the ace of spades!

Black eyes were uncommon at Greyfriars. Occasionally, very occasionally, some fellow happened to collect one. Now it seemed that Bunter had collected one—and it was a striking specimen. Never had a black eye been blacker. It was an eye that leaped to all other eyes. Like the sable arms of the rugged Pyrrhus, it did the night resemble.

Bunter blinked at a staring crowd of juniors. Then he squeaked:

"I say, you fellows! Is Skinner here?"

"I'm here, you fat funk," snapped Skinner, "and I'm jolly well going to boot you for not lending me a hand when those Highcliffe cads ducked my napper."

"Here's your cap."

"Wha—a—t?"

Billy Bunter hooked out a Greyfriars cap from under his jacket, and tossed it across to Skinner.

Skinner stared at it blankly and it fell to the floor at his feet.

"Skinner's cap?" said Bob Cherry, staring. "Skinner told us that Pon bagged his cap——."

"I got it back," said Bunter.

"You got it back!" roared Bob. "And Pon let you!"

"I fancy he'd had enough when I was done with him!" said Bunter, calmly. "I wasn't going to let those Highcliffe cads walk off a Greyfriars cap."

"Oh, my hat!"

"Great pip!"

"The great-pipfulness is terrific."

"Mean to say you tackled Pon, and made him hand over Skinner's cap?" gasped Johnny Bull.

"He didn't hand it to me on a plate!" answered Bunter, sarcastically. "It was pretty tough going, I can tell you, with the two of them: but I got that cap back all right."

"Gammon!" snarled Skinner. "That fat funk was skulking while those Highcliffe cads ragged me—catch him tackling Pon and Gadsby! That isn't my cap—it's all gammon."

Frank Nugent picked up the cap.

"It's yours, Skinner," he said.

"I tell you——."

"Your name's in it."

"Oh!" Skinner took the cap, and looked inside it. All Greyfriars fellows had to have their names in their caps. And there was "H. Skinner" staring him in the face. Undoubtedly it was his cap: the cap he had left in Cecil Ponsonby's hands when he fled from the enemy. Skinner was quite taken aback. But he rallied. "I daresay Pon chucked it away, and that fat spoofer picked it up——."

"Oh, really, Skinner——."

"He seems to have picked up a black eye along with it," said Peter Todd, regarding his fat study-mate with wonder. "Look here, Bunter, tell us what's happened——."

"Cough it up, Bunter," said Harry Wharton.

"There ain't much to tell, so far as I know," answered Bunter, carelessly. "I was on the tow-path, and I saw Skinner running away from those Highcliffe chaps——."

"They were two to one!" howled Skinner, "and——."

"We've heard that!" snorted Johnny Bull. "Now let's hear what Bunter's got to say."

"Well, I wasn't going to let Ponsonby keep that cap, and make out that we're all funks here," said Bunter. "Not Greyfriars style, you know. I just put my specs. in my pocket, and pushed back my cuffs, and walked up to them, and said, 'Look here, you Highcliffe rotter, give me that cap'. Just like that."

"I can see you doing it!" jeered Skinner.

"Shut up, Skinner."

"Carry on, old fat man."

"Well, of course, there was a scrap," said Bunter. "I

79

got some hard knocks—I—I believe my eye's black——."

"I believe it is!" chuckled Bob Cherry.

"The believefulness is terrific."

"Couldn't be blacker," grinned Vernon-Smith. "You'll have to explain that jolly old eye to Quelch, when he sees it."

"Well, Quelch won't blame a chap for getting a Greyfriars cap back from a fellow who snatched it," said Bunter. "He wouldn't expect a fellow to be a funk like Skinner——!"

"You fat frump——!" hissed Skinner.

"I got a black eye," said Bunter. "Well, I don't care! I can stand it. I wasn't going to let a Highcliffe cad walk off with a Greyfriars cap! Not me! You'd have done the same, Bob."

"I jolly well would!" agreed Bob Cherry. "But—but——." He stared at the fat Owl. Bunter as a bold fighting-man, recklessly tackling odds in desperate combat, was quite a new Bunter—a very unexpected Bunter. Indeed, but for the black eye, the Remove fellows would have believed, like Skinner, that Pon had thrown away the captured cap, and that Bunter had happened to pick it up. But there was the black eye! That indubitable sign of combat told its own tale—or at least appeared to do so. A fellow did not get a black eye picking up a cap that had been thrown away! Desperate combat was indicated!

"Those Highcliffe chaps haven't much pluck, you know," said Bunter. "They soon had enough! If they'd had my pluck——."

"Oh!"

"——or anything like it, they could have piled on me and knocked me out," admitted Bunter, "but a few good punches were enough for them. I can tell you they were glad enough to clear off and leave me the cap. I can tell you fellows that I fought like a—a—a lion——."

"You would!" grinned Smithy.

"Well, there's the cap!" said Bunter. "I got it back all right! I—I think I'll go and bathe this eye now—it feels pretty bad——."

"It must, if it feels as bad as it looks!" said Bob. "Better go to the matron and ask her if she can do something for it."

"Oh, I can stand it," said Bunter, carelessly, "I'm not

made of putty—I can stand a knock or two! Still, I think I'll go and bathe it a bit."

"I'll come with you, old chap," said Peter Todd: much more cordially than he was accustomed to speak to his fat study-mate.

"Eh? Oh! No, don't you bother," said Bunter, hastily: and he rolled out of the Rag leaving the crowd of fellows there in a buzz.

"Well," said Bob Cherry, "who'd have thought it!"

"Wonders will never cease!" said Frank Nugent, laughing. "Fancy Bunter tackling Pon—and Gaddy too——!"

"Did he?" sneered Skinner.

"Where do you think he got that black eye?" demanded Bob. "Picked it up along with the cap? You shut up, Skinner! You let Pon walk off with a Greyfriars cap, and you didn't stop to collect a black eye——."

"I tell you——."

"Oh, pack it up! Look here, you men," said Bob. "Bunter's done a jolly plucky thing, and I for one think it's time he was let out of Coventry."

"Hear, hear!" said Nugent.

"The hear-hearfulness is terrific."

"I—I suppose he isn't pulling our leg," said the Bounder, thoughtfully.

"Oh, don't be a rotter, Smithy! A fellow doesn't get a black eye without a jolly good punch in it," said Bob, warmly. "Bunter's out of Coventry as far as I'm concerned, at any rate."

"And so say all of us!" said Harry Wharton, laughing. "Bunter's let off! You go and tell him so, Toddy."

"What-ho!" agreed Peter.

And Peter Todd went up after his fat study-mate. But he did not find Bunter bathing that black eye. Bathing a black eye may be beneficial: but William George Bunter had excellent reasons, known only to himself, for taking exceeding care not to bathe that particular black eye.

CHAPTER 17

ALL RIGHT FOR BUNTER

"PREP, old man!" said Peter Todd, quite gently.

"Old man" was quite an unaccustomed form of address from Peter and his fat study-mate. Neither was he accustomed to speak in gentle tones when Billy Bunter sprawled in the study armchair while the other occupants of No. 7 worked at prep.

But circumstances alter cases.

It was more usual for Toddy's remarks to be emphatic and personal: such as "Get a move on, you fat slacker!" or "Don't frowst, you lazy fathead;" And of late he had not spoken to the ostracised Owl at all. But now there was a change in No. 7 Study.

The black eye had done it.

That black eye was very conspicuous as Bunter sprawled in the armchair. It had a disarming effect on Peter.

For the first time—the very first time in history—William George Bunter was a credit to the study!

Hitherto, Peter had had a deplorably poor opinion of Bunter. Not only was he an unscrupulous raider of other fellows' tuck: not only was he a fibber compared with whom Baron Munchausen might have been called almost truthful: but only too often had he displayed funk. He had been seen in flight from Tubb of the Third. He had had his cap knocked off in quad by Nugent minor of the Second. Any fellow in the Remove would have expected Bunter to dodge round the nearest corner at the mere sight of Ponsonby of Highcliffe. It was clear now—or at least seemed clear—that Bunter had not had justice.

For there was the black eye!

Every fellow agreed that only a very hefty punch in the eye could have produced such midnight blackness. A fellow who could and would stand up to a hefty punch in the eye was no funk. Somewhere under Billy Bunter's layers of fat lurked a spot of pluck—indeed, quite a large spot.

Skinner had fled from the Highcliffians, leaving a Grey-friars cap as a trophy in the hands of the enemy, with the excuse that they had been two to one. Two to one had not deterred Bunter! Had he not recaptured the trophy, and a startling black eye along with it?

It was all the more impressive, because it was so very unexpected. Had Billy Bunter, like the elder Hamlet, possessed an eye like Mars, to threaten and command, it could not have produced more effect on the Remove fellows—not so much, in fact, as a discoloured eye collected in combat with the Highcliffe enemy.

Heedless of Peter's gentle admonition, Bunter sprawled in the armchair. He passed a fat hand over his black eye, as Peter looked at him, as if he had a pain there. It was in fact noticeable that whenever the fat Owl found eyes on him, his fat hand came up to that eye. Really it was almost as if he did not want it subjected to too close an inspection!

But if that discoloured eye was painful, the damage did not seem to affect Bunter's spirits. He was quite cheerful: no doubt because he was now well out of that dismal dwelling, Coventry. Every now and then, in fact, a fat grin illuminated his plump visage.

"Better get on with it, old chap," said Peter, still in the same gentle tone. "I'll lend you a hand with it."

"I think I'll chance it with Quelch in the morning, Toddy." The armchair, as often happened, appealed to Billy Bunter with a stronger appeal than prep. "I— I I don't feel like mugging up Virgil, with—with this eye, you know."

"That won't do for Quelch," said Peter.

"Oh, blow Quelch."

"He won't be pleased to see a black eye in his form," said Peter. "Better not skew in con as well."

"I— I —I suppose Quelch will notice it, in form!" said Bunter, apparently a little uneasy on that point.

"Sort of!" grinned Peter. "It's the blackest eye I've ever seen—black as soot——."

"As—as—as what, Peter?" gasped Bunter.

"Soot! My dear chap, that eye could be seen a mile off. It doesn't seem to be swollen——." Toddy scanned the black eye, and Bunter's fat hand came up to it once more, "but it's jolly black—Pon or Gaddy must have given you no end of a punch. Which of them was it?"

"Eh? I—I don't know—I—I mean, it was Pon! Pon put up rather a scrap," said Bunter. "He's bigger than I am, you know——."

"Endways," agreed Peter, "not sideways."

"Oh, really, Toddy! Well, I jolly well tackled him, and got in two or three jolly good ones, and he went down. And then Gaddy got me in the eye——."

"Eh? Didn't you say it was Pon?"

"Oh! Did I? Oh! Yes—I—I mean Pon! He got me in the eye—right in the eye you know! But did I care! Not me! I went for the pair of them, and they soon had enough, I can tell you."

"Beats me!" said Peter. "Old Bob could knock out the pair of them, easy: but you must have had no end of a tussle——."

"Oh, really, Toddy! If you'd seen me tackling them——."

"I wish I had!" said Peter.

"Oh! Yes! I—I wish you had, Peter! It was some scrap, I can tell you! It—it was worth seeing! I knocked them right and left! I said, 'Have you had enough, you Highcliffe cads?' Those very words! They'd had enough, Toddy. But—but I say, think Quelch will ask me about this eye? Smithy said he would, but——."

"Of course he will! Beaks don't like black eyes in their forms! Shouldn't wonder if he had something to say at Highcliffe about it."

"Oh, crikey!"

"You know what beaks are," said Peter. "I don't see how Quelchy can blame you for getting a Greyfriars cap back from those cads—you needn't worry, old chap. But he might ring up Highcliffe about two fellows setting on one and handing out a black eye——. What's the matter, Bunter?"

Peter stared at Bunter! The fat Owl had heaved himself upright in the armchair, and was blinking at him in consternation.

"Oh, lor'!" gasped Bunter. "Think—think—think Quelch might—might—might do that, Peter?"

"Why shouldn't he?"

"Oh, crikey!"

"Don't you worry, old fat man—you'll come through

it all right!" said Peter, reassuringly. "You got the black eye, you know."

"But—but—oh, lor' I—I don't want a lot of fuss with Highcliffe—I—I don't want to land those fellows in a row, Peter. I—I think I—I'll tell Quelch that I got this black eye running into something—suppose I—I ran into a tree, see?"

"You fat Ananias——."

"Oh, really Toddy——. I—I ain't going to land Pon and Gaddy in a row with their beak—'tain't playing the game!" said Bunter. "I shall stuff Quelch about it, if—if—if he notices it——."

"No 'if' about that," said Peter. "Quelch will spot that eye first thing in form, if he doesn't spot it sooner."

"It—it might be gone, Toddy——."

"Fathead! It won't be gone in a week, from the look of it."

"It—it might be cured quite—quite suddenly!" mumbled Bunter.

"Rot!" said Peter. "Black eyes can't be washed off, you fat chump! You've got that eye for a week! Now what about prep?"

"Blow prep!" said Bunter, irritably.

The fat Owl remained in the armchair while Toddy and Tom Dutton got through prep. It was not only laziness that supervened. Bunter seemed to be worried about something. Possibly he had strong personal reasons for feeling alarmed at the suggestion that that black eye might be reported at Highcliffe as the foul work of Pon and Gaddy! Undoubtedly, he was uneasy.

Prep over, Peter rose and put away his books. There was a tramp of feet in the passage, a thump at the door of No. 7, and it flew open. Five cheery faces looked into the study.

"Hallo, hallo, hallo!" roared Bob Cherry. "How's the jolly old eye, Bunter?"

"Oh! Pretty bad!" said Bunter. A fat hand passed over the black eye, as all the Famous Five looked at it. "Bit painful, you know——."

"Must be," said Frank Nugent. "You had a knock, and no mistake. Why not go to Mrs. Kebble? She might be able to do something."

"That's all right," said Bunter breezily. "I don't want

to make a fuss. I never was a chap to make a fuss about a knock or two, as you fellows know."

"Oh, my hat! " said Johnny Bull, involuntarily.

"Oh, really, Bull——."

"Coming down, old fat man?" asked Harry Wharton.

Bunter almost purred, like a plump cat. Coventry, clearly, was a thing of the past, when that cheery company called for him to go down after prep. And it was quite an attractive idea to march into the Rag in that distinguished company—a man they delighted to honour. He heaved himself out of the armchair.

"Coming! " he said.

And he came.

He marched off cheerily with Harry Wharton and Co., followed by Toddy and Dutton. Vernon-Smith and Tom Redwing joined them in the passage: Ogilvy and Squiff and Tom Brown and Lord Mauleverer on the landing: two or three other fellows on the staircase. It was quite a party. Skinner scowled at the fat Owl in the Rag, but nobody minded Skinner. It was all right for Bunter now: never had such happy results accrued from the acquisition of a black eye. Billy Bunter's fat face wore a wide grin of satisfaction: and it was a cheerful Owl that rolled off to the Remove dormitory that night.

CHAPTER 18

SPOOF!

"BUNTER!"

"Oh! Yes, sir."

"It appears that you have been fighting, Bunter."

Bunter did not immediately reply.

Peter Todd gave him an encouraging look. Bunter did not even see it. His eyes and spectacles were fixed rather uneasily on his form-master.

It was form in the morning. In the Remove form-room, Mr. Quelch's gimlet eye was fixed on Bunter's black one. Bunter could hardly have hoped that such an adornment would escape Mr. Quelch's notice. Quelch had not,

"It appears that you have been fighting, Bunter."
Bunter did not immediately reply.

apparently, observed it till the Remove came into form: possibly the artful fat Owl had been keeping out of his way as long as he could. But he observed it now: and the look he gave it, and its proprietor, was somewhat grim.

Quelch knew, of course, that schoolboys would sometimes get exc'ted, and sometimes row and rag, and even punch one another on occasion. But a black eye was over the limit: Greyfriars fellows were not expected to go about adorned with discoloured eyes. This was a matter into which Quelch had to inquire. Bunter could not help being aware that it had to come. No Remove fellow could see why he should be uneasy about it: for surely Quelch couldn't blame a Greyfriars man for recapturing a Greyfriars cap snatched from a Greyfriars head by a fellow belonging to another school? But the possessor of that darkened eye was undoubtedly uneasy.

"Do you hear me, Bunter?" rapped Mr. Quelch.

"Oh! Yes, sir!" stammered Bunter. "I—I—I haven't been—been fighting, sir! I—I ran into a tree, sir——."

"Was your eye discoloured in that shocking manner by accident, Bunter?" asked the Remove master.

"Yes, sir!" gasped Bunter.

Mr. Quelch eyed him. So did a good many of the Remove fellows. In the general opinion of the form, that black eye was a credit to Bunter, considering how it had been acquired. There was no reason for him to tell fibs about it: unless, indeed, it was force of habit, and he couldn't help fibbing. Peter Todd gave him a very expressive look—the Famous Five frowned at him—Lord Mauleverer shook his head sadly. Bunter heeded none of them. His uneasy and furtive gaze remained fixed on Quelch.

Quelch's brow cleared. While every fellow in the form-room knew that Billy Bunter was departing from the straight and narrow path of veracity, Quelch saw no reason to doubt. Bunter was no fighting-man: he was indeed the last fellow in the Remove whom Quelch would have suspected of engaging in strenuous combat, to the extent of collecting black eyes. It was in fact more probable that, if Bunter had a black eye, it was the result of accident, rather than of desperate combat—much more probable!

"Very well, Bunter," said Mr. Quelch, quite mildly, "if it was an accident——."

"Oh, yes, sir!" said Bunter, eagerly. "I—I was running, sir, and I—I ran right into the wall, sir——."

"The wall?" said Mr. Quelch, staring. "You said a tree, Bunter.

"Oh! Yes! I—I mean a tree, sir," gasped the fat Owl. "I—I ran right into the tree, sir, and banged my face on the wall—I mean the tree—and—and it—it blacked my eye, sir——."

"You should be more careful, Bunter! Such an accident might be very serious, as you wear glasses—you must take more care, Bunter."

"Oh, yes, sir! Certainly, sir."

"Were your glasses damaged, Bunter?"

"Oh! No, sir! I—I'd taken them off, as it happened——."

"That is very fortunate, in the circumstances," said Mr. Quelch, eyeing Bunter. "But it may have been the cause of the accident, Bunter. You should certainly not run about without your glasses, as you need them to aid your vision. You are a foolish boy, Bunter."

"Oh! Yes, sir! No, sir! I mean, yes, Sir."

Billy Bunter hoped that Quelch would leave it at that. But Quelch did not leave it at that. Quelch was too dutiful a form-master to think of leaving it at that!

"Have you seen the House-dame about this injury to your eye, Bunter?"

"Oh! No, sir."

"You should have done so immediately, Bunter."

"It—it's only a—a—a black eye, sir——."

"You are a stupid boy, Bunter. You should have gone to Mrs. Kebble at once. It may be necessary for you to see the school doctor——."

"Or, lor'!" gasped Bunter.

"The injury may be greater than you suppose, Bunter, from such a crash into a tree-trunk as you have described——."

"I—I didn't——."

"What?"

"I—I mean——."

"Well, what do you mean, Bunter?" asked Mr. Quelch, testily.

"Oh! N—n—nothing, sir," gasped Bunter. The fat Owl began to wish that he had not made it a tree-trunk, after all! Certainly he did not wish to see the House-dame about that black eye: still less the school doctor.

"Stand out here, Bunter."

Bunter jumped.

"Oh, lor'. I—I—I haven't done anything, sir!" he squeaked, in alarm. "It—it was an accident, running into the wall——."

"The wall?"

"I—I mean the tree! I—I couldn't help it, sir! I—I——. 'Twasn't my fault, sir——."

"You foolish boy, do you suppose that I think of punishing you for an accident?" snapped Mr. Quelch. "Come here at once."

"B—b—b—but, sir——," babbled Bunter.

"I shall look at your eye, Bunter, and judge whether you had better see the school doctor about it or not."

"Oh, crikey!"

"You are wasting time, Bunter! Come here at once," rapped Mr. Quelch. Quelch was getting annoyed. Minutes were being wasted: the lesson was delayed. The Remove, certainly, did not mind how much the lesson might be delayed. But the Remove master did!

To Quelch's surprise, and his further annoyance, Bunter did not immediately emerge from his place. He remained as if glued to it, blinking at his form-master in utter dismay. Other fellows stared at him in surprise. What was the matter with Bunter they could not guess. Quelch had swallowed his story of an accident: and there was no reason, so far as they could see, why he should object to Quelch giving that black eye the once-over at close range. But Bunter evidently had an objection, and a strong one.

"Do you hear me, Bunter?" Quelch's voice rumbled. "Come out of the form immediately! Come here."

Peter Todd gave the fat Owl a poke.

"Get a move on, you fat ass," he whispered. "What on earth's the matter with you? Quelch is getting shirty."

"Oh, crikey!"

"BUNTER!"

Unwillingly, but inevitably, the fat Owl dragged himself out before the form, all eyes following him. The Remove fellows could only wonder at his reluctance, and Quelch undoubtedly was getting "shirty". Bunter approached him, as slowly as if the Remove master had

been a ravenous lion instead of an elderly Master of Arts.
His podgy feet dragged.

He stood before Mr. Quelch at last, right under the
gimlet-eyes. Those eyes almost bored into him.

"Turn your face to the light, Bunter. How can you be
so stupid as to turn your face away from the light when I
desire to examine your injury? Now, look up—and let
me see your injured eye quite plainly."

There was no help for it!

Often had Bunter trembled under that gimlet-eye. Now
he fairly quaked under it. He could almost feel it on him
like a gimlet! For some mysterious reason known only
to himself, Bunter did not want that black eye scanned
closely, especially by the keenest eyes at Greyfriars. But
it had to be.

Quelch bent his tall head and scanned that eye. Then
an expression came over his speaking countenance that
made the Remove fellows stare. It was quite an extraordinary expression. For a moment, Quelch seemed unable to believe his eyes, keen as they were. What he discerned, now that he scanned that black eye at the distance
of only a few inches, seemed to take him quite aback.

"Bless my soul!" ejaculated Mr. Quelch.

"What the dickens——!" muttered Bob Cherry.

"Something's up——!" whispered the Bounder.

"But what——."

"BUNTER!" Quelch's voice was almost a roar.
"Bunter! What does this mean? How dare you play such
a prank in the form-room?"

"Oh, lor'!"

"Your eye is not damaged at all! It is blackened with
soot. You have rubbed soot round your eye, Bunter, to
give it the appearance of a black eye! Why have you
played this insensate prank, Bunter?"

"I—I—I haven't—I—I—I mean—I—I——."

"Soot!" gasped Peter Todd, like a fellow in a dream.
"Soot! Oh, my only hat! Not a real black eye at all——!"
Spoof!"

"Oh, crumbs!"

"The fat spoofer——."

"He never got a black eye at all——."

"All gammon——!"

It was quite a buzz in the Remove. For the moment

91

they forgot that they were in form, in their amazement at that startling discovery. No one had suspected it—no one had even dreamed of it! Even Quelch's gimlet eye had not detected it, at a distance. Only at close range had he discerned that the black eye was not caused by a jolt, but by the much less painful process of rubbing soot into the skin round the eye. The Remove fellows knew now why Bunter had not gone to the House-dame with that eye: and why he had not even bathed it! Bathing it would have bathed it off!

"Silence in the form!" Quelch's voice gave a good imitation of thunder. "Silence! Bunter, why have you played this extraordinary prank?"

"Oh, jiminy!"

"You have deliberately darkened your eye with soot, to give it the appearance of a black eye, and have ventured to play this insensate trick in the form-room—to play this trick on me! On ME! I shall cane you for this foolish prank. Hand me the cane from my desk, Bunter."

A dismal fat Owl handed Quelch the cane from the desk. It swished in the air.

"Now bend over, Bunter, and touch your toes."

"Oh, lor'!"

Swipe! swipe! swipe!

"Yow—ow—ow! Wow! Oh, crikey! Wow!"

Mr. Quelch laid down the cane.

"Now go out and wash your face immediately, Bunter."

"Yow—ow—ow—ow!"

A fat Owl in the lowest possible spirits rolled out of the form-room, wriggling as he rolled: he was followed by expressive looks from the Remove. There was no sign of a black eye about Bunter when he rolled in again. Billy Bunter's black eye had vanished like the baseless fabric of a vision!

CHAPTER 19

BUNTER, BEHAVE!

"HERE, Bunter!"

Coker of the Fifth called to Bunter of the Remove as
Achilles might have called to a myrmidon, or as Nero
might have called to Tigellinus, "Veni, Tigelline!"

It was one of Horace Coker's manners and customs to
speak as one having authority. That he, Horace James
Coker, was nobody in particular, was a fact never quite
borne in upon Coker's rather solid brain.

Billy Bunter blinked round at him.

On Saturday afternoon. Bunter was haunting the tuck-
shop. He did not enter that establishment, because Mrs.
Mimble required cash in exchange for sticky eatables,
and the Owl of the Remove had been disappointed about
a postal order. And there was not the slightest, faintest,
remotest chance of any Remove man standing him so much
as a currant bun. But apparently he drew some comfort
from the mere vicinity of foodstuffs.

Bunter was not feeling bright or bonny that afternoon.
Indeed he was feeling rather that life was a delusion and a
snare: and, even at Greyfriars, that it was weary, stale,
flat, and unprofitable.

He was back in Coventry, of course. His escape from
that chilly habitat had been brief.

Pluck covers a multitude of sins. His supposed exploit
had made it all right for Bunter—for a brief space! But
Quelch had put paid to that!

Skinner had looked for him, after class, and kicked him.
Skinner had cut a very inglorious figure, in comparison
with Bunter, in the affair with the Highcliffians. And it
had turned out that Bunter's bold exploit was "spoof" from
beginning to end: merely a figment of the fat Owl's fertile
imagination. He had picked up that cap somewhere, and
invented a black eye to give colour to a tale of derring-do.

Everyone had been taken in except—unfortunately—
Quelch! Now everyone knew, and the hapless Owl's last

state was worse than his first. Skinner kicked him: the other fellows were content with relegating him once more to the cold shades of Coventry. Once more Billy Bunter knew what it must have been like on Crusoe's island.

Most Remove fellows were enjoying life that afternoon. Harry Wharton and Co. were playing the soccer match with Shell, unavoidably postponed on Wednesday. Football fellows not in the team were gathered round the field. Bunter, like Gallio of old, cared not for these things. He could hear distant shouts from the football field, but they did not interest him: even a roar of "Goal! Good old Smithy!" did not make him lend a fat ear. It was a dismal fat Owl that afternoon: and he was almost grateful when Coker of the Fifth threw a word to him: though Coker threw it as Achilles might have to a myrmidon, or Nero to Tigellinus.

Coker had come out of the tuck-shop. He had quite a considerable parcel under his arm.

Bunter blinked at him—and at the parcel. He did not need telling that there was going to be a spread for tea, in Coker's study. Coker had heaps of money, and spent it royally, for which his study-mates, Potter and Greene, were duly thankful.

Coker gave him a look, and held out the parcel.

"Take this up to my study!" he said. "Be careful with it."

That was Coker all over! The Remove did not fag even for the Sixth: and the bare idea of fagging for the Fifth would have been repudiated with scorn. Almost any other Remove man would have told Coker at once exactly where he had to get off. But Billy Bunter was too interested in Coker's parcel, to think of telling Coker what he thought of him.

"All right, Coker," he answered.

He took the parcel from Coker's hands, and rolled off to the House. Coker, giving him no further thought, walked away in the direction of the football ground. A senior match was going on there, Fifth and Sixth, and his friends, Potter and Greene, were in the Fifth-form team. Coker was going to take them off to the spread in the study when the game was over.

Billy Bunter rolled into the House with Coker's parcel under a fat arm.

Bunter did not, like any other Remove man, resent being called upon to fag for the lofty Horace. Bunter's thoughts were dwelling on the contents of Coker's big parcel. He was only too glad to get it into his fat hands. He was going to take it to Coker's study, as bidden: but it was improbable that it would be quite so large a parcel, when Coker arrived later with Potter and Greene.

The fat junior mounted the stairs with the parcel. Skinner was lounging on the landing, and at sight of Bunter, he came towards him, with the very evident intention of landing an additional kick.

"Here, you keep off, you beast!" Bunter backed away. "You make me drop this parcel, and you'll have Coker after you—I'm taking it to his study—Yaroooh! Leave off kicking me, you beast! Wow!"

The parcel dropped. Probably there were eggs in it, for there was a cracking sound. Bunter squirmed from a lunging foot.

Luckily for him, Lord Mauleverer came out of the Remove passage, as Skinner was delivering a second and third kick.

"Stop that, Skinner," called out Mauly.

Skinner stared round.

"Mind your own business," he suggested.

"Makin' it mine," explained Lord Mauleverer, amiably. "Leave Bunter alone. Don't hit a man when he's down, you know."

"I'm going to boot the fat spoofing slug all round the landing."

"You're not!" said Mauly, cheerfully, and he stepped between Bunter and Skinner, pushing back his spotless cuffs.

Skinner looked at him, and decided not, after all, to boot the fat Owl all round the landing. He scowled and went down the stairs instead. Billy Bunter picked up Coker's parcel.

"I say, Mauly——!" he squeaked.

Lord Mauleverer walked on.

"Mauly, old chap——!"

No reply. Mauleverer walked on to the stairs.

"Beast!" hissed Bunter, no doubt by way of thanks for Mauly's intervention, and he rolled on his way with Coker's parcel.

Lord Mauleverer, about to go down the stairs, paused and glanced round. His eyes dwelt thoughtfully on Bunter's fat back, as the Owl of the Remove rolled into the Fifth-form passage.

Heedless of Mauly, Billy Bunter landed the parcel on the table in Horace Coker's study.

His next step should have been to quit the study, leaving it there. But he did not take that next step.

He did not quit the study. Instead of that, he shut the door, and stood blinking through his big spectacles at the parcel on the table.

A fat hand was stretched out to the string that secured it. Then it was withdrawn. Then it was stretched out again.

Bunter paused. He hesitated. Just as he had paused and hesitated the previous day, before walking off with Bob Cherry's paper-bag, so he now paused and hesitated in Coker's study.

There was a struggle in his plump breast.

Billy Bunter was not very bright. His fat brain moved in mysterious ways, when it moved at all. But even Bunter realised, by this time, that if he was ever going to emerge from "Coventry", he had to emerge as a reformed Bunter. It was a case of "Bunter, behave!"—the alternative being a continuation of his present Crusoe-like existence. He had made up his fat mind to it—or almost! But——.

There was a "but": and it was a large size in "buts". The lure of tuck was too strong for Billy Bunter's powers of resistance.

He hesitated: but it was said of old that he who hesitates is lost! To his credit be it said, that for a whole long minute he hesitated. Then the fat hand stretched out again to the string on the parcel: and this time it clutched! Once more the Owl of the Remove was falling to temptation!

But even as he clutched the string, the study door opened. Bunter, with a squeak of alarm, spun round, dreading to see Coker.

"Oh, crikey! I—I say, Coker, I—I wasn't going to— Oh! It's you—what do you want here, Mauly, you beast?" gasped Bunter.

It was not Coker. It was Lord Mauleverer who stepped into the study.

"I—I thought it was Coker!" gasped Bunter. "I—I say,

look here, Mauly, you get out—I—I ain't going to open that parcel—'tain't your business, anyway—Leggo my ear, will you?" yelled Bunter.

Lord Mauleverer did not speak. He fastened a finger and thumb on a fat ear, and led Bunter towards the door.

His kind-hearted lordship doubtless compassioned the hapless fat Owl in the dolorous shades of Coventry. Bunter did seem rather a hopeless case: but Mauly was willing to help him on the path of reform. He helped him with that pincer-like grip on his fat ear, leading him doorward.

"Will you leggo?" hissed Bunter. "I ain't going—yaroooh! Leggo my ear! Can't you mind your own business, Mauly?"

Apparently Mauly couldn't! At all events, he continued to pull that ear doorward: and Bunter had to follow the fat ear.

"Beast!" howled Bunter.

He was led out of the study. Mauly closed the door with his free hand, and still gripping the fat ear, led Bunter down the passage. Not till they reached the landing was the fat ear released.

Then Mauly drew back his foot.

Billy Bunter did not wait for the next act! He bolted into the Remove passage. Lord Mauleverer, smiling, went down the stairs.

He had saved Coker's parcel from Bunter—and Bunter from himself! But whether that parcel would still be intact, when Coker came in with Potter and Greene after the football match, was still on the knees of the gods. Mauly had done his best, and no fellow could do more.

CHAPTER 20

BUNTER—AS USUAL!

"RESCUE!" yelled Billy Bunter.

He yelled as he hurtled into the Rag.

It was uncommon to behold Billy Bunter in rapid motion. But his speed, as he shot into the Rag, was almost supersonic.

D

A crowd of fellows stared round at him.

The Remove footballers were all there, after the match with the Shell. Most of them were discussing the game. They had drawn with the Shell: and a draw with an older form, especially with Hobson and Co., who were great men at soccer, was not too bad.

But there had very nearly been an odd goal in favour of the Remove. Smithy had shot from the right wing, and just failed to pot the pill: and the general consensus of opinion was, that Smithy ought to have centred to Wharton, and left him to take the shot. The Bounder was sometimes a selfish player: but often his long shots came off brilliantly: and a goal covered a multitude of sins. But a long shot that did not come off made quite a different impression. So there was a vigorous and emphatic argument going on in the Rag, when Billy Bunter happened. The fat Owl's frantic yell interrupted it.

"Hallo, hallo, hallo!" exclaimed Bob Cherry. "What——?"

Really Billy Bunter looked, at the moment, as if a mad bull might somehow have penetrated into the scholastic precincts of Greyfriars School, and was hot on his track!

"I say, you fellows, rescue!" yelled Bunter, charging breathlessly and frantically in.

The next moment the cause of his frantic flight and wild alarm was discerned: in the shape of a burly Fifth-former, who charged into the Rag after him.

It was not a mad bull that was at Bunter's heels: it was Horace Coker of the Fifth Form. But Coker looked almost as dangerous as the maddest bull. His rugged face was red with wrath, his eyes gleaming: there was a fives bat in his hand, and what he was going to do with that fives bat, when he reached Bunter, was clear! It had, in fact, already landed twice on Bunter's fat person before he dodged into the Rag: but it had to land a good many more times before Horace Coker was likely to be satisfied.

"I say, you fellows!" Bunter, yelling, dodged round the long table. "I say, rescue! Keep him off! It—it wasn't me! I never——."

"Here, get out, Coker!" called Harry Wharton.

"Outside, Coker!" roared Bob Cherry.

"Barge him out!" exclaimed the Bounder.

Soccer argument was forgotten. The Rag belonged to

the juniors. Senior men who came in were expected to remember their manners, and certainly not to throw their weight about. Hostile looks were cast at Coker from all sides. Even Lord Mauleverer detached himself from an armchair, prepared to lend a hand in dealing with Coker of the Fifth.

Unheeding, Coker charged after Bunter.

Still at almost supersonic speed, the fat Owl raced round the long table, with Coker raging on his track. He yelled as he raced. Two from that fives bat were more than enough for Bunter.

But Coker's lengthy legs would certainly has beaten Bunter's short fat ones in the race, had not Johnny Bull interposed a timely foot.

Over that foot Horace Coker stumbled, landing on old oak planks with a yell louder than Bunter's.

A crowd surrounded him as he sprawled.

"Collar him!"

"Bag him!"

"Boot him out!"

Coker sat up dizzily. He gasped for breath, and glared at inimical faces. Coker was not going to carry matters with a high hand in the juniors' own territory, if they could stop him! And they could! Even Coker, perhaps, realised that he could not handle more than a dozen Remove fellows at once! He condescended to explain.

"Look here, that fat villain's raided my tuck!" he spluttered. "I'm going to whop him, see?"

"Oh!" said Harry Wharton, "Bunter, you bloated brigand——."

Bunter had come to a breathless halt, leaning on the table and spluttering for breath. He squeaked in alarm.

"I—I say, you fellows, I—I never! I—I didn't! I—I haven't been in Coker's study at all! I—I—I Coker never saw me there——."

"Why, you fat tick!" roared Coker. "Didn't I send you up to my study with a parcel? And when I came in, it was open on my table, and half the stuff gone——."

"Oh! Yes! But—I—I—I——."

"Looks a clear case," said Johnny Bull. "Serve you jolly well right, Coker, for your cheek, fagging a Remove man——."

"Yes, rather!" said Nugent.

"The ratherfulness is terrific." said Hurree Jamset Ram Singh. "Give the esteemed Coker the bat on his ridiculous trousers for fagging a Remove man."

"Hear, hear!"

"Good egg!" Bob Cherry jerked the fives bat from Coker's grasp "Collar him and jam him on the table!"

"Why, you cheeky ticks!" roared Coker. "I—I'll smack your heads a.l round—I'll pulverise the lot of you—I tell you he had my grub, and I'm going to—whooop! Leggo my ears, Bull—leggo my hair, Todd, you young ruffian—leggo my neck, Nugent——. Yaroooh! Oh, crumbs, I'll smash you—I'll——."

Coker struggled in many hands. But he struggled in vain. Few fellows, if any, were likely to doubt that Billy Bunter, having conveyed Coker's parcel to Coker's study, had sampled the contents thereof. He had not—yet at all events—learned new manners and customs in "Coventry". But all agreed, without a dissentient voice, that Coker of the Fifth, by fagging a Remove man, had asked for a batting.

"Will you let me go?" bellowed Coker, struggling frantically.

"Not at all!" answered Bob Cherry. "Keep quiet, Coker! If you keep on wriggling I shall tap your nose with this fives bat—like that——."

"Wow!" howled Corker.

"Ha, ha, ha!"

"Slam him on the table!" exclaimed Vernon-Smith.

Corker, in spite of strenuous resistance, was slammed half-over the table, in a favourable position for batting. Billy Bunter grinned approval.

"I say, you fellows, whop him!" he squeaked. "Cheek, you know, fagging a Remove man! I never touched his parcel—I mean, after I put it in his study! Mauly knows—you know, don't you, Mauly?"

"I know I lugged you out of Coker's study by your ear," answered Lord Mauleverer. "Did you go back afterwards?"

"Not till you were gone down, Mauly—I—I mean, I—I never went back at all. I—I wouldn't you know! If Coker's missed the meringues from that parcel, I don't know anything about them. I never knew there were any meringues in it! I never touched the cake, either—not so much as a plum—there weren't many plums in it, either——."

"Oh, gad!"

"Will you leggo?" roared Coker. "You touch me with that bat, young Cherry, and I tell you I'll—yaroooooop!"

Whop! whop! whop!

"Whooooop!"

"He, he, he!" chuckled Bunter. "How do you like it yourself, Coker? Making out I snooped your tuck! I say, you fellows, I never——."

"You fat villain, your turn comes after Coker's!" said Harry Wharton. "Go it, Bob—make it six!"

"Oh, crikey!" gasped Bunter.

Whop! whop!

"Oh, crumbs! Oh, scissors!" spluttered Coker. "I—I—I—stoppit! Will you stoppit?"

Whop! The fives bat fairly rang on Coker's trousers in the final whop.

"Wow! wow!"

"That's six!" said Bob, cheerfully. "When you want another six, Coker, start fagging Remove men again! You can have your bat now—I'll shove it down the back of your neck——!"

"Ha, ha, ha!"

Many hands held the infuriated Horace, as the fives bat was crammed down the back of his neck. It was rather a close fit, but Bob Cherry drove it well home, to an accompaniment of almost fiendish yells from Coker.

Then the whole crowd of juniors joined in booting Coker out of the Rag. Coker went into the passage in a yelling heap. It was a dusty, dizzy, dilapidated Coker that tottered away, with a fives bat down his back.

"Now it's Bunter's turn!" said Bob.

"I—I say, you fellows——!"

"We've sent that fat snooper to Coventry for snooping tuck!" said Bob. "It hasn't done him any good so far, but a spot of booting may help!"

"Oh, really, Cherry——"

"Collar him!" said Johnny Bull.

"I—I say, it wasn't me!" yelled Bunter. "I keep on telling you that it wasn't me! I—I never touched Coker's parcel! Besides, he jolly well deserved it for fagging a Remove man, as you jolly well said yourself, Bull! I—I

101

wouldn't have touched it if he hadn't fagged me, carrying his parcels for him! Besides, I—I never touched it at all!"

"Oh, my hat!"

"Not a single thing," asseverated Bunter. "I—I haven't tasted meringues to-day, or cake either—and I never took any of the apples, and I haven't got one in my pocket now——."

"Ha, ha, ha!"

"Bag him!" said Bob Cherry. "Hold him by the ears while I kick him into the passage——."

"Yaroooh!" roared Bunter, in anticipation. The prospect of being kicked into the passage by the largest and heftiest foot in the Remove seemed to alarm him. "I say, you fellows——."

"Good egg!" said Harry Wharton. "I'll hold one ear——."

"Aand I'll hold the other," grinned Nugent.

"Leggo my ears!" wailed Bunter, as he was led towards the door by those appendages, which were large enough to give quite a good hold. "I tell you I never——."

"Now stand steady!" said Bob.

"Beast!" gasped Bunter.

Vernon-Smith, grinning, set the door wide open. Billy Bunter stood facing the doorway. Gladly he would have bolted through it, and cut for his fat life, now that Coker was gone. But a grasp on either fat ear held him where he was: wriggling in dire anticipation. Bob Cherry stepped behind him, and drew back his right foot.

"Ready, Bunter?" he asked.

"Ow! No!" yelled Bunter. "Don't you kick me, you beast! I say, you fellows, leggo my ears! I say——."

"Now, I'll count three," said Bob Cherry. "When I say three, let go his ears, and I'll land him right across the passage. One!"

"Ow! Help!" yelled Bunter.

"Ha, ha, ha!"

"Two!" said Bob.

"I—I—I say, Bob, old chap, stoppit!" yelled Bunter. "I—I say, I'll give you the apple—it's a jolly good apple—the best one there was in Coker's parcel——."

"Ha, ha, ha!"

"Three!" said Bob.

Harry Wharton and Frank Nugent released the fat ears.

The next item on the programme should have been a tremendous kick from Bob Cherry, lifting the fat Owl through the doorway, and landing him in the passage. But as Bob had not the remotest intention of delivering that kick, his foot remained where it was. But the anticipation was enough for Bunter. It had not dawned on the fat Owl that his podgy leg was being pulled.

The moment his ears were released, he bounded. An arrow in its flight had nothing on Bunter, and he shot through the doorway of the Rag. He fairly whizzed.

"Ha, ha, ha! "

"Hallo, hallo, hallo! He's gone! "

"Ha, ha, ha! "

"Come back, Bunter! " roared Bob.

Billy Bunter was not likely to come back He vanished into space: and soccer argument was resumed in the Rag. Billy Bunter was not seen again for quite a long time: and when he did reappear in the public eye, it was to find that "Coventry" had clamped down again. The Owl of the Remove was booked for a "quiet week-end".

CHAPTER 21

THE WORM TURNS

"I SAY, you fellows! "

Probably Billy Bunter did not expect to receive a reply. He did not, at all events, receive one.

It was a clear, cold, sunny morning. Five fellows had come out of the House, all of them looking extremely neat and tidy. It was Sunday morning, and the Famous Five were going on a "Sunday walk": and as that walk was to take them in the direction of Cliff House School, at Pegg, with the possibility of falling in with Marjorie Hazeldene and her friends, they were all, so to speak, in their best bibs and tuckers. Shakespeare's schoolboy with his shining morning face could not have looked more spotless.

Mr. Quelch, crossing the quad from the chapel, glanced at them, and his glance was approving. Quelch liked to see his boys looking a credit to their form. His glance at Billy Bunter was not so approving. Bunter, as usual, looked as if he would be none the worse for a wash: and a sticky smear round his capacious mouth indicated that he had been somewhere where there was jam.

Bunter, however, did not heed Quelch, who passed on without receiving a single blink from the fattest member of his form. Bunter's eyes and spectacles were fixed on those five "posh" juniors: who, however, seemed to have no use for Bunter. If they heard his fat squeak, as doubtless they did, they heeded it not.

"I say, you fellows, you ain't keeping this up?" pleaded Bunter. "I say, are you going for a Sunday walk?'

No reply.

"I'll come, if you like," said Bunter. Sunday walks, or any other walks, had little appeal for Bunter. But Coventry was weighing heavily upon him.

Bob Cherry spoke: but not to Bunter. The Famous Five in fact did not seem aware of his fat existence.

"How long is that ass Hazel going to be?" said Bob. Apparently Hazeldene was joining the Famous Five in that Sunday walk. Apparently too, he was in no hurry to start.

"Oh, we can wait," said Harry Wharton. "No hurry, Bob."

Grunt from Bob Cherry! Hurree Jamset Ram Singh closed a dark eye at Johnny Bull, who grinned. Bob, catching both the wink and the grin, reddened.

"No good hanging about," he said gruffly.

"None at all," said Frank Nugent, laughing. "Cut in and tell Hazel to get a move on, or we may miss seeing his sister at Pegg."

Another grunt from Bob. For reasons best known to himself, Bob Cherry was anxious to get as far as Pegg Lane at least: that being the region where a chance meeting with Marjorie was most likely to materialise. Otherwise, there was no special hurry to start: and Hazel evidently saw no reason for not taking his time.

"I say, Bob, old chap!" squeaked Bunter.

"We'll take the cut through Friardale Wood," said Bob. "That's the shortest way. Bother that slacker, Hazel."

"Look here, if you can't answer a chap——."

"I think I'll cut in and call him," said Bob. And he

104

cut back into the House, his friends smiling as he went. Billy Bunter did not smile. He frowned.

"I say, you fellows, if you think I had Coker's tuck, I jolly well didn't!" he pleaded. "I—I said I—I wouldn't, and I—I didn't——."

Stony silence.

If there had been a chance of the Owl of the Remove escaping from Coventry, the tuck-raid on Saturday had knocked it on the head. It was the same old Bunter at the same old game: and as Coventry had done him no good so far, it was going on till it did!

"I say, you fellows——."

Four fellows walked away, without a word, to wait in another spot for Bob to come out with Hazel. Billy Bunter glared after them.

"Beasts!" he hooted.

Billy Bunter would really have liked to roll after them, and punch four heads one after another! But that was not practical politics.

But a gleam came into the little round eyes behind the big round spectacles, as another and more practicable idea came into Bunter's fat mind. And the frown on his fat visage was replaced by a grin.

"Beasts!" he breathed. "I'll show 'em!"

The fat junior revolved on his axis, and rolled away to the gates. He knew the way the chums of the Remove were going, when they started: and as they were waiting for Hazel, he had ample time to get ahead of them on the footpath through Friardale Wood. A deep dark scheme was working in Bunter's fat brain. He was, in fact, going to "show 'em!"

He rolled away down Friardale Lane at quite a good speed, and clambered over the stile into the footpath through the wood.

At a distance from the lane, that footpath crossed Friardale Water, a woodland stream, a tributary of the Sark, by means of a plank bridge. Anyone walking from Friardale to Pegg, or from Pegg to Friardale Lane, had to cross the stream by that plank. It had rested there for years, and was perfectly safe—if left alone. It was not going to be quite so safe when the Sunday walkers came along!

A party of Greyfriars fellows, dressed in their Sunday

best, would shortly be coming across that plank. Their Sunday best would not look quite so spick and span, if they had a ducking in the stream!

Such was the nefarious scheme working in Billy Bunter's fat brain. Even the worm will turn! Bunter, perhaps, was rather a worm! Anyway, he was turning!

He arrived at the plank bridge breathless, and rolled across it. Then he blinked back watchfully the way he had come.

There was not sign yet of the Famous Five. The vengeful Owl was well ahead of his intended victims.

"He, he, he!" chuckled Bunter.

He was quite cheered by the prospect. The beasts deserved it, and more, for sending Bunter to Coventry and keeping him there!

He bent down to grasp the end of the plank, and heave it from the stone on which it rested.

The bright idea was to leave just a tip of it resting on the stone, so that it would look safe from the other side, but would inevitably tip over when walked across. Some of the party, probably all of them, would go splashing into the water and into the mud. When they emerged, they would assuredly be in no state for presenting themselves to the gaze of the Cliff House girls.

Billy Bunter grinned from ear to ear, as he pictured what they would look like, after they had scrambled out. The woodland stream, which in summer was low, was now full to overflowing, even lapping a little over the plank. and over its grassy banks. There was mud in abundant quantities at the margin: deep, thick mud: Bunter's shoes were already caked with it, as he grasped the end of the plank. But the fat Owl did not mind a little mud, so long as those beasts had a lot!

He heaved and heaved at the plank.

But it was long and heavy, and well set in its place. It was far from easy for the fat Owl to shift. He tugged and tugged at it, with both fat hands, panting for breath and still it did not stir.

Bunter had not foreseen that spot of difficulty. But now that he had set his fat hand to the plough, as it were, he was not going to turn back. He was going to shift that plank somehow. Really it was worth a little exertion, to give those beasts a ducking in their Sunday best for keeping him in Coventry.

The fat Owl exerted himself, going all out, with the perspiration trickling down his plump brow. With both hands gripping that obstinate plank, and his feet firmly planted in mud, he tugged and tugged and tugged. Suddenly, the plank yielded to the tug—very suddenly: so very suddenly that the tugging fat Owl was taken by surprise.

Bunter's idea was to shift that plank a foot or so, leaving it in a favourable position for tipping over when walked on. Instead of which, that terrific tug suddenly dislodged the plank altogether, and it flew.

"Ooooogh!" gasped Billy Bunter, as he went over backwards, and sat down.

Splash!

The plank slipped from the fat hands, and splashed into the stream. Caught by the current, it floated away downstream, in the direction of the Sark. But Billy Bunter was no longer heeding the plank. Billy Bunter was sitting on the margin of the stream, in a foot of water and a foot of mud, yelling.

CHAPTER 22

JUST LIKE BOB

"HALLO, hallo, hallo!"

"What the dickens——?"

"It's Bunter!"

"Looks a bit muddy."

"The muddifulness is terrific!"

Half-a-dozen Greyfriars juniors came up the footpath from the direction of Friardale Lane. They had arrived at the woodland stream with the intention of walking across the plank bridge. That plank bridge was no longer available: it was well on its way to the wide waters of the Sark. Half-a-dozen pairs of eyes fixed on a woebegone figure on the further bank.

It was Bunter—they recognised it as Bunter. But the

hapless Owl was so clothed in mud, clothed in it as in a garment, that really they might not have known him, but for the unmistakable circumference, and the glimmer of muddy spectacles.

Not very much of Bunter was in view. Water was flowing over a good half of him. On the margin of the stream, where the fat Owl had sat down so suddenly, the water was shallow, but the mud was deep. Under the water, Bunter sat deep in mud, and the water flowed round him. He was in no danger of being washed away by the current. He was too deeply anchored in mud for that. Water eddied and splashed round him as he wriggled in mud. Muddy hands sawed the air and splashed in water. Mud daubed the fat face and spotted the spectacles. He was making frantic efforts to free his fat legs from clinging mud, and get on his feet. But he couldn't! That thick bed of viscous mud held him in a vice-like grip. It was a glad sight to Billy Bunter's eyes when the fellows he had planned to duck came along to the stream. They were his only present help in time of need.

"I say, you fellows!" yelled Bunter.

"Poor old Bunter!" gasped Bob Cherry. "Does he look damp?"

"Ha, ha, ha!"

"The dampfulness is terrific."

"The plank must have slipped," said Harry Wharton, "it's always been safe——."

"Bunter's weight, perhaps——."

"Well, it's gone!" said Johnny Bull, glancing down the stream. "We shall have to walk round by the village, if we're going to Pegg. Come on."

"Jolly long walk!" grunted Hazel.

"What about jumping it?" suggested Bob.

"I can see myself trying to jump it, fathead."

Harry Wharton laughed.

"You won the long jump last time, Bob," he remarked. "You might be able to clear it—but I wouldn't advise it, in your Sunday bags. We'd better walk round by Friardale."

"Yes, rather," said Frank Nugent. "I'm not looking for a ducking, for one."

"The duckfulness would be preposterous," said Hurree Jamset Ram Singh, with a shake of his dusky head. "The walkfulness round is the proper caper. What cannot be cured must make Jack a dull boy, as the English proverb remarks."

"I say, you fellows, I'm all wet!" yelled Bunter.

"You look it!" agreed Bob.

"Beast! I'm soaked to the skik—skik—skin!"

"Well, why don't you crawl out, you fat ass?" demanded Johnny Bull. It had not occurred to the juniors, for the moment, that Bunter was stuck fast in mud and could not disengage his fat limbs from it. Any other Remove man, no doubt, could have dragged himself out. But Bunter was firmly anchored.

"You silly idiot!" yelled Bunter. "Think I should be sticking here if I could get out? I'm stuck!"

"Oh, my hat!"

"I'm stuck in the mud!" shrieked Bunter. "I kik—kik—kik—can't get out! I say, you fellows, help!"

They gazed at him. They realised now that Bunter was at anchor in the mud, stuck fast by his embedded fat legs. But how he was to be helped out was another matter. For the moment, at least, they forgot that he was in Coventry: and were quite willing, indeed anxious, to help. How, was the problem.

In summer, when the stream was low, any of them could have jumped it, at the cost of collecting a few spots of mud. But it was very different now. The woodland stream was full to its very brim, and at its widest. All the Famous Five were pretty good at the long jump. But it was very doubtful whether any of them could have cleared that wide stretch of rippling water. And they were all in their Sunday best, too—newly swept and garnished, as it were, for a possible encounter with the Cliff House girls.

"Are you going to stand there like a lot of boobies staring at a fellow stuck in the mud?" yelled Bunter. "I tell you I'm stuck, and can't get out! Help!"

"And how are we to help you, you fat chump?" snorted Johnny Bull. "Think we can fly across?"

"Oh, crikey!" gasped Bunter.

From the bottom of his fat heart, Billy Bunter repented that he had meddled with the plank bridge. That plank had drifted far out of sight by this time. Six fellows, on the opposite bank, would have helped him, if they could. But they couldn't!

"Look here, try and crawl out, you fat ass!" called out Bob Cherry.

"Think I haven't tried?" howled Bunter. "I tell you I'm stuck! I say, you fellows, you've got to help me somehow. I never meant it for you, you know."

"What?"

"I—I—I didn't really!" spluttered Bunter. "I—I never shifted the plank, and that isn't why I fell in——."

"Oh, suffering cats!"

"I—I—I just slipped!" gasped Bunter. "I wasn't pulling at the plank, or—or anything! I never even thought of giving you fellows a ducking for sending me to Coventry! It was a—a—a pure accident! I was—was walking across, you know, when it slipped—I wasn't tugging at it——."

"You fat villain!" roared Bob.

"Oh, really, Cherry——!"

"Well, that does it!" grunted Johnny Bull. "That fat scoundrel was going to duck us, was he, and tumbled in himself! Leave him to it."

"What-ho!" said Hazel.

"I say, you fellows——!"

"You piffling, pie-faced, pernicious porpoise!" roared Bob Cherry. "You've asked for it, and now you can make the best of it!"

"Beast!"

"Come on," said Johnny Bull. "If we're going round by the village, we shall have to put it on. We're wasting time."

"I say, you fellows, you can't go and leave me like this!" yelled Bunter. "I shall kik—kik—catch kik—kik—old—Help!"

"We can't get across without the plank," called back Harry Wharton. "There will be somebody along from the other direction—somebody from Pegg——."

"Beast!" roared Bunter.

"There's nothing we can do," grunted Johnny Bull, "and we've got a jolly long way to go round. Come on." He gave Bob Cherry a glare. "Thinking of trying to jump it, you ass?"

Bob, gazing across the flowing stream, was calculating the distance, with a careful eye. Bunter, no doubt, had asked for it: no doubt, too, some pedestrian would be coming along from Pegg sooner or later, who would be

110

Bob put all his beef into that leap, and cleared the stream—just!

able to help him out. Still, it went against the grain with the kind-hearted Bob to leave the hapless Owl stuck in the mud, with the stream washing round him.

"Look here, I think I could do it," said Bob. "May mean getting spotted a bit——."

"It means a ducking, and getting as muddy as Bunter!" grunted Johnny. "Is that how you want to look when we meet the girls?"

"Um! No! But—I think I'll try it on."

"More ass you, then!"

Bob had made up his mind. Certainly, he did not want to get into Bunter's muddy state: and it was only too likely that, even clearing the stream, he would land in splashing mud. But he hoped for the best.

He walked back along the path, to take a run for the leap. His friends waited and watched. If any member of the party could make that jump, it was Bob: and it was like him to risk a mud-bath for a fellow whom he would much rather have booted.

He came back at a rapid run, and leaped.

His friends watched the take-off anxiously, more than half-expecting him to splash in. But Bob put all his beef into that leap, and cleared the stream—just! He landed on the further side—but it was in thick mud that he landed, and there was a mighty, muddy splash! Mud flew up all round him, and his feet sank into it over the ankles.

"Good man!" exclaimed Harry Wharton.

"Silly ass!" grunted Johnny Bull.

"He's done it——."

"The donefulness is terrific."

"Looks a bit muddy!" grunted Hazel.

Bob Cherry gasped. He had done it: and he was safely landed. His shoes and trouser-ends were caked with wet mud, and spots and splashes were all over him. There was a yell from Bunter.

"Ow! Look out, you idiot! You've splashed mud right in my eye! Wow!"

"Oh, you fat tick!" gasped Bob. "Look at me—nice state I'm in——."

"Urrggh! Splashing mud all over a fellow——."

Bob Cherry breathed hard. However, he had jumped the stream to rescue Bunter, and he proceeded to rescue

112

him. He grasped a collar behind a fat neck, and dragged. There was another howl from Bunter.

"Wow! Mind what you're at, you dummy! You're chook—chook—choking me! Do you want to throttle a fellow! Urrrggh!"

Unheeding, Bob dragged. There was a squee-geeing sound as Bunter was extracted from mud. He came out at last, like a cork from a bottle. He rolled in the grass, drenched with water, smothered with mud, and spluttering for breath.

Bob looked down at his clothes, with a rueful face. Then he looked back at his friends across the stream. They were grinning. Bob's Sunday best had suffered sadly. He was not nearly so muddy as Bunter: but he was muddy from head to foot: and certainly in no state for a Sunday walk with the Cliff House girls.

"You fellows had better cut," he called out. "I'm going back—can't go on like this."

"You look rather a picture!" said Nugent.

"Br—r—r—r—r!" grunted Bob.

There was not help for it. That Sunday walk was over, so far as Bob Cherry was concerned. Harry Wharton and Co. turned back along the footpath, to go round by the village, leaving Bob scraping off mud, and Billy Bunter sitting in wet grass and spluttering. Bob tramped away up the stream, looking for a spot where it was easier to cross: leaving the fat Owl still spluttering: and with considerable self-restraint, refraining from kicking Bunter before he went. Billy Bunter was not thinking of trying to negotiate that stream at any point whatsoever: there was a long, long tramp ahead of Bunter, to get back to Greyfriars. It was a weary fat Owl that rolled in at last: and there was no doubt that, by that time, the worm was deeply regretting that it had turned!

CHAPTER 23

UNSYMPATHETIC!

CLANG! Clang!
  Groan!
  Clang!
  Groan!

It was quite startling, in the Remove dormitory, when the rising-bell rang in the misty morning.

Bob Cherry, generally the first to stir in that dormitory, sat up in bed, rubbed his eyes, yawned, and looked at the glimmering windows. It was not an inviting morning. Seamist had rolled inland, and the windows were clammy. It was cold. It was altogether a morning when a warm bed seemed extremely attractive.

But sticking in bed till the last possible moment was not Bob's way. He hurled bedclothes right and left, and came out with a bound.

  Clang!
  Groan!

Bob stared round. From one of the beds came the sound of a dismal groan, as if in answer to the clang of the bell.

"Hallo, hallo, hallo!" ejaculated Bob. "Who's that? What's up?"

  Groan!

Then Bob located the dismal sound. It proceeded from Billy Bunter's bed. He stared at that bed, and at a fat face on the pillow.

Billy Bunter did not always awake with the clang of the rising-bell. It was not unusual for him to snore on, till some kindly fellow jerked off his bedclothes, or dabbed a wet sponge on his fat little nose. But he was awake now —and his little round eyes blinked at Bob dolorously from his pillow.

Remove fellows were turning out all along the dormitory. But Bunter made no move to turn out. He remained where he was, and groaned.

"What's the trouble, old fat man?" asked Bob: for-

114

getting for the moment that the fat Owl was in Coventry.

Groan!

"Stop that row, you fat ass! " called out Vernon-Smith.

"Ow! I'm ill! " groaned Bunter.

"Gammon! "

"Beast! "

Bob came towards Bunter's bed. If Bunter was ill, Bob was prepared to be sympathetic and helpful. "Coventry" could hardly be applied strictly to a fellow who was ill. Bob even forgot that Bunter had "dished" him out of that Sunday walk with Marjorie the previous day: though several times since that occurrence he had been strongly tempted to reward him with a booting. He looked down at the dolorous fat face on the pillow.

"What's the matter?" he asked. "Too many suppers last night?"

"Oh, really, Cherry——."

"Pain in the middle of your circumference?" asked Bob. "You should go easier on the gruh, old fat bean."

" 'Tain't that! " yapped Bunter. "I—I—I'm ill! It was getting soaked with water yesterday—oh, lor'! I've caught a fearful cold—wow! I've been suffering fearfully all night —ow! wow! "

There was a chuckle from Skinner.

"It didn't keep him awake! " he remarked. "I woke up twice, and each time I heard him snoring."

"Beast!" groaned Bunter. "I may have dropped off, now and then. I'm awfully ill. I—I don't think I can get up! Oh, crikey! "

The fat Owl followed this up with a dismal, almost hair-raising groan. A dozen fellows gathered round his bed. Harry Wharton and Co. regarded him dubiously. Like Bob, all the Co. were prepared to be sympathetic if Bunter was ill. But there was always an "if" where statements from Billy Bunter were concerned. Billy Bunter's reluctance to turn out of bed on a cold morning was well known. Also, it might have occurred to the wily fat Owl that illness was an easier way out of Coventry than the steep path of reform! On the other hand, Bunter certainly had sat in cold water after his mishap with the plank at the woodland stream, which might very easily have caused any fellow to catch a chill. True he had shown no sign of it till now. But it might be a case of delayed action, so to speak.

"You were all right last night," said Peter Todd, suspiciously.

"I hadn't thought——."

"What?"

"I mean it hadn't come on then!" said Bunter, hastily. "I—I wasn't going to say that I hadn't thought of it then——."

"Oh, my hat!"

"I'm not spoofing, you know," said Bunter, blinking at the staring juniors. I'm awfully ill. Quelch saw me when I came in yesterday, and he made me go and change at once—he said I should be ill if I didn't get out of my wet clothes immediately——."

"And that put it into your head?" asked Skinner.

"Oh, really, Skinner——."

"Ha, ha, ha!"

"Blessed if I see anything to cackle at!" exclaimed Bunter, indignantly. "I think you fellows might be a bit sympathetic, when a fellow's ill—lying at death's door for all you know."

"Dash it all, wouldn't you even stop lying at death's door?" asked Johnny Bull.

"Ha, ha, ha!"

"Oh, really, Bull——."

"So you've caught a fearful cold, have you?" asked the Bounder.

"Ow! Yes! Awful!"

"People generally sneeze when they catch cold," said Smithy. "Anybody heard Bunter sneeze?"

"I heard him snoring, but I never heard him sneezing!" grinned Skinner.

"I—I——!" stammered Bunter. He realised that he had overlooked a not unimportant detail. A fellow catching a fearful cold was practically certain to sneeze. Bunter hadn't sneezed. A fellow could not think of everything: Billy Bunter hadn't thought of that! "I—I—I think it's interneral——."

"It's whatter?" gasped Bob Cherry.

"Interneral——!"

"Do you mean internal, you fat chump?"

"I don't care whether it's internal or interneral, but that's what it is," yapped Bunter. "I've got an awful pain

116

in my legs—I—I can't move! I—I think it's turned to pneumonia——."

"In the legs?" yelled Nugent.

"Ow! Yes! I—I think it runs in the family. My—my grandfather was—was lame with it——."

"Oh, suffering cats and crocodiles!" said Bob Cherry. "If Bunter's got pneumonia in the legs, it's a jolly serious case."

"Ha, ha, ha!"

"The pain is awful!" groaned Bunter. "You fellows wouldn't cackle, if you had a pain like burning daggers in your feet——."

"In your feet?" exclaimed Harry Wharton.

"I—I—I mean in the legs! That is, I mean in the legs and the feet as well. It's like burning daggers and red-hot pincers!" said Bunter, pathetically. "I—I—I say, Harry, old chap, will—will you tell Quelch that I'm fearfully ill, and—and can't get up this morning?"

Harry Wharton laughed.

"I think I'll leave you to tell Quelch!" he answered, "I'm sure he will sympathise with a fellow who's got pneumonia in his legs and feet."

"Ha, ha, ha!"

"Oh, really, Wharton——?"

"Sure you haven't got a broken leg in the back of your neck?" asked Skinner.

"Ha, ha, ha!"

"Oh, cackle!" said Bunter, bitterly. "You see me lying here——."

"And hear you, too!" said Skinner.

"Beast! You see me lying here, fairly doubled up with plumbago—I mean pneumonia—and all you can do is to cackle! You—you go and tell Quelch, Wharton. It's up to you as Head Boy, you know! And—and he mightn't believe me——."

"He might not!" chuckled Bob.

"The might-notfulness is terrific!" chortled the Nabob of Bhanipur.

"It was that soaking in Friardale Water yesterday," groaned Bunter. "Quelch said I might be ill, and—and I am! Awfully ill! You fellows can cackle, but I—I couldn't stir from this bed if the house was on fire. I—I

117

couldn't stir a limb if—if there was a wild tiger coming in at the door! "

"Too jolly bad! " said Bob Cherry. "Don't you think that anything could make you jump out of that bed, Bunter?"

"Nothing at all!" groaned Bunter. "I—I can't move! "

"Not if I took my bolster——."

"Eh?"

"And walloped you with it——?"

"Look here, you unsympathetic beast—yaroooh! Keep that bolster away!" yelled Bunter. "Whooop! Stoppit! Oh, crikey! Wow—ow—ow! Yoooop!"

"Ha, ha, ha!"

There was a roar of merriment in the Remove dormitory. Bunter had stated that he could not stir a limb, even in the improbable event of the house catching fire, or the still more improbable event of a wild tiger coming in at the door! But although those two extreme and improbable contingencies could not make him stir. Bob Cherry's bolster undoubtedly could—for it did! He stirred at the first swipe—and at the second, rolled over to escape—and at the third, bounced out of bed in a tangle of bedclothes. He rolled on the floor in sheets and blankets and roared.

"Ow! Keep off, you beast! Yaroooh! Stoppit! Oh, crikey!"

"Ha, ha, ha!" yelled the Removites.

Bob Cherry came round the bed, flourishing the bolster.

"Feel better now?" he asked.

"Ow! No! Worse! " yelled Bunter.

Swipe!

"Yarooooop! "

"Better now?"

"Ow! wow! No—Yes! I—I mean yes!" howled Bunter. "I—I think I can gerrup! Keep that bolster away, you beast! "

"Ha, ha, ha!"

"Well, if you're better, O.K.," said Bob, "but if you feel that plumbago and pneumonia coming on in your legs and feet again, just give me the tip, and I'll give you some more of the same."

"Beast! "

"Ha, ha, ha! "

Billy Bunter, apparently, did not feel those dread com-

118

plaints coming on again. Certainly he did not want any more of Bob Cherry's drastic remedy. It was a wrathy and morose fat Owl that rolled down from the dormitory with the Remove—the recipient of not a single spot of sympathy, and still in Coventry.

CHAPTER 24

THE GENUINE ARTICLE?

"AYTISHOOOOH!"

Mr. Quelch started, and looked round from his desk. All the Remove looked round, as that loud, prolonged Gargantuan sneeze woke the echoes of the form-room.

"Atchooooh!" went on Billy Bunter. "Choo—choo—achooh! Aytichoo!"

Bunter sneezed, and sneezed, and sneezed.

In the dormitory that morning, not a fellow had believed that Bunter had caught a cold. There had not been a sign of sneezing about him then—not the ghost of a sneeze. Neither at breakfast had he sneezed—he had been intent, as usual, on the foodstuffs: to which at mealtimes Bunter was accustomed to give concentrated and undivided attention. Not till lessons were about to begin in the form-room did Bunter sneeze.

Then he made up for lost time, as it were. He sneezed, and sneezed, and sneezed, almost frantically. Indeed, he seemed almost bent on sneezing his fat nose off his fat face.

It came on suddenly. He had rolled into the form-room, and taken his place in the form, unsneezing. Sitting there, he had dabbed his nose with his handkerchief: and the sneezing immediately followed. Sudden as it was, it was very emphatic. It almost roared.

"Oh, gum," murmured Bob Cherry, "has that fat ass got a cold after all?"

"He hadn't one in the dorm," said Harry Wharton, shaking his head.

"Well, he's sneezing now——."

"The sneezefulness is terrific."

"Gammon!" murmured the Bounder.

119

All eyes were on Bunter. Every fellow believed that he had been "spoofing" in the dormitory. They could hardly help suspecting that he was spoofing now. But looking at him, they had to admit that it looked genuine.

"Aytishooooh!" sneezed Bunter. "Urrrggh! Oooogh! Atchoooh! Atchooh!"

It was genuine sneezing! There could be no mistake about that. Not only was the fat Owl sneezing as if for a wager: but his fat little nose was crimson, and his eyes watering under his spectacles—almost streaming. "Spoof" was Billy Bunter's long suit: but this could scarcely be "spoof": unmistakably the fat Owl was in the throes of a terrific fit of sneezing. He sneezed, he gasped, he gurgled, he guggled, and he sneezed again, and yet again.

"Bunter!" exclaimed Mr. Quelch.

"Urrrrggh! Aytishooo! Oooogh!"

"You foolish boy!" exclaimed Mr. Quelch, really concerned for the suffering Owl, "I warned you that you might catch a severe cold if you did not change your clothes when you came in wet yesterday. Did you not do so, Bunter?"

"Urrrggh! Yes, sir! Atchooooooh!"

"You have caught a cold, Bunter——."

"Aytishoooh!"

"You should have gone to the House-dame at once, when you felt it coming on," rapped Mr. Quelch. "You had better go to her now. You cannot remain in class in that state."

Skinner winked at Snoop.

"That's the game!" he whispered.

And Snoop grinned and nodded.

"Go to Mrs. Kebble at once, Bunter," said Mr. Quelch. "You will carry out any directions she may give you. You seem to have a very bad cold."

"Groogh! Yes, sir! I—I think I've got a temperament——."

"A—a—a what?" ejaculated Mr. Quelch.

"A temperament, sir—a very high temperament——."

"Oh! I presume that you mean a temperature, Bunter. Ask Mrs. Kebble to take your temperature! Go to her at once, and you need not return to the form-room. You may go to your study, and remain there."

"Urrrrgh!" Yes, sir."

"Lose no time, Bunter."

"Atchoooh-chooh—choooh! Yes, sir! Chooooooooh!"

Billy Bunter left his place, and rolled to the door. All eyes in the Remove followed him. He sneezed, as he went —sneeze! sneeze! sneeze! The most doubting fellow had to admit that those sneezes were genuine.

There had been no sympathy for Bunter in the dormitory that morning. Really, a complaint of pneumonia in the legs was not calculated to elicit sympathy! But quite a number of glances were sympathetic now.

The Remove fellows were used to "gammon" from Bunter: but "gammon" would hardly have made his fat little nose burning red, and his eyes stream with water. Even Skinner could hardly doubt, as he watched the hapless fat Owl, almost doubled up with sneezing, totter to the door. He looked an extremely woebegone object as he tottered.

"Aytishooh! aytishooh!" sneezed Bunter, as he turned the door-handle. "Oh, crikey! Oooogh! Oytishoooooh!"

He rolled out of the form-room, and the door closed on him. Lessons in the Remove began minus the fattest member of the form.

Bunter sneezed, and sneezed, and sneezed again, as he rolled down the corridor. He took the direction of the House-dame's room, as bidden by his form-master. But as he entered the passage leading to that apartment, he came to a stop.

He seemed dubious.

"That old cat Kebble's jolly sharp!" he murmured, uneasily. "I—I jolly well ain't going to her."

He turned to roll away. For some reason, best known to himself, Billy Bunter did not want to interview the House-dame, or benefit from her ministrations. It was true that Mrs. Kebble was "sharp" and not easily imposed on, as Bunter knew by experience. Perhaps that was his reason!

But he turned back again. Quelch would very likely ask the House-dame about him, and it would come out that he had not gone as bidden: and that would spell trouble with Quelch. He realised that he just had to go to Mrs. Kebble, "sharp" as she undoubtedly was.

For a whole minute the fat Owl stood thinking it out. Then, apparently, he made up his fat mind. He took his handkerchief from his jacket pocket: the hanky with which he had dabbed his fat little nose in the form-room: which dab had been followed by that Gargantuan outbreak of sneezes. His next proceeding might have astonished any beholder. Holding his nose with the finger and thumb of his left hand, he shook the handkerchief in the air with his right—giving it a succession of vigorous shakes, as if to shake something out of it.

He was thus engaged when the door of Mrs. Kebble's room opened, and Trotter, the House page, came out, and came down the passage.

Trotter came to a sudden halt, staring at Bunter.

No doubt he was surprised to see a Remove junior out of form while lessons were going on. He was still more surprised to see him holding his nose with his left hand, and shaking out a handkerchief with his right. It was really quite a remarkable performance on the part of any Greyfriars fellow.

But the next moment, Trotter forgot to be surprised, as he began to sneeze! It seized him suddenly, as it had seized Bunter in the form-room.

"Aytishoooh!" sneezed Trotter. "Ooogh! Atchooh! Oooogh!"

Bunter jumped, and blinked round at him.

"Oh!" he gasped. "I—I say——."

Trotter sneezed loud and long.

"Ooogh! Atchoooh! Aytishooh! Tishoo! tishoo! tishoo! What are you doing, Master Bunter? What have you got pepper on your hanky for? Oooooch! Atchoooh! Tishoo! tishoo! tishoo!"

"Oh!" gasped Bunter. "Tut—tut—'tain't pepper, Trotter! I've got a kik—kik—cold in the nun—nun—nose! Tut—tut—'tain't pepper——."

He shoved the handkerchief hastily in his pocket, and sneezed. He had caught a whiff, as well as Trotter.

"It's pepper!" gasped Trotter. "Oh, crikey! Tishoo! tishoo! tishoo! Why, you've shaken out pepper—tishoo! tishoo—all over the shop—tishooo! You've made me sneeze—aytishoo! tishoo!"

Billy Bunter glared at him, with a glare that might almost have endangered his spectacles. It was rather unfortunate that Trotter had detected pepper in his handkerchief—a circumstance which William George Bunter desired to keep a deep, dead, dark secret!

122

"Look here, Trotter, don't you be cheeky!" yapped Bunter. "You mind your own business, see?"

"Tishoo! tishoo! tishoo!" was Trotter's only reply: and he passed Bunter, and went on his way, the fat Owl frowning after him.

Not till Trotter had quite disappeared, did Billy Bunter extract that handkerchief from his pocket again, and, holding his fat little nose, shook it in the air, to rid it of the last trace of pepper. Mrs. Kebble being so very sharp, obviously it was only prudent to have nothing about him scented with pepper, when he presented himself. She might have traced the sneezes to their source! Satisfied at last that it was all clear, Bunter rolled on to the House-dame's room.

Sympathetic fellows, in the Remove, wondered how poor old Bunter was getting on. Poor old Bunter was, as a matter of fact, getting on quite well. He found frowsting in an armchair before a study fire ever so much more enjoyable than lessons in the form-room!

CHAPTER 25

BEASTLY FOR BUNTER

"WHAT about Coventry?" grunted Johnny Bull.

"Oh, rot!" said Bob Cherry.

"Um!" said Harry Wharton, doubtfully.

The Remove were out in break. A fat figure, usually seen rolling towards the tuck-shop in break, was now conspicuous, as it were, by its invisibility. Nothing was to be seen of Billy Bunter. No doubt he was keeping in his study, nursing that cold: and Bob suggested giving him a look in, to see how he was getting on. Bunter had rolled out of the form-room in a paroxysm of sneezing, and Bob had a sympathetic heart. Johnny was more uncompromising.

"Well, he's ill!" argued Bob. "At least, he's got a fearful cold! You saw him sneezing his fat head off! He was gammoning in the dorm this morning—but——."

Grunt, from Johnny Bull.

"Did he snaffle our spread last week, and did old Wingate have to go away without any tea?" he demanded.

"Well, yes! But——."

"Isn't he in Coventry for tuck-raiding, till he learns to behave? Has he learned yet?" further demanded Johnny.

"Well, no: but——."

"That's that!" said Johnny Bull.

"True, O King!" admitted Bob. "All the same, let's go up and see how the fat old fathead is getting on, and whether we can do anything. Temper the wind to the shorn lamb, you know. If a fellow's knocked out with a fearful cold——."

"If!" snorted Johnny.

"Well, there's no 'if' about that," said Frank Nugent. "We all saw him doubled up with sneezing, in the form-room. Come on."

Bob Cherry led the way, and Harry Wharton, Nugent, and Hurree Jamset Ram Singh followed him. Johnny Bull, having expressed his feelings with another snort, followed on. Perhaps Johnny's bark was worse than his bite.

On the Remove landing they came on Lord Mauleverer, heading for the studies. Apparently Mauly also was going to give the sad sufferer a look-in. The half-dozen juniors went up the Remove passage together.

Bob Cherry opened the study door, and they looked in.

"Hallo, hallo, hallo!" roared Bob.

"Oh!" came a startled gasp.

Billy Bunter was reclining, not to say sprawling, in the study armchair, before the study fire. He had loaded the fire with the whole supply of coal, and the study was as warm as toast. Under the influence of the warmth, combined with laziness, the fat Owl seemed to be nodding. But he sat up and took notice, as Bob's cheery roar impinged upon his fat ears, and blinked round at the juniors in the doorway through his big spectacles.

"Oh! I say, you fellows——."

"Feelin' better?" asked Lord Mauleverer.

"Eh! Oh! No! Worse—much worse!" answered Bunter, promptly.

"You're not sneezing now!" remarked Johnny Bull, with a suspicious look at the fat Owl.

"Oh, really, Bull——."

"Looks as if that cold's gone!" said Johnny.

124

" 'Tain't!" howled Bunter. "It's worse than ever! I—I—I've been sneezing like—like billy-o—right up to this minute! The House-dame thinks it's a feverish cold, and—and so it is! You—you have to feed a cold, you know. You fellows got any chocs or toffee?"

"You have to feed a cold, and starve a fever," said Johnny Bull.

"Oh, Yes! Well, if I feed the cold now, I can starve the fever afterwards," said Bunter.

"Ha, ha, ha!"

"I'm fearfully hungry," said Bunter pathetically, "and—and I'm too ill to go down to the tuck-shop——."

"That's all right," said Bob. "I'll fetch anything you like, old fat man. Trot out the tin——."

"I—I've been disappointed about a postal order. I—I think I told you fellows, days ago, that I was expecting a postal order——."

"I think you did!" admitted Bob.

"The thinkfulness is terrific," chuckled Hurree Jamset Ram Singh.

"It—it hasn't come," said Bunter sadly. "Why, I don't know—it's from one of my titled relations, you know—but—but it hasn't come! If you fellows could lend a fellow ten bob till the postal order comes——."

"This year, next year, some time, never!" remarked Johnny Bull.

"Beast!"

"Look here, is that fat spoofer on the sick list at all?" grunted Johnny Bull. "He was sneezing in the form-room, but he seems to have jolly well got over it now——."

"What would you like, Bunter?" asked Lord Maulverer. His lordship did not seem to share Johnny's doubts.

Bunter's eyes glistened behind his spectacles.

"I—I think I could eat a cake, Mauly," he answered. "I—I think some toffees would do me good, too. And—and some jam-tarts. And—and a few dough-nuts——. I'll—I'll settle when my postal order comes, of course——."

"Oh! Yaas! Of—of course! Back in two ticks!" said Mauly, and he detached himself from the group at the door of No. 7 Study, and cut away down the passage.

The Famous Five gazed at Bunter, not exactly suspiciously, but dubiously. Except that his fat little nose was still red, they could discern no signs of that fearful cold about him now. Bunter's fat hand went to the handkerchief in his pocket. No doubt the artful fat Owl had replenished that hanky for action, since his visit to the House-dame.

"I say, you fellows, don't come too near," squeaked Bunter. "You might catch my cold, you know—I can feel the sneezing coming on again. Mind you don't get the microbobes——."

"The whatter?"

"The airs full of microbobes when a fellow with a cold sneezes," explained Bunter. "Better keep a safe distance."

"Oh! Microbes!" gasped Bob Cherry. "Do you mean microbes?"

"No, I don't—I mean microbobes! Keep at that door, and don't come too near—it's just coming on—oooooggh!"

Bunter put his handkerchief to his nose. Harry Wharton and Co. having no desire whatever to pick up any microbes if any were about, remained at the doorway: but they eyed the fat Owl still more dubiously. But the next moment they had to admit that Bunter was right—the sneezing was coming on again! There was no doubt about that: not a shadow of doubt: for a sudden tremendous sneeze fairly roared out in the study.

"Aytishoo! Tishoo! tishoo! Atchooooooooooooh!"

"Oh, my hat!" ejaculated Bob.

"Sounds like sneezing, Johnny!" remarked Frank Nugent, a little sarcastically.

Johnny gave a grunt. He had to admit it.

"Ooooogh!" spluttered Bunter. Perhaps he had overdone the pepper a little. "Oh, crumbs! Yooooch! Atchooh—aytishoo—sho—sho—shooooh! Wooogh!"

"Poor old Bunter?"

"The poorfulness of the esteemed old Bunter is terrific."

"Tishoo! tishoo! tishoo! tishoo!" Bunter went on, as if for a wager. He sneezed, and sneezed, and sneezed. "Aytishoooooh! Tishoooooh! tishoooooh! Wooogh!"

Harry Wharton and Co. gave him sympathetic looks—even the doubting Johnny. They could not help sympathising with a fellow in the grip of so tremendous a fit of sneezing. Luckily for Bunter, they were not close enough to detect the scent of the pepper parked in the folded hanky. Bunter had the whole benefit of the pepper, and

126

the fearfullest of fearful colds could not have made a fellow sneeze more wildly and frantically.

"Tishoo! tishoo! aytishoooooooooooooooo!" Bunter's little fat nose glowed red, his little round eyes streamed with water: his whole circumference shook with sneezes. It was like Bunter to overdo it. He had, certainly, convinced the Famous Five: but he was not enjoying the process.

There was a somewhat heavy tread in the Remove passage, and the juniors looked round as they heard it. An angular figure was coming up from the landing.

"Quelchy!" breathed Bob.

The juniors stood respectfully aside for their form-master to enter the study. Quelch, apparently, also wanted to know how Bunter was getting on !

He stepped into the study and was greeted by a terrific sneeze!

"Aytishoo—shoo—shoo—wooogh—tichoooh—oooh!"

"Bless my soul!" said Mr. Quelch. He gazed at that suffering member of his form, and his usually crusty countenance was quite concerned. "Bunter——."

"Oooooogh! Grooogh! Tishoo—tishoo—tishoo——." Bunter gave his form-master a watery blink through damp spectacles. A moment ago he had been regretting that he had overdone the pepper in the hanky. Now he was glad of it! It was more important to convince Quelch than to convince the Famous Five: the bare thought of Quelch discovering the "spoof" was unnerving! But those tremendous sneezes might have convinced Doubting Thomas himself.

"Your cold is no better, Bunter! It seems worse——."

"Tishoo—tishoo—tishoo——."

"I am sorry to see you like this, Bunter." Quelch's tone was kind. "It must be due to your immersion yesterday. You cannot possibly attend classes in this state. Neither can you remain here, Bunter. The other boys would be in danger of infection—indeed, it might spread over the whole form. I will speak to Miss Prim at once——."

Bunter jumped.

"M—m—miss Pip—pip—pip—Prim!" he stuttered. Miss Prim was the school nurse. She was a most efficient lady: whose efficient hands were the very last into which

127

William George Bunter desired to fall. "I—I say, sir——."

"A bed will be prepared for you immediately in the sanatorium——."

"Oh, crikey! "

"Where you will have every care, and, I trust, a rapid recovery," said Mr. Quelch. "Come with me now, Bunter."

"Oh, lor'! "

"Wharton, perhaps you will kindly get Bunter's overcoat and scarf and cap——."

"Oh! Certainly, sir."

"Tishoo! tishoo! tishoo!" Bunter, from the bottom of his fat heart, wished that he had parked a little less pepper in the hanky. Certainly he wanted to convince Quelch: but not to the extent of being walked off to the school sanatorium. He had been there before: and he knew what hospital diet was like! "I—I—I say, sir—groogh! —I say, I—I think I feel a little—tishoo—tishoo—tishoo—a little better, sir—Aytishoooooooooh!"

"Not at all, Bunter——."

"Oh! Oh, yes, sir! I—I think it—it—it's passing off, sir!" gasped Bunter, utterly dismayed by the prospect of coming under Miss Prim's hands. "I—I—I'd rather not go into sanny, sir—tishoo! tishoo!"

"That is absurd, Bunter! In the school sanatorium, you will be well cared for, and your diet will be carefully supervised, and you will be allowed nothing that would not be good for you in your present state—a very important matter, Bunter."

"Oh, crumbs! But, sir, I—I say—aytishhhhooooooh!"

"Here you are, old bean." Lord Mauleverer came into the study, unaware for the moment that Mr. Quelch was there. "Here you are, Bunter—a plum cake, a bag of doughnuts, and another of jam-tarts, and—Oh! I beg your pardon, sir—I—I didn't know you were here——!" Mauly became aware of Quelch.

His form-master frowned at him.

"Mauleverer! Have you brought those sticky and somewhat unwholesome comestibles here for Bunter?" he exclaimed.

"Oh! Yass, sir."

"You are a very thoughtless boy, Mauleverer," said Mr.

128

Quelch, severely. "Such comestibles may be quite harmful to Bunter now he is ill. Take them away."

"Oh, gad! I—I mean, yaas, sir," stammered Mauly.

"Oh, lor'! If—if you please, sir," gasped Bunter. "I—I think the cake would do me good, sir—tishoo—tishoo—tishoo——."

"Nonsense, Bunter."

"Oh, really, sir——."

"Miss Prim will decide your diet, Bunter. I doubt very much whether anything of that kind will be permitted. At all events the decision rests wholly with Miss Prim. Ah! Thank you, Wharton." The captain of the Remove came back with coat, and cap, and scarf." Put on your coat, Bunter——."

"I—I say, sir——!" groaned the hapless fat Owl.

"You are wasting time, Bunter. Put on your overcoat at once," said Mr. Quelch, sharply. "Now your scarf! You must be careful of the cold wind, in your present state. You have a very severe cold, Bunter—I have seldom or never heard such prolonged fits of sneezing——."

"I—I—I—I—tishoo—tishoo—tishoo——."

"Come!" said Mr. Quelch.

"Oh, crikey!"

The Remove master stepped out of the study. Billy Bunter blinked at the Co. with an expression that might have moved a heart of stone.

He had to turn a fat back on Mauly's cake, and tarts, and doughnuts, untasted! He had to accompany Mr. Quelch to a dolorous spot where he would be allowed to eat only what was good for him, and only so much as was good for him! The prospect was harrowing. Even "Coventry" was better than that!

Not for the first time in his fat career, the Owl of the Remove wished that he had not been quite so artful a dodger! But it was too late to think of that! He limped after Mr. Quelch, with an expression on his fat face compared with which that of the Knight of the Sorrowful Countenance might have been called merry and bright.

E

CHAPTER 26

FOOD SHORTAGE

"You fellows comin'?"

Lord Mauleverer asked that question, in break the following morning. It was addressed to Harry Wharton and Co.

"Whither bound?" asked Bob Cherry.

"Bunter——!"

"Oh!" said Bob, without enthusiasm. Bob had an old footer under his arm, which the juniors had intended to punt about in break. On a fine, clear, cold morning, punting a footer interested them much more than a visit to the sanatorium. But Mauly's thoughts, it appeared, dwelt on the visitation of the sick.

"Um!" said Johnny Bull.

Bunter had not been seen since Quelch had walked him off to "sanny" the previous day. Sad to relate, he had not even been missed. There had been a vacant place in form that morning: there was no fat Owl to supply his usual "howler" in "con". Fellows, of course, sympathised with anyone laid up with a severe cold: and Bunter, on a diet prescribed by Miss Prim, was perhaps a special object of sympathy. Nevertheless, absence in Bunter's case did not seem to have had the effect of making hearts grow fonder. It was like old Mauly to remember him when everyone else seemed to have forgotten his fat existence.

"It's a bit rotten for him, you know," said Lord Mauleverer. "Sneezing his head off in sanny, with no company but Prim's. She's a good sort, and a jolly dutiful nurse, but not what a fellow could call exhilaratin'. I've asked Quelch for leave, and we can go in if we like."

"You seem to have forgotten that that fat frump is in Coventry!" said Johnny Bull, sarcastically.

"Yaas! Let's go on forgettin' it!" suggested Lord Mauleverer.

Harry Wharton laughed.

"Let's go," he said. "Might cheer him up a bit. Chuck

130

that footer over to Smithy, Bob, and let's go with Mauly."

"Oh, all right!'

And the Famous Five accompanied Lord Mauleverer. Break lasted only fifteen minutes, and nobody wanted to lose that respite from Quelch: still, it was possible that a visit from his form-fellows might cheer up the sad sufferer, and they presented themselves cheerfully to Miss Prim, prepared to sacrifice ten of the fifteen minutes to the fat Owl.

"Bunter better, I hope, Miss Prim?" asked Lord Mauleverer.

Miss Prim, a somewhat severe-looking lady of uncertain age, gave a slight—a very slight—sniff.

"Very much better, I think," she answered.

"Still sneezing?" asked Bob.

"He has not sneezed once since he was admitted yesterday."

"Oh, that's good."

"Very!" said Miss Prim, in a very dry manner. "If you have your form-master's leave, you may see him. Come this way."

The juniors exchanged glances, as they followed Miss Prim. They gathered from her manner that she was taking a rather dim view of her patient. Johnny Bull gave a shrug of the shoulder. He still had a lingering doubt about that fearful cold from which Bunter was suffering: and now he had an impression that Miss Prim had doubts on the subject also.

They found Bunter in bed, sitting up against the pillows, blinking from a window into the garden. He turned a fat head as they came in, and blinked at them instead, with a dolorous blink. Bunter was getting out of lessons, getting out of prep, and, temporarily at least, getting out of Coventry. But he did not look as if he enjoyed it all. Probably Miss Prim's views on the subject of diet were beginning to tell on him.

"Ten minutes!" said Miss Prim, briefly: and she left the visitors with the suffering Owl, retiring to the further end of the room: where she sat down. Her keen eyes, however, remained on them. Possibly Miss Prim had had experience of thoughtless schoolboys smuggling indigestible comestibles to friends in "sanny".

Billy Bunter eyed the juniors eagerly, but did not speak

131

till Miss Prim was out of hearing. Then he whispered:

"I say, you fellows, got any chocs?"

Six heads were shaken. It was, of course, strictly against all rules for tuck to be smuggled into sanny: neither would it have been easily practicable under Miss Prim's keen eyes.

"Any toffee?" breathed Bunter.

"Not a spot."

"Oh, crikey! Haven't you got anything to eat at all?"

" 'Tain't allowed, old chap——."

"Well, you silly idiots!" said Bunter. "What have you come for, then?"

Lord Mauleverer coughed.

"Hem! We thought you'd rather like us to give you a look-in, old tulip——."

"You might have brought a fellow something to eat. I've had nothing since Quelch hiked me in here yesterday —practically nothing! That old cat——."

"Eh? Who?"

"That old cat Prim won't let me have so much as a doughnut! I had one egg for brekker—ONE!!" groaned Bunter. "I'm to have a cup of broth at eleven! Nothing else till tiffin—and I can guess what that will be like, under Prim's eye! I—I say, you fellows, sure you haven't got even a bull's-eye?"

"Sorry, old bean! We couldn't hand you anything with Prim's eye on us——."

"You could manage somehow if you had any sense!"

"Hem! Miss Prim says you're getting better," said Bob. "You won't be in here long, at this rate."

"Fat lot she knows about it," grunted Bunter. "I don't believe she really believes I've got a fearful cold at all. Suspicious cat, you know! Eyes a fellow! She's got an eye on us now. I—I wonder what she did with my hanky."

"Your hanky!" repeated Harry Wharton, blankly. The juniors had not expected a fellow suffering from a fearful cold, combined with the horrors of a restricted diet, to be bothering about a handkerchief. But it seemed that the fat Owl was worried on that subject.

"You see, Quelch hooked me in here, and I was bundled into bed at once," explained Bunter. "Prim gave me a clean handkerchief, and took away the old one. I—I couldn't say anything, or——."

"Oh what?"

"Oh! Nothing! I—I never had a chance to—to——."

"To what?"

"Nothing! But—but what do you think they've done with that hanky?" asked Bunter, blinking at the juniors anxiously.

"Put it in the wash, I expect," said Harry. "What does it matter?"

"Oh, it doesn't matter at all—not a bit! Not if it went straight into the wash, anyhow! But if Prim happened to notice——."

"What was there to notice?" asked Harry, quite astonished.

"Oh! Nothing! Still, if she told Quelch——."

"If she told Quelch what?"

"Nothing, of course," stammered Bunter.

The juniors gazed at him. Why he was worrying about the handkerchief that had been in his pocket when Mr. Quelch walked him into sanny, was a mystery to them.

Naturally Miss Prim had given him a clean handkerchief, and taken the old one away, doubtless to give it a spot of disinfectant and pass it on to the laundry. There was nothing in that to worry Bunter, as far as they could see. They were not aware that that grubby handkerchief contained an unmistakable clue to the source of Bunter's sneezing—if anyone happened to spot it!

"Suspicious old cat, you know," mumbled Bunter, "she might think——"

"What might she think?" asked Harry, quite mystified.

"Oh! Nothing!" Bunter changed the subject. "I say, you fellows, you must be silly idiots not to bring in something for a fellow to eat—I think you might have brought a chunk of toffee, at least——."

"But it isn't allowed——."

"What does that matter, so long as I get the toffee?" yapped Bunter. "You could sneak it in somehow! I'm hungry. I say, you fellows, come and see me again, will you—you needn't stay now, but come and see me again, and bring something in your pockets next time——."

The Famous Five grinned. It seemed that Bunter had no particular use for their company, so far as that went.

"We'll come again if you like——," said Frank Nugent.

"Good!" said Bunter.

"But we can't smuggle in any tuck——."

"Beast!"

"My esteemed and ludicrous Bunter——!" murmured Hurree Jamset Ram Singh.

"Oh, pack it up!" yapped Bunter. "If you ain't going to bring anything to eat, what's the good of coming at all? I say, Mauly, you'll come again, won't you——?"

"Yaas."

"And bring me something to eat," said Bunter, anxious. "Of—of course I—I want to see you, old chap, but I specially want something to eat. If you could wangle some chocs or toffee without that old cat spotting you, you know——."

"She's got a jolly sharp eye," said Johnny Bull.

The sharpfulness of her absurd eye is terrific," remarked Hurree Jamset Ram Singh, "and the spotfulness means a row with the esteemed Quelch."

"Mauly ain't funky of Quelch, like you fellows! You leave Mauly alone! I say, Mauly, old chap, you won't let me down, will you? You can manage it somehow without Prim spotting you——."

"I—I'll do what I can, old fat bean," said Lord Mauleverer, "but——."

"Cave!" whispered Bob Cherry: as Miss Prim rose from her chair and came across the room to the sufferer's bedside. Time was up.

The juniors had to take their leave—Billy Bunter's eyes and spectacles following them anxiously as they departed. He was left with a glimmer, at least, of hope and comfort. Lord Mauleverer was going to do his best, at any rate, to satisfy the fat Owl's deep and heart-felt yearning for sweet and sticky things, though whether he would succeed in eluding the eagle eye of Miss Prim was another matter. But the mere possibility of toffee and chocs was a comfort! Billy Bunter had, at least, something to hope for.

CHAPTER 27

WILY

FISHER T. FISH glanced up with an irritated frown, as a tap came at his study door, and it opened. After third school, Fisher T. Fish, not disposed to join other Remove fellows in putting a footer in the quad, had gone up to his study, having more important matters, of a financial nature, on his Transatlantic mind. That elusive threepence in his accounts was still eluding him, and it had worried him for days. But the frown on his bony brow changed at once into the most amiable grin of which his sharp features were capable, as he saw that the visitor to No. 14 Study was Lord Mauleverer.

Mauly was the kind of fellow with whom the business-man of the Remove delighted to deal. Generally he had few opportunities: his lordship having no use whatever for Fisher Tarleton Fish. Now, however, he had come to Fishy's study of his own accord, and he was as welcome as the flowers in May. The fact that he was accustomed to keep Fishy at arm's length did not diminish the affa-bility of Fishy's greeting. Mauly was, in Fishy's opinion, a goob, a goof, and a bonehead, and dealing with goobs, goofs, and boneheads, was the way for a guy to turn his dimes into dollars.

"Say, push in, big boy," said Fisher T. Fish, amicably, and Lord Mauleverer pushed in. "Squat!"

Lord Mauleverer did not "squat". He had called on busi-ness, as Fishy guessed: and if he wanted anything that Fishy had to sell, Fishy was prepared to treat him with the distinction due to a nobleman, and charge him three times the value instead of merely twice that amount as was his custom.

"Books, is it?" asked Fisher T. Fish. "If it's a noo dictionary you want, old-timer, I've got one here that's practically noo—only the covers gone——."

"Thanks! No——."

"Lost your keys? This hyer bunch——."

"Oh! No! I haven't lost my keys——."

"Mebbe your ticker's stopped? I've got a watch here——."

"Nunno! I want that jig-saw puzzle of yours."

"Gee-whiz!" ejaculated Fisher T. Fish. He was pleased, but surprised. Fisher T. Fish had bought that jig-saw puzzle, in its wooden box, from a hard-up fag in the Third, weeks ago. He had bought it so very, very cheap, that he had not been able to resist it: but he had doubted since whether he had not, perhaps, got "left" on the transaction. He had hawked that jig-saw puzzle up and down the Remove without finding a single taker. In the Greyfriars Remove there seemed to be absolutely no demand for jig-saw puzzles, and the article was still on Fishy's bony hands. Mauly, among others, had had the offer of it, which he had declined without thanks. So why he wanted it now, was really as great a puzzle as the jig-saw itself. But apparently he did: and the businessman of the Remove was very glad to hear it. He had feared that he never would be able to "trade" that jig-saw puzzle: which made the two shillings he had given for it a very painful memory indeed.

"You've still got it?" asked Lord Mauleverer, rather anxiously.

"Yup!"

Fisher T. Fish bounced out of his chair, and bounced to the study cupboard. He reached therein, and jerked out a wooden box.

Lord Mauleverer looked at it. The box was about fifteen inches by ten, and rather deep. It had a sliding wooden lid. On that lid was a coloured picture, and the inscription:

LITTLE GEORGIE'S JOLLY JIG-SAW

Fishy could not help being surprised. Lord Mauleverer really did not seem the kind of guy to find entertainment in piecing together little Georgie's Jolly Jig-Saw. But Mauly was more than welcome to the article, of which, with all his gifts of salesmanship, Fishy had not yet been able to dispose.

He slid back the sliding lid with a bony thumb.

"Seventy-five pieces, same as it says on the box!" he remarked. "Like to count 'em, big boy?"

"Oh! No! Not at all!"

"Keep you amused for hours!" said Fisher T. Fish. "Nothing better for a rainy day, I guess! Yourn for seven-and-six."

Fisher T. Fish's manner was hearty and genial: but he gave Mauly a rather stealthy look, wondering whether the goob would remember that he had last offered that article for five shillings.

But if Lord Mauleverer remembered that circumstance, he made no remark upon it. He laid three half-crowns on the study table, so readily, that Fisher T. Fish was immediately smitten with remorse for not having asked more. But it was too late now: Little Georgie's Jolly Jig-Saw was gone for seven-and-six.

"Thanks!" said Lord Mauleverer. He put the box under his arm, and turned to the door.

"Say! Anything else I could show you, Mauly?" asked Fisher T. Fish. "I guess I've got a box of card tricks here that would amoose you no end——."

"Not at all."

"Can I interest you in a ping-pong set——?"

"Not in the least."

Lord Mauleverer quitted No. 14 Study, with the box under his arm. Fisher T. Fish picked up the three half-crowns, bit each of them in turn, and slipped them into his pocket, and grinned.

"I'll say that dumb-clucks and their dough are soon parted!" he remarked. Then he returned to his accounts, and his bony brows concentrated once more in a frown over the elusive threepence.

Lord Mauleverer ambled gracefully down the passage to his own study, No. 12. Inside that study, he shut the door carefully, and laid the box on the table.

If Fisher T. Fish had been surprised by the purchase, he would probably have been still more surprised, could he have witnessed Mauly's next proceedings.

The box was turned over on the table, and seventy-five irregularly-shaped pieces of thin wood tumbled out. Then it was set upright again, and Lord Mauleverer proceeded to pack it with something quite unlike a jig-saw puzzle.

He opened a large box of chocolate-creams, and with careful fingers, arranged a layer of the same at the bottom of the puzzle-box. Mauly was himself rather indifferent

137

to the attractions of sticky things: but that ample array of "stickers" would have delighted Billy Bunter's heart, and made his capacious mouth water. There were almost as many as even the fat Owl could have negotiated at a single sitting.

Having carefully arranged that layer of plump chocolate-creams, each in its silver foil, at the bottom of the puzzle-box, Lord Mauleverer proceeded with equal care, to cover it up with a layer of jig-saw pieces.

The chocolates did not leave room for all the seventy-five: but that was a matter of no moment. Mauly packed in a layer that covered the chocolates, and completely hid them from sight. The remainder he left on the table.

Having now packed the puzzle-box to capacity, he slid the sliding-lid into its place, closing it.

Then, with a cheery smile on his face, he put the puzzle-box under his noble arm again, and left the study. Skinner, on the Remove landing, stared at it, as he passed him. He had seen that jig-saw puzzle box before.

"Oh, crumbs! Has Fishy landed that on you, Mauly?" he asked.

"Yaas."

"Sort of ass you are, ain't it?" said Skinner, agreeably.

"Thanks."

Lord Mauleverer went down the stairs, leaving Skinner grinning. Skinner's grins did not affect his lordship's equanimity, however. He strolled out into the sunny quad with the box under his arm.

"Hallo, hallo, hallo!" A cheery roar greeted him. "Join up, Mauly, and help us punt this footer! Great pip!" Bob Cherry stared at the wooden box under Mauleverer's arm. "What's that?"

"Something for Bunter," explained Lord Mauleverer.

"Oh, suffering cats and crocodiles!" ejaculated Bob. "Think that fat cormorant can eat a jig-saw puzzle? What he wants is something to stuff!"

"Well, we ain't allowed to take in a box of chocolates," said Lord Mauleverer, "but Miss Prim will let a jig-saw puzzle pass, I suppose."

"Of course she will," assented Bob, "but what's the use of that to Bunter? He can't eat jig-saw puzzles."

"Nunno! But he could eat what's underneath the pieces,

138

when he takes them out and finds it!" murmured Lord Mauleverer.

"Eh?"

"More in it than meets the eye, you know."

"Oh, my hat!"

Bob Cherry stared blankly at Lord Mauleverer, for a moment. Then he burst into a roar.

"Ha, ha, ha!"

"A fellow hates breakin' the rules," murmured Lord Mauleverer, "but poor old Bunter's simply perishin' for something sticky."

"Ha, ha, ha! You deep, wily old Machiavellian plotter!" gasped Bob. "You wily old schemer! So that's it, is it?"

"Yaas."

"Best of luck!" grinned Bob: and he returned to the punt-about, leaving Lord Mauleverer to amble on to the sanatorium, with Little Georgie's Jolly Jig-Saw box under his arm—with more in it than met the eye; and which, it was to be hoped, would not meet the penetrating eye of Miss Prim.

CHAPTER 28

NO GO!

BILLY BUNTER blinked at Lord Mauleverer, through his big spectacles. His little round eyes glistened behind those spectacles, as he blinked. Mauly, true to his word, had come again, after third school: and that, Bunter hoped at least, meant that Mauly was playing the part of a bold bad smuggler—smuggling "stickers" to a hapless invalid laid up in "sanny" on a regular and restricted diet. Even Mauly, Bunter considered, couldn't be quite idiot enough to come without something edible for a hungry Owl.

Bunter was not looking as if he enjoyed his sojourn in "sanny". Indeed, he was inclined to recover and get out: only he had a misgiving that so very sudden a recovery might awaken suspicion.

The bare idea of Quelch discovering that it was all "spoof" made him feel quite cold down his fat spine.

Prim, he knew, was dubious and suspicious already. She had heard from Quelch of Bunter's frantic outbreaks of sneezing. But these had entirely ceased after his admission to sanny. Bunter, certainly, would have been willing to oblige Miss Prim with a few sneezes, if that was what she wanted: but he couldn't, without the assistance of his peppered handkerchief. Still, Prim didn't matter much, so long as Quelch had no doubts. Prim could give him grim glances, and speak with a voice that seemed to come out of a refrigerator: but Quelch could wield the cane—and was quite certain so to do if he discovered that the fattest member of his form had pulled his majestic leg.

Bunter was uneasy about that handkerchief. If Prim captured so much as a sniff or a whiff from it, the game was up. Quelch had marched him off to sanny so suddenly, that he had had no chance at all of taking precautions, as he had done before calling on the House-dame. But he had heard nothing about it so far: and he fervently hoped that he was going on hearing nothing about it.

In the meantime, while sanny was not a bed of roses, there were consolations. He was cutting lessons: which from Bunter's point of view, was distinctly to the good. He was getting out of Coventry, which was even better. Half-a-dozen sympathetic fellows had been in to see him, and seemed to have forgotten all about "Coventry". Could they begin it all over again when the invalid recovered? Hardly! Prospects seemed good to Bunter. "Sanny" was a blow: he would have preferred to have his illness in No. 7 Study, with the pepper-pot at hand to help him keep up appearances. Still, it certainly made the thing look genuine.

Bunter, in fact, would not have been dissatisfied, but for the food question. That, unfortunately, was a question of the greatest and most far-reaching importance: transcending any other problem that existed within the wide limits of the universe. A fellow had to eat!

A cup of broth at eleven was to Billy Bunter like unto a drop of water in the ocean, or a single grain of sand on the sea-shore.

And there was nothing else coming till dinner: and at

dinner Bunter was accustomed to annexing many helpings. He could dismally foresee that helpings would be few and sparse under Prim's eye.

His hope was in old Mauly.

Mauly was ass enough to risk getting into a row for breaking the rules, in his sympathy for a fat and suffering Owl. Mauly had lots of money, which he never counted. He had said that he would do his best: and surely even that ass Mauly would have sense enough to smuggle in something good, and somehow wangle it into Bunter's possession without catching Prim's sharp eye!

So at the sight of Lord Mauleverer coming in with Miss Prim, the fat Owl's eyes glistened behind his spectacles, in anticipation.

He noted that Mauly had something under his arm. That could hardly be tuck, as it was in full view of Prim as she showed him in. It looked to Bunter like a rather long flat box, and he wondered what it was, without much interest. Food filled his thoughts.

"A few minutes," Miss Prim was saying. "No doubt a jig-saw puzzle will help the patient to pass the time——."

"I—I think Bunter will like it, ma'am," murmured Lord Mauleverer. "If—if I may leave it with him——."

"Certainly you may," said Miss Prim.

Billy Bunter's eyes and spectacles fixed on Lord Mauleverer with a look that was almost ferocious. A jig-saw puzzle, was it?

That Mauly was an ass, Bunter knew. He was ass enough to break the rules and risk a row with Quelch. But was he, could he be, ass enough to bring Bunter a jig-saw puzzle to pass the time, instead of the supply of stickers for which the fat Owl yearned?

"Feelin' better, Bunter, old thing?" asked Lord Mauleverer.

"Eh? Oh! Yes! No! I say, have you——?" Bunter broke off in time. Miss Prim was not retiring to a distance now. She was waiting to take Mauly away when he had presented his gift to the invalid. Possibly a second visit on the same day had made Miss Prim wary. Anyhow, there she was, well within hearing, and Bunter dared not breathe a word about tuck for her ears to catch.

"I've brought you this, old chap," said Lord Mauleverer.

141

He held out the flat wooden box. "I hope you'll find it amusin'."

Bunter breathed hard through his fat little nose, as he blinked at "Little Georgie's Jolly Jig-Saw" box.

He had one remaining hope! Perhaps, under cover of that box, Mauly was going to slip him something edible.

That hope proved delusive. Except for the puzzle-box, Mauly's hands were empty. That was all he had—nothing else! He was ass enough, idiot enough, blithering fathead enough, to bring Bunter a jig-saw puzzle, instead of something to eat! He wasn't after all, risking breaking the rules: Bunter was going to be left with the food shortage as severe as ever, with a jig-saw puzzle to console him! Bunter's feelings were almost too deep for words.

"Here you are, Bunter," said Mauleverer, cheerily. He slid open the lid of the puzzle-box, for Miss Prim's behoof. Nothing of a suspicious nature was revealed: only jig-saw pieces.

"You silly idiot!" breathed Bunter. He guessed no more than Miss Prim did!

Lord Mauleverer looked at him. Billy Bunter was not quick on the uptake, and evidently he did not catch on. However, he would catch on fast enough when he found the chocolates under the jig-saw pieces! Mauleverer placed it in his fat hands.

"I'm sure you'll like it, old chap," said Mauly.

Billy Bunter looked at him. To Billy Bunter, Little Georgie's Jolly Jig-Saw was a jig-saw puzzle: merely that and nothing more. Mauly wasn't going to bring him any tuck—he had brought him that utterly idiotic jig-saw puzzle! It was too much! The wrath of Achilles, to Greece the direful spring of woes unnumbered, was merely a passing breeze, compared with Billy Bunter's wrath at that moment. Words failed him! It was a time for action, not words.

He grasped that long flat box with both hands. He leaned across towards Lord Mauleverer, his eyes gleaming through his spectacles.

What happened next startled Miss Prim, and astonished Lord Mauleverer. It was quite unexpected.

With both fat hands, Billy Bunter brought that box down on Lord Mauleverer's startled head! Its contents flew in the air.

142

*With both fat hands, Billy Bunter brought that box
down on Lord Mauleverer's startled head.*

143

Crash!

"Oh!" yelled Lord Mauleverer. "Ooogh! Oh! Oh, gad! Oh!"

"Master Bunter——!" gasped Miss Prim.

"Oh, gad! Ow!"

"There, you idiot!" hissed Bunter. "There, you fathead! There, you noodle! There, you blithering, blethering chump! There!"

Lord Mauleverer tottered in a rain of jig-saw pieces—and of other objects that were wrapped in silver foil! Jig-saw sections and chocolate creams scattered round Mauly on the floor.

Billy Bunter glared at him, his very spectacles gleaming wrath.

"There, you silly chump!" he hooted. "There, you fathead! There, you—Oh! Oh, crikey! Oh, crumbs! Oh!" He glimpsed the chocolates among the jig-saw sections: and at long last—rather too late!—understood. "Oh! Oh, scissors!"

"You fat ass!" gasped Lord Mauleverer, rubbing his head.

"Upon my word!" Miss Prim's eyes were on the chocolates. "Mauleverer! What does this mean?"

"Bunter, you fat ass—."

"Oh, crikey!"

"Mauleverer, I shall report this to your form-master. You will not be permitted to come here again! Go away at once," snapped Miss Prim. "Upon my word! Actually smuggling sweets to a boy in sanatorium! Go away immediately."

"Yaas, ma'am!" gasped Lord Mauleverer.

He went away immediately: rubbing his head as he went. Billy Bunter blinked after him: and blinked at the chocolates on the floor. Miss Prim, with a severe brow, gathered them up.

"Oh, lor'!" moaned Bunter.

There were dozens of the chocolates. But there was not a single choc for Bunter. Miss Prim gathered them up and departed with them while Bunter's eyes and spectacles followed her and the chocolates, as Dido's sad eyes followed the departing sails of Æneas. He groaned. Only a groan could express his feelings. Miss Prim walked off with the chocolates and left him to groan.

CHAPTER 29

FOR IT

"HALLO, hallo, hallo!"

"Bunter!"

"Turned up like a bad penny!"

"Sudden recovery!" grunted Johnny Bull.

"The suddenfulness is terrific."

All eyes turned on Billy Bunter. The bell had rung for class, and the Remove had gathered at the door of their form-room, for Mr. Quelch to let them in as usual. So far as they thought of Billy Bunter at all—which was not, perhaps, very much—they supposed that he would be absent from class that afternoon as he had been in the morning. So it was quite a surprise to see him. Mr. Quelch came up the corridor, as expected: Billy Bunter followed him up, which was unexpected.

"Henry looks shirty!" murmured Bob Cherry; taking exceeding care that that murmur did not reach "Henry's" ears as he came.

Henry Samuel Quelch certainly did look grim. Something, it was clear, had stirred his ire. Billy Bunter looked dismal, dolorous, and apprehensive.

There was no sign of a fearful cold about him. Apparently he was quite restored to his normal fat self. A fellow who had had a fearful cold, and had recovered so suddenly and completely, might have been expected to feel, and look, bucked. But Bunter plainly was not enjoying his remarkable recovery. Seldom or never had he looked so pessimistic.

Mr. Quelch unlocked the door: and Billy Bunter gave his form-fellows a dismal blink as they went in.

"Glad to see you up again, old fat man," whispered Bob Cherry.

"The gladfulness is preposterous, my esteemed fat Bunter."

"O.K. now?" asked Harry Wharton.

"Cold quite gone?" asked Peter Todd.

145

It looked as if "Coventry" was quite forgotten! Sympathetic hearts had been touched by Bunter on the sick list. The artful dodger had, in fact, got away with his artful dodging!

That was what the wily fat Owl had schemed. Apparently he had succeeded! Yet he failed to look happy about it. Something seemed to be weighing on Bunter's fat mind: and he responded to those kind and friendly remarks only with a dismal, dolorous mumble.

"Bunter!" rapped Mr. Quelch.

"Oh, lor'! I mean, yes, sir," stammered Bunter.

"You will not go to your place yet, Bunter! I have to deal with you first."

"Oh, crikey!"

The Remove went to their places, leaving Billy Bunter standing before his form-master. Quelch's brow was grim: indeed at its grimmest: and his gimlet-eyes almost bored into Bunter.

The juniors looked on, wondering. Clearly there was a "row" on: but what the matter was, no one could guess so far. But it looked as if Bunter, for some unknown reason, was "for it".

"Bunter!" said Mr. Quelch, in a very deep voice, "I have to deal with you, and I shall deal with you severely. In all my career as a schoolmaster, I have never known of such a deception."

"I—I—I——!" mumbled Bunter.

"You deliberately led me to believe, Bunter, that you were suffering from an extremely severe cold, due to your immersion in the stream in Friardale Wood," said Mr. Quelch, sternly.

"Oh! Yes, sir! It was—was—was fearful, sir——." gasped Bunter.

"You have not suffered from a cold at all, Bunter!"

"Oh, really, sir——."

"Oh, my hat!" murmured Bob Cherry, and Johnny Bull gave a grunt. Johnny had had a lingering doubt all along.

"Spoof all the time!" whispered Skinner.

"But he was sneezing his head off!" muttered Nugent. "What——."

"Silence in the class!" rapped Mr. Quelch. "Bunter, you have deceived me—deceived and deluded me. I had

146

no doubts, Bunter, after the paroxysm of sneezing I saw with my own eyes. I find that Miss Prim had doubts, and those doubts, Bunter, have been confirmed by a discovery she has made. Do you now deny, Bunter, that your fits of sneezing were produced, deliberately, by packing pepper in your handkerchief?"

"Oh, crumbs!" gasped Bob Cherry.

"Pepper!" repeated Frank Nugent. "Pepper! Oh, my hat!"

"The fat spoofer——."

"Pulling our leg all the time——."

"Might have guessed——."

"Silence in the form! Bunter, the handkerchief you were using before being admitted to the sanatorium was taken from you. Miss Prim noticed nothing at the time. But as you were supposed to have a bad cold, Bunter, Miss Prim set it aside, to be sprinkled with disinfectant, before it was sent to the wash. She was about to do this to-day, when the scent of pepper from the handkerchief attracting her attention, she examined it, closely and carefully. She found, Bunter, that it had been impregnated with pepper—indeed, she has informed me that it caused her to sneeze, herself, in examining it! You have not had a severe cold, Bunter—you have not had a cold at all—you have resorted to this deceitful device to escape your lessons!" thundered Mr. Quelch.

"Oh, crikey!"

"And now, Bunter——." Mr. Quelch picked up the cane from his desk.

"Oh, lor'! I—I—I didn't, sir!" gasped Bunter. "I—I wasn't! I—I never thought of getting out of lessons, sir——."

"Silence, Bunter! I will hear no more untruthfulness from you."

"But—but—really, sir——."

"Silence!"

Some of the Remove were grinning now. Mr. Quelch, now that he was aware of the trick played by the fat Owl, concluded as a matter of course that it had been a dodge to get out of lessons. The Removites could guess that it had been a trick to get out of Coventry! Getting out of lessons too had no doubt been welcome to Bunter, but it had been only a by-product, as it were.

147

Mr. Quelch swished the cane.

"Bunter! Bend over that form!"

"I—I—I say, sir—I—I didn't—I—I wasn't—I—I never!" gasped Bunter. "I—I—I don't know how the pepper got in my hanky, sir—I—I mean I—I spilt it there entirely by accident, sir, and—and——."

"Bend over that form, Bunter."

"Oh, crikey!"

In the lowest possible spirits, Billy Bunter bent over. His masterly scheme had gone awry: his artful dodgery had come home to roost! In fact there seemed to be always a technical hitch somewhere in Bunter's scheming.

Whop! whop! whop!

"Yow—ow—ow!" roared Bunter.

Whop!

"Yaroooh!"

Whop!

"Oh, crumbs! wow! ow!"

WHOP!

"Yoooo—hooooooop!" bellowed Bunter.

Mr. Quelch laid down the cane.

"You may now go to your place, Bunter! I trust that this will be a lesson to you. Cease that absurd noise at once, and go to your place."

Bunter went to his place. But he did not find it easy to cease the absurd noise. "Six" from Quelch had almost doubled up the fat Owl. But there was no doubt that it would be, as Quelch trusted, a lesson to him. Never again was Billy Bunter likely to invent a fearful cold with pepper in his handkerchief.

CHAPTER 30

PLAYFUL PON

"I say, you fellows!"

There was no hopeful note in Billy Bunter's fat squeak.

He did not expect the Famous Five to heed: and they did not.

On Wednesday afternoon, a half-holiday, most Greyfriars fellows were looking cheery. That afternoon the chums of the Remove were going out on their jiggers, and Bunter waylaid them on the way to the bike-shed, where Bob Cherry had a puncture to mend before they could get get going.

Five fellows walked on regardless of a squeaking fat Owl.

The hapless Owl was back in Coventry. His escape from that chilly region had been brief. Twice, by knavish tricks, had Bunter shaken the dust of Coventry, so to speak, from his podgy feet. In neither case had his success lasted. Fellows who had sympathised with a sick Owl sneezing his head off, had no sympathy to waste upon an artful dodger who had pulled their leg. "Coventry" had clamped down once more on Billy Bunter, and his last state was worse than his first. He cast a doleful blink after the Famous Five as they disappeared into the bike-shed.

"Beasts!" mumbled Bunter.

He bore down on Peter Todd. In No. 7 Study, since the facts had come out about Bunter's fearful cold, Peter had been giving him what Fisher T. Fish called the marble eye and the frozen mitt. The eye was still marble, and the mitt still frozen, as Bunter rolled up.

"I say, Toddy, old fellow—I say, lend me a tanner, old chap! I'm going over to Cliff House, and——. Beast!" Bunter addressed that final remark to Peter's departing back.

He blinked round at Vernon-Smith, coming out of the House with Tom Redwing.

"I say, Smithy——."

Smithy and Redwing walked on.

Bunter breathed hard through his fat little nose. He was sorely in want of a word to break the solitude of Coventry. Still more he was in want of a small loan. Once more he had been disappointed about a postal order. He was going over to Cliff House that afternoon: not so much because as an affectionate brother he yearned to see his sister Bessie, but as a rest from Coventry. Bessie Bunter might or might not be pleased to see Brother Billy: but at any rate she would not remain dumb.

But there was a lion in the path! Unless he could borrow the bus fare to Pegg, he had to walk to Cliff House School. Even by the short cut through Friardale Wood it was a long walk. And Bunter did not like even short walks! So it was necessary for a victim to be found.

He had a faint access of hope, as his spectacles fell on Lord Mauleverer, leaning on the tree near the tuck-shop, with his hands in the pockets of his elegant bags. He rolled up to Mauleverer.

"I say, Mauly, old chap——."

Lord Mauleverer did not speak. His gaze passed Bunter by unseeingly.

"I—I say, Mauly, you ain't shirty, are you?" pleaded Bunter. "I—I never knew there were chocs in that box yesterday—I—I thought—I thought you'd let me down, old chap, bringing me that silly jig-saw instead of something to eat. It—it—it was jolly decent of you, Mauly."

No reply.

"I—I hear that Quelch gave you a hundred lines, old chap! I—I say, shall I help you do the lines?"

Silence.

"I say, Mauly." It was an almost despairing squeak: "I say, I've got to go over to Cliff House to see my sister Bessie—I—I haven't seen her for a long time—I say, old boy, do lend me a tanner for the bus fare, will you?"

A faint grin dawned on Lord Mauleverer's expressionless face. He did not speak: but a hand came out of a pocket, with sixpence in it. That sixpence, still in silence, was dropped into a fat grubby palm.

Billy Bunter's fat face brightened. He would have liked a word, no doubt: but the bus fare was really more important. He rolled away with the sixpence clutched in fat fingers.

150

It was rather unfortunate, for Bunter, that he had borrowed that "tanner" so near the school shop. He passed the open door of that establishment as he rolled away.

At that door he paused.

He needed that "tanner". Its expenditure on tuck meant that he would have to walk to Cliff House School after all. He had borrowed it with the intention of expending it on a bus fare. But——!

The lure of tuck was too strong. For a few moments Bunter hesitated. Then he rolled into the tuck-shop: where the next few minutes were spent in absorbing exactly as much stickiness as could be obtained for the moderate sum of sixpence!

He emerged with a smear of jam round his mouth: minus a bus fare!

There was now nothing for it but to walk it. But was there not? Lord Mauleverer was still leaning on the tree: and hope springs eternal in the human breast. The fat Owl rolled over to Mauly again.

"I say, Mauly, old chap——."

Mauly stared stonily.

"I say, I—I—I've lost that tanner, Mauly: I say, old fellow, lend me another tanner, will you?"

Lord Mauleverer did not speak. He detached himself from the tree, grasped the fat Owl's collar, and slewed him round. Bunter gave an anticipative squeak.

"Ow! Leggo, you beast! Look here—yarooooh!"

Thud!

It was quite an elegant foot that landed on Bunter's tight trousers. But once was enough for Bunter. He departed in haste, giving up all hope of further tanners from Mauly.

He had to walk it! But he paused again, at the sight of his form-master in the quad. There was quite a pleasant expression on Mr. Quelch's face. As a matter of fact, he was thinking of his expected visitor that afternoon, and of a happy discussion in his study on the subject of alcaics, sapphics, asclepiads, with trochees and spondees galore, when Professor Pawson arrived—if that absent-minded gentleman did not get into the wrong train, or get out at the wrong station, and arrive somewhere else!

Billy Bunter had long since forgotten that talk on the telephone in Quelch's study, and had no clue to the be-

151

nignity in Quelch's countenance. But he noted that Quelchy was looking unusually good-tempered: and he debated in his fat mind whether he could venture to "touch" Quelch for the much-needed sixpence! It was worth trying on, at any rate: Quelch could only say no, anyway. So that fat Owl rolled up to his form-master with his most respectful smirk.

"If you please, sir——."

Mr. Quelch looked at him. The benign expression faded from his face, and he frowned—and interrupted.

"Bunter! Your face is smeared with jam——."

"Oh! I—I—I——."

"I have spoken to you many times, Bunter, on the subject of this slovenliness," said Mr. Quelch, severely.

"I—I—I——." Bunter wished that he had given Quelch a wide berth! He wished it still more fervently the next moment.

"Go into the House at once, Bunter——."

"Oh, really, sir——."

"——and wash!" snapped Mr. Quelch.

He walked on, leaving it at that. Billy Bunter, with deep feelings, rolled into the House: his last hope of a "tanner" gone.

When he rolled out again, he headed for the gates, having made up his fat mind to walk it! His plump face was a little less grubby, if that was any comfort.

He rolled away down Friardale Lane, heading for the stile that gave on the footpath through the wood: the way he had followed on Sunday morning, with such muddy results to himself.

By the time the stile came in sight, Bunter was feeling the need for a rest. It was rather irritating, as he drew nearer, to observe that someone was already sitting on the stile, in the shade of the spreading branches of the massive old beech that grew beside it.

Whoever it was, was sitting with his back to the lane, facing the wood, so the fat Owl could not see his face, or whether it was a Greyfriars fellow or not. It was not till he was quite near, blinking at the back of a head, that he noted the yellow-and-black in the cap, and realised that it belonged to a Highcliffe junior.

Bunter came to an abrupt halt.

As he did so, the fellow sitting on the stile glanced round, no doubt having heard him coming.

"Oh!" gasped Bunter, as he recognised Cecil Ponsonby, of the Fourth Form at Highcliffe School.

Ponsonby stared at him, and then grinned.

Bunter did not grin. He had not forgotten Skinner's encounter with Pon a week ago. He backed away. The playful Pon was about the last person in Kent whom Billy Bunter desired to meet in a lonely spot. Pon was only too likely to be playful with Bunter, as he had been with Skinner.

"Oh! You!" said Pon, agreeably. "Haven't I seen you before somewhere?"

"Oh, really, Ponsonby——."

"Must have been in the Zoo, I think! How did you get away from the other porpoises?"

"Look here——."

"Don't go!" grinned Pon, as the fat Owl backed further away. He slipped from his stile and followed Bunter up. Pon, as usual, was in a mischievous mood, and a fat helpless fellow like Bunter was just his game.

"I—I say——!" stammered Bunter. "Oooogh! Leave my cap alone, you beast!" He grabbed, too late, as Pon snatched the cap from his head. "Look here, you gimme my cap! I—I'm going over to Cliff House, and I can't go without my cap!"

"Dear me!" said Ponsonby. "What about climbing for it?"

"I—I——!"

Pon, with a swing of his arm, tossed the Greyfriars cap into the branches of the beech. Bunter's eyes, and spectacles, followed it, in dismay. The cap came to rest on a leafy branch, and stayed there.

"Beast!" roared Bunter.

Ponsonby chuckled.

"Going up for it?" he asked.

"Oh, you Highcliffe rotter!" gasped Bunter.

"Mustn't call a fellow names!" said Ponsonby, chidingly. "If a fellow calls me names I boot him—like that!"

"Yarooooh!"

"And like that——!"

"Ow! Keep off, you beast!" yelled Bunter.

"And like that——!"

Bunter made a frantic rush for the stile, and clambered over. He was not thinking of climbing to recover his cap. He was only thinking of getting out of reach of Cecil Ponsonby's lunging foot.

He clambered over in hot haste, a final kick from Ponsonby helping him over. He rolled in the grass of the footpath: Pon looking at him over the stile, and roaring with laughter.

"Ooogh! Oh, crikey! Ooooh!"

"Ha, ha, ha!"

Billy Bunter scrambled to his feet, and, capless, tore up the footpath through the wood: leaving Ponsonby still roaring. That little episode had amused Pon immensely. He laughed loud and long, as Bunter disappeared into the wood: so immensely amused that he did not hear or heed a whirr of bicycles in the lane behind him, or realise that others had arrived on the scene till a sudden grip fell on the back of his neck.

CHAPTER 31

SAUCE FOR THE GANDER

"Look!" ejaculated Bob Cherry.

"Pon——!"

"And Bunter——!"

"That Highcliffe cad——."

"Put it onfully, my esteemed chums!"

Five fellows exclaimed together, as a bunch of cyclists swept round one of the winding turns in Friardale Lane, and came in sight of the stile, and the little scene that was being enacted thereat.

From a distance, Harry Wharton and Co. beheld the playful Pon toss Bunter's cap into the beech branches, and help the fat Owl over the stile with his foot. And they put it "onfully", as Hurree Jamset Ram Singh recommended. The bicycles fairly flew.

Bob Cherry, with his sinewy legs driving like machinery,

shot ahead: and an arrow in its flight had simply nothing on him, as he whizzed on towards the stile.

It was a matter of seconds, before he jumped off, leaving his jigger to run where it would, and jumped at Ponsonby, and grabbed him by the back of the neck.

Up to that moment, Pon had been immensely amused. But at that moment, he ceased to be amused with startling suddenness. He spun round, wriggling in the grip on his collar: and there was not the faintest hint of merriment in his face as he stared at Bob Cherry.

"Oh!" he gasped. "Let go!"

"Don't let that cad bolt, Bob!" yelled Johnny Bull, as he scrambled off his machine.

"I've got him!" grinned Bob.

"Will you let go my collar, you Greyfriars ruffian?" breathed Pon.

"Like to cut?" asked Bob. "Why, you were as bold as brass when you ducked Skinner last week, and as brave as a lion ragging that fat ass Bunter. My dear man, now's your chance to put in some more ragging. Pick your man and begin."

He hooked Ponsonby away from the stile by the collar. A few moments ago, Pon had been roaring with laughter at Billy Bunter's frantic flight. But there was no doubt that he would gladly have emulated the fat Owl at the present moment. The Famous Five were made of sterner stuff than Skinner and Bunter: and the dandy of Highcliffe did not like the outlook at all. But there was no escape for Pon.

Bob released his collar when he was surrounded by the five Greyfriars juniors. Pon had had his spot of fun with Bunter. Now he had to stay for a further spot. He scowled from face to face.

"Look here——!" he muttered.

"Looking!" grinned Bob. "Don't you worry—we're not going to handle you two to one, as you and Gaddy did with Skinner. Pick out your man!"

"I'm not goin' to row with you——!" muttered Ponsonby.

"Your mistake—you are!" assured Bob. "Exactly what you're going to do."

"What-ho!" said Johnny Bull, emphatically.

"The rowfulness is going to be terrific, my esteemed

and execrable Ponsonby," grinned Hurree Jamset Ram Singh.

"Dash it all, you were full of beans, a minute ago, Pon!" said Harry Wharton. "Has all the gas escaped already?"

"Looks like it!" chuckled Nugent.

Evidently the "gas" had escaped! Pon was looking completely deflated. A rag on Billy Bunter was one thing: on a member of that strenuous Co. it was quite another. Ponsonby drove his hands deep into his pockets, as an outward and visible sign that he did not intend to use them.

"Not feeling like a scrap?" asked Bob.

"I tell you I'm not going to row with you," said Ponsonby, sullenly. "Now let me get out of this."

"Not just yet!" said Bob. "You've chucked Bunter's cap into that tree. He's scooted without it. Fetch it down."

"I'll do nothin' of the kind."

"I rather think you will!" said Bob, cheerfully. "You were ragging a fat ass who can't put up his hands, and you ought to have a jolly good hiding. You'll get it, if you don't fetch down Bunter's cap."

"Boot him!" growled Johnny Bull. "He was booting Bunter, wasn't he? Let him have some of his own medicine."

"The footfulness is the proper caper!" declared Hurree Jamset Ram Singh, with a nod of his dusky head. "Turn roundfully, my esteemed and funky Pon."

Ponsonby breathed hard.

"I—I tell you——!" he muttered.

"You needn't tell us—we know you're in a blue funk," said Bob. "Are you fetching down Bunter's cap?"

"No!" hissed Ponsonby.

"You'll be booted till you do! Go it, you men!"

Thud! thud! thud! thud! thud! Each member of the Co. delivered one, and the hapless Highcliffian yelled and dodged and wriggled as he received them. It was, as Johnny Bull had said, his own medicine: but clearly Pon did not like its taste.

"Stoppit!" he yelled. "I—I—I'll fetch down the cap, if you like! It—it—it was only a joke on that fat fool—I—I'll get it——."

"Better," agreed Bob.

Ponsonby, panting, looked up at the tree. He had pitched Bunter's cap as high as he could, and he rather regretted now that he had done so. It was no easy task to climb that high beech, and crawl out on the branch to recover the cap—and clambering in trees was rough on a fellow's clothes, and Pon was very particular about his elegant clobber.

But there was no help for it. He was in the hands of the Amalekites, and five boots were ready to lunge again. He had to make up his mind to it.

With deep feelings, the Highcliffe junior clambered into the beech, the Famous Five watching him from below with smiling faces. Autumn winds had stripped the beech of many of its leaves, and they were able to follow Pon's progress as he hooked himself up breathlessly from bough to bough.

He reached, at last, the branch on which the cap was lodged. There he paused to pant for breath. The look he cast down at the Greyfriars juniors was rather like that of a demon in a pantomime.

He crawled out on the branch at last, and reached the cap. He grabbed it up, and pitched it down. Bob Cherry caught it as it fell, and tucked it into his pocket, to be restored to its owner later.

"Thanks!" he called out. "You can come down now, Pon!"

Ponsonby crawled back to the main trunk. But he did not descend. He sat there astride of the branch, scowling down at the Greyfriars juniors. Apparently his idea was to remain up the tree till they were gone.

"Waiting for you!" called out Harry Wharton.

"You can wait!" snarled Pon.

"But we're not finished with you yet!" explained Bob Cherry. "You booted Bunter as he went. Don't you want to travel the same way!"

Ponsonby answered only with a black scowl. Evidently he did not want to depart from the spot, like Bunter, with a boot behind him.

"Look here, are you coming down?" demanded Bob.

"No, you Greyfriars rotter."

"O.K. I'll come up for you!"

Bob Cherry stepped towards the beech. Pon glared down at him. The prospect of a tussle in the tree, in Bob's hefty grasp, was too alarming. Pon changed his mind all of a sudden, as Bob put his hands to the trunk.

"I'm comin' down!" he howled.

"Buck up, then! You're wasting time."

Ponsonby, with a face more than ever like that of a demon in a pantomime, slithered down the tree. He landed in the midst of the Co. Bob Cherry grasped his collar, and hooked him out into the lane.

"Now, then, all together——!" said Bob.

"Look here, chuck it!" panted Pon, "I—I——."

"Didn't you boot Bunter?" snorted Johnny Bull. Johnny was a believer in making the punishment fit the crime!

"I—I—I——!"

"Whoever is saucy to the goose, must be saucy to the gander, as the English proverb remarks," said Hurree Jamset Ram Singh!

"Ha, ha, ha!"

"Sauce for the goose is sauce for the gander, Pon! You shouldn't ask for these things if you don't want them!" chuckled Bob. "This is a lesson for you, my dear boy. I won't say it hurts us more than it does you, because it jolly well doesn't——."

"Ha, ha, ha!"

"But it will do you good! Go it, you men."

The Co. "went" it! Ponsonby bolted down the lane yelling, with lunging feet behind him. The Highcliffe junior disappeared in a cloud of dust: and the Co., laughing, returned to their machines, to resume their interrupted spin.

CHAPTER 32

UNEXPECTED!

BILLY BUNTER came to a sudden halt.

"Oh, lor!" he ejaculated.

He stared through his big spectacles at a swollen, rushing woodland stream, in dismay.

Bunter had kept on the run for quite a considerable distance. He was tired and he was breathless: but the possibility that Ponsonby might be on his track spurred him on. Not till he was quite, quite sure that there was no pursuit, did he drop into a walk. Then he plugged on, at the pace of a very old and fatigued snail, till he reached Friardale Water. And there, as stated, he came to a sudden halt, and ejaculated "Oh, lor'!" in utter dismay.

To get to Pegg, and Cliff House School, by that route, Bunter had to cross the woodland stream. Dozens of times he had crossed it, by the plank bridge. But there was no crossing it now by that plank bridge. The plank bridge was gone!

Billy Bunter had almost forgotten the episode of the Sunday walk. So far as he had thought about it at all, he had taken it for granted that the plank bridge had been replaced, during the days that had since elapsed. It was the duty of the Rural District Council to keep that footpath open to the public: and the plank having floated away to the river, it was up to that R.D.C. to recover it and put it back. No doubt, in the fullness of time, the Rural District Council were going to do it. But, evidently they had not done it yet—for there was the woodland stream, swelling against its banks, rushing on to the Sark, rippling through the rushes, glistening in the autumn sunshine—a pleasant scene to the view, but absolutely uncrossable.

"Oh, lor'!" repeated Bunter.

Nobody could get across that rushing stream, unless by swimming, jumping, or flying! These resources were not at Billy Bunter's disposal. Certainly he had no idea of emulating Bob Cherry's exploit, and jumping it: he would hardly have reached the middle before he splashed in. Caesar, of old, paused long on the bank of the Rubicon before he crossed. Bunter was booked for a longer pause than Caesar's. Bunter couldn't cross at all!

"Oh, crikey!" said Bunter.

Those fatheads—thus disrespectfully did the fat Owl think of the Rural District Council!—ought to have replaced that plank bridge. He did not reflect, for the moment, that he ought not to have shifted it.

Anyhow, the plank was not there! Whosoever was to blame, whether the Rural District Council, or William George Bunter of Greyfriars Remove, or both, there was no bridge over Friardale Water: and Billy Bunter had to come to a full stop.

"Oh, crumbs!" moaned Bunter.

He blinked dismally at rushing water.

He was tired. He could have plugged on, at a snail's pace, to Pegg and Cliff House School: had the plank bridge been there. But the mere thought of the long way round by the village made him moan. Certainly, he wanted to get to Cliff House and Bessie, as a change from "Coventry": and it was possible, too, that Bessie might have a cake. But——!

For a long dismal minute, he stood blinking at the rushing stream. Then he blinked round in search of something on which to sit and rest. Whether he would go the long way round, or walk back to the school, was a problem to be thought out: in the meantime, what he wanted was a rest for his little fat legs.

He found a log among the willows on the bank, and sank down on it. With a dolorous fat face, he sat on the log, leaning back against a tree, gazing at the impassable stream, and the footpath winding on through the wood beyond. The glistening stream, the ripples among the rushes, the woods rich in their autumn tints, did not comfort him: he was not thinking of the picturesque. If he had had a chunk of toffee, or even one of those chocs that Mauly had packed in the jig-saw box, it would have been a comfort. Willingly Bunter would have swopped all the beauties of Nature for a single, solitary bull's-eye! But no such consolation was available. It was a doleful Owl!

After half-an-hour or so, a pedestrian came into sight under the branches over the footpath on the opposite side of the stream.

Bunter gave him an uninterested blink as he appeared in view.

The newcomer, a stranger to Bunter's eyes, was a little old gentleman, with silvery hair showing under his hat. He was reading a book as he walked, and Bunter caught a glimmer of gold-rimmed glasses. So intent was the old gentleman on that book, that he did not lift his eyes from it for a moment, and looked neither to the right nor the left as he came slowly onward. Once he bumped against a low branch that projected over the footpath. Even then he hardly looked up from his book as he disengaged himself from the branch.

Billy Bunter grinned.

That pedestrian, coming from Pegg, was going to meet

with the same disconcerting surprise as the fat Owl. He could no more cross the stream than Bunter could.

With his eyes and his gold-rimmed glasses fastened on his book, evidently not thinking for a moment of looking ahead, he did not yet know what was in store for him. Indeed, if he was a stranger in the locality, probably he did not even know that there was a stream in the wood to be crossed at all.

He was going to make that discovery when he arrived at uncrossable water: which rather amused Billy Bunter.

"Old ass!" murmured the fat Owl.

Bunter had never seen the silver-haired gentleman before: but had he remembered the talk on Quelch's telephone a week ago, he might have guessed that this was his form-master's expected visitor.

Mr. Quelch at the school, expecting the visitor who had not arrived, might have surmised that the absent-minded Professor had, after all, omitted to get out of his train at Courtfield, and had gone on to the terminus at Pegg: landing himself in a walk to Greyfriars. That did not occur to Bunter, who had forgotten Professor Pawson's existence.

The fat Owl watched, and grinned.

"Old ass!" he murmured again. "He'll be walking into the water if he doesn't look out! He, he, he!"

That idea quite amused Bunter.

At the distance, he could see the book the old gentleman was holding up close to his gold-rimmed glasses, but he could not discern the title on the cover. Had he been able to do so, it might have reminded him of Quelch's friend the Professor.

That title was "Le Odi di Orazio: Traduzione Metrica"—though Billy Bunter would hardly have been able to construe that into "The Odes of Horace: Metrical Translation".

It was, in fact, the Italian translation of Horace's Odes that the Professor was reading as he walked, which Bunter had heard him mention on the telephone, and about which he was going to have a happy and enjoyable discussion with Quelch.

He was deeply immersed in it: indeed, utterly absorbed. Possibly he was spotting trochees, where according to the Horatian mode there should have been spondees!

161

F

Anyhow he was as deep in that book, as Billy Bunter had ever been in a bag of juicy jam-tarts.

Billy Bunter's fat grin widened as the walking reader came down to the bank of the woodland stream, still without looking up.

In fact, unless he knew that the stream was there, it was natural for him to suppose that the footpath continued as before. And Bunter could see that he did not know that the stream was there. It was going to give him a jump, when he suddenly found himself on the edge of it! Grinning, the fat Owl watched, to see him jump!

Splash!

"He, he, he!"

The old gentleman did jump, when he suddenly trod in shallow water on the margin of the stream. In fact, he bounded. Water flowing over his shoes startled him even out of Le Odi di Orazio!

"Ooooooooogh!" Bunter heard him gasp.

He jumped wildly, and the book flew from his hand as he jumped, and splashed into the water.

Up to that moment, Billy Bunter had been amused. But what happened next wiped the fat grin off his face. His eyes almost popped through his spectacles.

The silver-haired gentleman reached after the book in the water. It was out of reach of his grasp, bobbing away on the current: and in his anxiety to recover it, the Professor over-reached.

Splash!

"Oh!" gasped Bunter.

He jumped up from the log.

Splash! splash! splash! The old gentleman had tipped over, and plunged headlong in. In a moment, he was swept by the current: and the fat Owl, in utter horror, stared at a white face that glimmered on deep water and then disappeared. It happened so suddenly that the horrified Owl could only blink, spell-bound. A few moments ago, that old gentleman had been reading Horace: now, helpless in swirling water, he was being swept away to death!

"Oh!" panted Bunter.

The book sank—a hat floated away. A face white as chalk glimmered on the surface again, and a hand was flung up from the water.

It caught the trailing tip of a long drooping branch of

the willow under which Bunter had been sitting. It closed there in a convulsive grip.

The branch sagged down. The current, rushing on to the Sark, tugged at the man who was hanging on, almost tearing him away. But he held on desperately: and a panting cry came from him:

"Help!"

"Oh, crikey!" groaned Bunter.

The old gentleman was holding on. That trailing branch was all that held him back from drowning. But it was only too clear that he could not hold on for very long. Perhaps he had glimpsed the horrified schoolboy on the bank, for he called again:

"Help!"

Billy Bunter's teeth chattered. He cast a wild look round him. There was no one in sight on the footpath, in either direction. There was no help—no help for the man who, in a matter of minutes, would be drowning helplessly. Unless——!

An active fellow, with plenty of nerve, could have crawled out on that branch, and reached the drowning man, and helped him up. Bob Cherry, or Harry Wharton, or Smithy, or even old Mauly—they would have risked it. But if the branch broke——!

Bunter shuddered.

The hapless Owl who had hunted cover while Highcliffe fellows ragged Skinner, who less than an hour ago had fled yelling from Ponsonby's foot: he was not the man for desperate risks. The bare thought of it made his head swim! The branch would break—if it did not break under the weight of one, it would break under the weight of two— he could not, he would not, he dared not!

"Help!"

The call came faintly.

"I—I—I can't!" breathed Bunter. "I—I can't—I can't do a thin. I—I——."

Was there, hidden deep under Billy Bunter's layers of fat, some lingering spot of genuine British pluck? It looked like it, for, frightened almost out of his fat wits as he was, in a moment more he was clambering out on the swaying, sagging branch over deep water, at the risk of his fat life!

CHAPTER 33

BUNTER'S LATEST

MR. QUELCH stared: and frowned.

A crowd of fellows in the Greyfriars quad stared: and some of them grinned.

Gosling stared, from his lodge.

Harry Wharton and Co. back from their bike spin, and strolling in the quad, ceased to stroll, and joined in the general stare.

Wingate and Gwynne, chatting on the Sixth-form green, ceased to chat, and stared. Coker of the Fifth stared. Temple, Dabney and Co. of the Fourth stared.

In fact. every Greyfriars man within staring distance, stared—at the wet, weary, drenched, dripping, bedraggled object that crawled in at the school gates.

"Upon my word!" exclaimed Mr. Quelch.

He frowned portentously.

Quelch was in a rather perturbed frame of mind already. His expected visitor had not arrived, and Quelch was pacing in the quad, with an eye on the gates, hoping every moment to see Professor Pawson blow in. The visitor was late: and Quelch could not help fearing that absent-mindedness had supervened: and that the Professor might be very late, or indeed might not arrive at all. Professor Pawson was incapable of error in such matters as spondees, trochees, and dactyls: but in such commonplace matters as railway trains and railway stations, he was very liable to error indeed. With that spot of worry on his mind, Quelch was not likely to be pleased by the sight of a member of his form crawling dispiritedly in at the gates, soaked from head to foot, hatless, with wet hair plastered over a fat head, squelching water as he crawled. "Only "crawling" could describe Billy Bunter's motions: for he was evidently in the last stage of fatigue, and could hardly drag one weary, podgy foot after the other.

Quelch bore down on him at once. Greyfriars fellows

*A wet, weary, drenched, dripping, bedraggled object
crawled in at the school gates*

165

converged from all sides. Billy Bunter was the cynosure of all eyes. He "had the house" as it were.

"Bunter!" Quelch almost hooted.

The fat Owl came to a halt, blinking dizzily at his form-master through damp spectacles. Water trickled down him as he stood.

"Bunter! What does this mean? Why are you in such a state as this? Only a few days ago you came in wet and muddy, after falling into the stream in Friardale Wood. Now you are in a still worse state. Where is your cap?"

"I—I—I——!"

"Have you been so stupid, so insensate, as to meet with a similar accident a second time?"

"Nunno! I—I got wet——."

"I can see that you are wet, Bunter! Your clothes are drenched! Have you fallen in the water again?"

"Oh! No! I—I never fell in—I——."

"You did not fall in?" exclaimed Mr. Quelch. "Then why are you in this state?"

"I—I couldn't help——."

"You should have helped it, Bunter. Precisely the same accident, a second time within a few days! If you did not fall in, how did this happen?"

"The—the branch dipped, and—and——."

"Upon my word! Are you tell me, Bunter, that you were so foolish as to climb a tree overhanging water?"

"Yes, sir! You see, I—I——."

"Such foolishness—such unthinking folly—such stupidity——."

"But you see, sir——."

"Go into the House at once, Bunter, and dry yourself and change your clothes. You are in a shocking state—a disgraceful state—a revolting state——."

"Yes, sir, but I——."

"Wharton!" rapped Mr. Quelch.

"Yes, sir!" Harry Wharton ran up.

"Kindly take this stupid boy in, Wharton, and see that he dries himself immediately and changes out of his wet clothes——."

"Oh, certainly, sir."

"But you see, sir," gasped Bunter, "I——."

"Go in with Wharton at once, Bunter."

"Yes, sir, but——."

"Go!" thundered Mr. Quelch. "Do you desire to catch cold, you stupid boy? Wharton, take him in at once."

"Yes, sir! Come on, Bunter!" Harry Wharton slipped a hand under the Owl's fat arm, and led him away towards the House.

Mr. Quelch frowned after them as they went: much annoyed, indeed exasperated. But his thoughts returned to his expected visitor, and he resumed his pacing, with the corner of his eye on the gates, and dismissed Bunter from mind.

Others, however, did not dismiss him from mind. The Co. followed Harry Wharton and his fat charge, and quite a number of other fellows followed on, curious to know what had happened to Bunter. The dismal fat Owl trailed into the House: and on the stairs, Bob Cherry slipped a hand under his other arm, to lend aid. Whatever had happened to Bunter, it was clear that he was at the end of his tether, and could hardly totter on his way. Once more "Coventry" was temporarily forgotten.

"Brace up, old fat man!" said Bob, kindly, as Bunter was propelled into the Remove dormitory. "You look all in, and no mistake."

"Oh, lor'! I feel all in!" moaned Bunter. "I'm just soaked——."

"Been playing potty tricks with that plank again, at Friardale Water?" asked Johnny Bull, with a grunt.

"Oh, really, Bull——."

"Is that it?" asked Frank Nugent.

"No, it ain't!" yapped Bunter. "The plank wasn't there —they haven't put it back yet, blow 'em——."

"You didn't try to jump it?" exclaimed Bob Cherry.

"Oh, my esteemed hat!" ejaculated Hurree Jamset Ram Singh. "The jumpfulness would have been terrific."

"Of course I didn't!" yapped Bunter. "I—I daresay I could, if you come to that. You ain't the only fellow in the Remove that can jump, Bob Cherry. But—but I didn't jump it!"

"Guessed that one!" grinned Vernon-Smith.

"Ha, ha, ha!"

"Blessed if I see anything to cackle at! Help me off with these wet things, blow you—gimme a towel—I'm all wet——."

"Here you are, old fat man," said Lord Mauleverer.

167

Mauly sorted out towels, and other fellows helped the fat Owl off with his wet clothes, while others sorted out a change. In Bunter's dismal and disastrous state, everyone was willing to lend a helping hand. Bob, in the kindness of his heart, lent assistance with the towelling: with so vigorous a hand that Bunter yelled in protest.

"Ow! Stoppit! Do you want to rub my skin off, you silly idiot! Wow!"

"But how did it happen?" asked Harry Wharton, when the fat Owl, sufficiently towelled, plunged into dry clothes. "You told Quelch that you didn't fall in——."

"Of course I didn't!" yapped Bunter. "Think I'm idiot enough to fall in?"

"Yes! I mean, if you didn't fall in——."

"The branch I was on dipped, and ducked me, of course——."

"But what on earth were you doing on a branch over-hanging Friardale Water?" exclaimed Bob.

"Saving a man's life——."

"WHAT?"

"Which?"

"Great pip!"

"Ha, ha, ha!"

"Oh, cackle!" said Bunter bitterly. "Cackle, when a chap's got wet through, and jolly nearly drowned, and may get pneumonia in every limb, saving a man's life—cackle!"

"Thanks, we will!" chuckled Bob. "Ha, ha, ha!"

"Ha, ha, ha!"

There was quite a roar. Billy Bunter, sitting on the edge of his bed, putting on dry socks, paused, with one sock on, and the other in a fat hand, and gave the hilarious Removites a devastating glare through his spectacles.

Apparently he had not expected such a reception of his startling statement: though really, he might have. His former tale of derring-do had been credited—until his black eye was washed off! A second and still more heroic exploit was really too heavy a strain on the credulity of the Removites. The juniors did not even think of beginning to believe a word of it. They roared.

"Look here——!" yelled Bunter.

"Ha, ha, ha!"

"I tell you I saved his life——."

"Ha, ha, ha!"

"At the risk of my own——!"

"Ha, ha, ha!"

"Blessed if I see anything to cackle at? Think it's funny?" howled Bunter.

"The funnifulness is terrific," chuckled Hurree Jamset Ram Singh.

"Your funniest, old fat man," chortled the Bounder. "This beats knocking out Pon and Gaddy and getting a black eye from the study chimney——."

"Ha, ha, ha!"

"Bunter the life-saver!" grinned Skinner.

Ha, ha, ha!"

"Beasts!" roared Bunter.

"Ha, ha, ha!"

The hapless Owl could only sit and glare. He had done it! Undoubtedly he had done it! Bunter knew that, if nobody else did! But nobody at Greyfriars was going to believe that he had done it. Bunter was rather in the position of the boy in the fable who cried "Wolf" so often when there was no wolf, that he was not believed when the wolf really came. So often, so very often, so invariably, indeed, had Bunter departed from the truth, that now he was stating the fact, it was received only as one of his wildest fictions. It was true: but to the Remove fellows it was only the latest of Billy Bunter's funny stories!

CHAPTER 34

CHUCK IT, BUNTER!

"I SAY, you fellows——."

"Ha, ha, ha!"

"If you'll let a chap speak——!" howled Bunter.

"Oh! do!" gasped Bob Cherry, "tell us all about it, Bunter! It will be worth hearing!"

"Pile it on!" said Johnny Bull.

"I'll tell you the exact facts——."

"Never mind the facts," said Smithy. "Keep to the fiction."

"Ha, ha, ha!"

"Beast! I tell you it really happened!" almost wailed Bunter. "I tell you I saved that man's life in Friardale Water. It was like this! You see, I was going over to Cliff House, but when I got to Friardale Water, I found the plank wasn't there, so I couldn't go on. I sat down to rest——."

"That sounds true!" agreed Bob. "That's more in your line than life-saving."

"Ha, ha, ha!"

"Yah! Well, then that old johnny came along the foot-path from Pegg, and fell into the water. The current washed him away at once, but he caught hold of the end of a branch—you know that tree near where the plank used to be, with a big branch sticking out right over the water——."

"We know it!" grinned Nugent. "Might really have happened, so far."

"It did happen!" yelled Bunter. "Right under my eyes! Well, there he was, hanging on for his life, jolly well half-drowned, and hardly able to hold on, and he couldn't do a thing to help himself. He couldn't have climbed on to that branch to save his life, and I can tell you that he was a goner, if I hadn't rushed to the rescue—I didn't hesitate for a single second——."

"You wouldn't!" grinned Bob.

"Hardly!" chuckled the Bounder.

"Couldn't see Bunter hesitating, at a time like that!" said Peter Todd. "Not Bunter! Other fellows might have, but never Bunter!"

"Ha, ha, ha!"

"Oh, really, Toddy——."

"So you plunged in and saved him!" said Skinner. "There's ten feet of water there at this time of the year, and we all know how Bunter swims!"

"I didn't plunge in," howled Bunter, "I couldn't go out of my depth—I—I mean, I'm a jolly good swimmer, but—but—but I didn't plunge in! I got into the tree and climbed along the branch to help him!"

"Active lad!" said the Bounder. "Nimble as a monkey, and all that! Doesn't he look it?"

"Ha, ha, ha!"

"Well, I jolly well did! And—and the branch sank under my weight, and dipped——."

"It would, if it happened at all!" agreed Bob. "Stout lad!"

"Ha, ha, ha!"

"But I got him!" went on Bunter, with another devastating glare at grinning faces. "I jolly well got hold of him, and dragged him up. I can tell you it was touch and go—I—I was afraid——."

"That sounds true!"

"Ha, ha, ha!"

"Beast! I was afraid he might drag me off the branch, and—and I thought it might break, too! But—but I helped him to get his arms over it, and then he was able to struggle out of the water—and—and we both got back along the branch to the bank. And then——."

"Then you woke up?" asked Skinner.

"Ha, ha, ha!"

"Oh, really, Skinner——."

"Is that all?" asked Bob Cherry.

"All?" hooted Bunter. "Isn't that enough? I tell you I saved his life—he would have been gone in another minute if I hadn't got hold of him and helped him up into the tree——."

"Didn't you grip him, and swing him to the bank with a single swing of your arm?" asked Vernon-Smith.

"Of course I didn't, you silly ass!' I couldn't, could I?"

"I know you couldn't—any more than you could have done what you've just told us! You might as well have put it in, though."

"Oh, really, Smithy——."

"So that's the lot, is it?" asked Harry Wharton, laughing. "You crawled out on a branch over deep water, you a fellow that swims like a stone, and a fellow whose weight might snap any branch in Friardale Wood—and saved a man's life——."

"I jolly well did!"

"Well, tell us next who the man was. You say he was coming along from Pegg. Anybody we know?"

"I—I think he was a stranger——."

"Sure to be!" chuckled the Bounder. "If it was anybody we'd seen around Pegg, we could ask him about it."

"Ha, ha, ha!"

"Well, strangers come to Pegg sometimes, don't

they?" hooted Bunter. "I'd never seen him before, that's all I know. He happened to be a stranger——."

"He would!" chuckled Skinner.

"Where is he now?" asked Bob. "Anywhere where a chap could give him the once-over?"

"I—I don't know——."

"The knowfulness would not be terrific," agreed Hurree Jamset Ram Singh.

"How should I know where he is?" howled Bunter. "I can tell you he was all in when we got to the bank. He asked me if there was a doctor's anywhere near, so I told him Dr. Pillbury in the village—our school doctor—and he told me to run home as fast as I could and get out of my wet clothes before I caught cold, and—I—I—I did!"

Bob Cherry winked at his comrades.

"How did you lose your cap?" he asked.

"Oh! It—it fell off, when—when I was—was reaching down to him from the branch, you know——."

"Oh, jiminy! It fell off into Friardale Water, did it, while you were saving that johnny's life?" yelled Bob.

"Yes. You see——."

"Ha, ha, ha!" roared the Famous Five.

"What are you cackling at now?" howled Bunter. The fat Owl was reluctant to relate precisely how he had lost that cap: and he was quite unaware, so far, that the episode had been witnessed from afar by five fellows on bicycles. It was like Bunter to prevaricate on the subject: but it was rather unfortunate, for if his startling tale had had the remotest chance of being believed, that final detail would have knocked it out. "My—my cap fell off, you know—it would——."

"Ha, ha, ha!"

"Look here, you cackling beasts——."

"You fat Ananias!" roared Bob. "We saw Ponsonby chuck your cap into the beech at the stile——."

"Eh?"

"And you scuttled off without it, you fat fraud, with Pon booting you," hooted Johnny Bull, "and we saw it all, on our bikes."

"Oh, crikey! I—I mean—I—I——."

"And here it is!" exclaimed Bob, jerking a crumpled cap from his pocket. "Here's your cap, you bloated fabricator, that fell off your head in Friardale Water——."

172

"Ha, ha, ha!"

"And we jolly well made Pon climb that beech and fetch it down," added Bob. "Here it is, you fat fibber—catch!"

"Wow!" howled Bunter, as Bob tossed the cap to him, and he caught it with his fat little nose. "Beast! Ow! I say——."

"And now, aren't you going to tell us how you got wet?" asked Harry Wharton.

"I've told you——!" shrieked Bunter. "I've told you all that happened——."

"I mean what really happened."

"Beast!"

"Did you fall in?"

"I tell you I got wet shaving a man's wife—I mean saving a man's life——," raved Bunter. "If you fellows don't believe me——."

"Believe you! Oh, crumbs!"

"The believefulness is not terrific, my esteemed fabricating Bunter."

"Ha, ha, ha!"

"Chuck it, Bunter!"

"Think out a better one."

"I say, you fellows——."

"Rats! Chuck it, Bunter!"

And the Removites, laughing, left Bunter sitting on the bed, his exasperated glare following them as they went. That afternoon Billy Bunter had saved a man from drowning. He had run the risk of it himself. And not a fellow believed a word of it! Bunter, for once, if for once only, was telling the truth. But nobody in the Remove could be expected to guess that one—and nobody did!

CHAPTER 35

NOTHING DOING

"PETER, old chap——."

No answer.

"I say, Peter——."

But for the fact that Billy Bunter was in Coventry, Peter Todd would have answered "Prep", or "Shut up!" Really it was not easy to get on with prep, with a fat Owl sitting in the study armchair, and persisting in talking.

As Bunter was in Coventry, Peter contented himself with looking up, giving him a warning glare, and then resuming prep.

That warning glare silenced Bunter for about a minute. But really he could not keep silent. Apart from the urge to wag his fat chin, which was always strong upon him, Bunter simply couldn't leave matters where they were. Somehow he had to make fellows understand that on this occasion, if on no other, he was stating facts—facts, no doubt, more surprising than his usual fictions: nevertheless, facts all the same.

If only fellows believed him, Bunter felt that all would be calm and bright! Bunter's sins were many: but pluck covers a multitude of sins. The black-eye episode had almost saved him—only unluckily the black eye had washed off! Now he actually had performed a much greater exploit than that imaginary one—if only fellows would believe that he had! But they wouldn't!

Billy Bunter was not the man to hide his light under a bushel. Some fellows, having done a plucky thing, would have said nothing about it. Bunter was not that kind of fellow. He was prepared—if he could!—to extract the very last ounce of glory from his exploit. Only, he couldn't!"

Not the smallest spot of glory came his way. The Remove fellows had roared with laughter over his startling tale. They had left it at that: only wondering how even

174

Bunter could be ass enough to pile it on so thick. Bunter was back in Coventry—and staying there. He was staying there till he learned to behave: and the incident of Coker's parcel revealed that he was as far as ever from behaving! Yet if only they believed him——!

"Peter, old chap, it's really true!" said Bunter, after about a minute had elapsed. "I—I—I really did it——."

Silence.

"Honest Injun, Peter!" pleaded Bunter.

Grim silence.

"I—I can't help the man being a stranger here, and nobody likely to see him," urged Bunter. "That's just one of those things, you know."

Peter Todd looked up again. He did not speak. He picked up a Latin grammar, and took aim.

"Beast!" roared Bunter.

He dodged just in time, and the Latin grammar missed by an inch.

Billy Bunter was silent for five minutes after that. He did not want any more of Peter's books to whiz across the study. When his fat chin resumed operations, he addressed his other study-mate.

"I say, Dutton, old chap!"

Tom Dutton did not answer: not because Bunter was in Coventry, but because he did not hear. Bunter put on steam.

"I say, Dutton!" he roared.

The deaf junior looked up.

"Eh? Did somebody speak?" he asked.

"I did!" yelled Bunter. "I say, Dutton, don't you believe I got that man out of the water?"

"What man's daughter?" asked Dutton.

"Not daughter—water!" howled Bunter. "Don't you believe I saved his life, Dutton?"

"I haven't got a knife——."

"Wha—at?"

"And there isn't any mutton in the study, that I know of. Why don't you get on with your prep, Bunter, instead of sitting there talking about mutton?"

"I'm not feeling up to prep, after what I've been through——."

"Eh? What did you throw?"

"Oh, crikey; I didn't say threw—I said through!" raved

175

Bunter. "I saved a man's life this afternoon, old chap."

"I know all about your cap," answered Dutton. "You let that Highcliffe cad snatch it, and Bob Cherry got it back for you. Funky!"

"Oh, you deaf dummy——."

"I don't call it rummy—I call it funky," answered Dutton. "I'd like to see Pon snatch my cap! Look here, Bunter, shut up. I've got prep to do, if you haven't—and you're in Coventry, too! Shut up!"

"Beast!"

Billy Bunter rose from the armchair. He did not take a seat at the table to get on with prep. Prep never attracted Bunter: he was rather given to chancing it with Quelch. Moreover, for the second time that day Bunter was telling the truth—he was not feeling fit for prep, after what he had been through! His wild adventure in Friardale Water had left him rather limp.

He rolled out of No. 7 Study, leaving Toddy and Dutton to prep. It was against the rules to go out of the studies in prep: but Bunter was not thinking about rules. He had more important matters on his fat mind. Somehow or other he had to convince the Remove fellows that he, William George Bunter, really was a fellow whom they ought to have delighted to honour.

The door of No. 4 Study was partly open, and Bunter blinked in at Vernon-Smith and Tom Redwing, both at work.

"I say, you fellows," he squeaked.

The Bounder looked round. He did not respond to the fat squeak in words. He reached for a cushion and hurled it.

Peter Todd's Latin grammar had missed Bunter by an inch. Smithy's cushion was truer to the target. It caught Bunter under a fat chin.

"Yaroooh!" roared Bunter, as it landed. He tottered back into the passage. "Ow! Beast!"

There was a chuckle in No. 4 Study. Billy Bunter was tempted to hurl that cushion back at the sender. But he did not want an irate Bounder rushing out after him. So he left it where it was, and rolled up the Remove passage to No. 13.

Bob Cherry, Hurree Jamset Ram Singh, Mark Linley and little Wun Lung were there, all at prep. They looked

176

up, as the door was pushed open, and a fat face and a big pair of spectacles looked in.

"I say, Bob, old fellow," squeaked Bunter.

"Prep!" answered Bob Cherry, forgetting Coventry.

"But I say——."

"Prep!"

"Blow prep!" howled Bunter. "Look here, Bob, you ain't such a beast as the other beasts, old chap—you—you do believe that I shaved that man—I mean saved him—in Friardale Water, don't you?"

"Not the least little bit in the world," answered Bob. "Are you still sticking to that yarn, you fat ass?"

"Oh, really, Cherry——."

"Make up an easier one!" suggested Bob. "Anyhow, it's no good telling the same funny story twice over! You've had the laughs."

"Beast!" I mean, look here, old fellow——!"

"Prep!"

"The absurd Bunter is in Coventry, my esteemed Bob!" murmured Hurree Jamset Ram Singh.

"Oh! I forgot." Bob Cherry rose from the table. "I'll kick you along the passage——."

"Beast!" roared Bunter.

He did not wait to be kicked along the passage. He closed the door with a bang, and rolled away.

His next visit was to No. 1 Study, where he found Harry Wharton and Frank Nugent deep in prep. They looked up at a dolorous fat face, and grinned, but did not speak.

"I say, Harry, old fellow, it all happened just as I told you!" said Bunter. "I—I think you might take a fellow's word! If—if you'd seen me up to the neck in water, helping that old johnny out——."

"Ha, ha, ha!"

"Blessed if I see anything to cackle at! Any minute that branch might have snapped off——."

"Ha, ha, ha!"

"Look here, you cackling beasts——!" Billy Bunter glared at two laughing faces. "I—I ain't making it up—it's all true——."

"Ha, ha, ha!"

Evidently, Billy Bunter's almost tearful asservations evoked only gaiety in No. 1 Study! With deep feelings,

177

the fat Owl banged the door shut, leaving Harry Wharton and Frank Nugent still laughing.

"Oh, lor'!" mumbled Bunter, in the passage. "Beasts! Rotters! Smears! Smudges——."

"Bunter!" rapped a sharp voice.

"Oh, crikey!" Billy Bunter spun round, as Wingate of the Sixth came into the passage from the landing.

"What are you doing out of your study in prep?" rapped Wingate.

"I—I—I——." Bunter blinked at the prefect in dismay. "I—I say, Wingate, I—I ain't feeling too well, you know, after—after what I've been through to-day——."

Wingate stared at him.

"Eating too much, as usual?" he asked.

"No!" howled Bunter. "I—I mean, I—I—I shaved—I saved a man's life in Friardale Water, Wingate——."

"What?"

"I—I did really, Wingate. It—it was jolly plucky, you know, wasn't it? I—I ain't making it up, Wingate, like all the fellows think——."

"You young ass!" said Wingate. "That will do. Go back to your study at once."

"But I—I—I really——!"

"I said that will do!" snapped Wingate: and taking a fat ear between finger and thumb, he led Bunter back to No. 7.

"Ow! wow! wow!"

"Whops, if I find you out of your study again in prep!" said Wingate, warningly. He walked away, and Bunter rolled dismally into No. 7 Study. Evidently, Wingate of the Sixth was as doubting a Thomas as any fellow in the Remove.

"Beast!" moaned Bunter, as he plumped into the study armchair again. "I—I say, Peter, old chap——."

Peter's hand strayed to the inkpot, and Bunter relapsed into silence. And grim silence still surrounded Bunter when the Remove went to their dormitory that night. Only by the route of reform, it seemed, could Billy Bunter hope to escape from Coventry: otherwise, there was nothing doing! Undoubtedly it was a bleak outlook!

CHAPTER 36

BUNTER! ! !

Tap!

If Mr. Quelch heard that tap at the door of the Remove form-room, in third school the next morning, he did not heed it.

The Remove master was concentrating, at the moment, in the fattest member of his form.

Billy Bunter, as not infrequently happened in that form-room, was under fire!

Quelch was, in fact, annoyed with Bunter. He was in a somewhat perturbed mood that morning, to begin with. His expected visitor had not arrived the previous afternoon. Instead of Professor Pawson, and a happy discussion of alcaics, sapphics, and asclepiads, Quelch had had a telephone-call from Dr. Pillbury at Friardale, apprising him that the Professor had had a ducking and a narrow escape from drowning. The venerable gentleman had been considerably upset by that experience, and was staying the night at the doctor's: but hoped to be sufficiently recovered to call at the school the next day. All of which was naturally very disturbing to Mr. Quelch.

In these circumstances, spots of bother in his form-room were superfluous and irritating. And Billy Bunter was a spot of bother.

A week ago Quelch had fancied that he had seen signs of amendment in the lazy fat Owl. Had not Bunter, wholly of his own accord, come to his form-master's study to seek assistance in elucidating a passage in the *Æneid*? Quelch had hoped that this improvement would continue.

But it had not continued. The incident had remained unique. Since then, Billy Bunter had not displayed the slightest interest in the adventures and misadventures of the good Æneas, or in the language in which the same were chronicled. His "con" was still the worst in the Remove.

This morning it was, if possible, worse than ever.

Only too clearly, Bunter had not only neglected his prep,

but had not even looked at it! Remove men were trusted to "prepare" in their studies: not under a master's eye like the Third and the Second. Bunter, undoubtedly, was in need of the master's eye!

No doubt Quelch failed to hear the tap at the form-room door. He was speaking at the moment: in a deep, deep voice.

"I have told you to go on, Bunter!"

"Oh! Yes, sir! I—I'm just going on!" mumbled the fat Owl, blinking despairingly at his book through his big spectacles. "I—I—I can't find the place for a minute, sir——."

That was merely to gain time, as Mr. Quelch was well aware. He had been there before, so to speak! However, he answered patiently.

"You will go on from 'Haec dum Dardanio Æneas miranda videntur', Bunter."

"Oh! Yes, sir!" gasped Bunter.

His eyes and spectacles were on 'Haec dum Dardanio Æneas miranda videntur", but what that might possibly mean, if indeed it meant anything at all, was a deep mystery to Bunter. Not for the first time, the fat Owl repented that he had not given a little attention to prep in the study.

Tap!

The tap at the door was repeated—still unheeded. Quelch was too concentrated on Bunter to hear or heed taps.

"I am waiting for you to construe, Bunter!" said Mr. Quelch, in a grinding voice.

"I—I—I——," stammered Bunter. He had to make a shot at it. "While Dardanian Æneas was seeing Miranda——."

"What?" Quelch almost bawled.

There was a chuckle in the Remove. Apparently Bunter had the impression that "miranda" was a name of a character in the *Æneid*, whom the good Æneas was seeing! Really it was one of Bunter's best "howlers": and it had quite an enlivening effect on the Remove.

Its effect on the Remove master was quite different!

"Bunter——!"

"I—I think I've got it right, sir," gasped Bunter.

"The translation of that line, Bunter, is 'While these wonders are seen by Dardanian Æneas."

"Oh! Is it, sir?"

"It is, Bunter! As it is plain that you have wholly neglected your preparation, Bunter, I shall cane you——."

"Oh, crikey!"

TAP!

The third tap at the form-room door was so emphatic, that Mr. Quelch had to hear it. In the act of picking up his cane from his desk, he paused, and looked round at the door, with a frowning brow. Quelch did not like interruptions in class, and he was annoyed. However, he snapped:

"Come in!"

The door opened, and Trotter the page appeared. He had not ventured to open the door before he heard "Come in" from Quelch, and there was a hint of trepidation about Trotter, as he met the frown and the glinting gimlet-eye.

"If you please, sir——," began Trotter.

"What is it, Trotter?" rapped Mr. Quelch, without giving the House page time to state what it was. "You are interrupting the class, Trotter! Why have you come here during lessons?"

"If—if you please——."

"Will you tell me immediately why you have come here, Trotter?"

"Oh! Yes, sir! A—a gentleman's called to see you, sir—he's here, sir—Professor Pawson, Sir——."

"Oh!"

Quelch was quite anxious to see his old friend Professor Pawson. But he was not anxious to see even his old friend Professor Pawson during class. Even an absent-minded old gentleman with his head full of trochees, spondees, and dactyls, ought really to have had sufficient tact not to call on a school-master while he was taking his form!

However, if Quelch thought of telling Trotter to show Professor Pawson to his study, to wait there till third school ended, it was too late! The Professor was already on the spot. A little silver-haired old gentleman pushed in past Trotter, who retired and left him to it.

"My dear Quelch!"

Professor Pawson came across to the Remove master with out-stretched hand. Quelch had to perform a kaleidoscopic change of mood. Annoyance had to be discarded, and a genial smile turned on in welcome of his old friend.

"My dear Pawson——!"

The Remove fellows looked up, not in the least sharing their form-master's objection to interruptions in lessontime. Indeed, they were prepared to be quite pleased if the Professor stayed talking to Quelch till the bell rang for the end of third school.

But while the rest of the Remove observed the Professor with casual interest, there was one member of the form who stared at him with little round eyes that almost popped through a pair of big spectacles.

Billy Bunter wondered whether he was dreaming!

"I am glad, my dear Pawson, to see you so recovered from your unfortunate experience yesterday. The telephone call from Dr. Pillbury was a great shock to me——."

"Quite! quite! I had a narrow escape, Quelch—a terribly narrow escape. By some mischance, I missed my station at Courtfield—I was in fact reading the Italian translation of the Odes, so you will easily understand that I forgot to look out at the station——."

"Oh! No doubt! But——."

"Luckily, the railway terminates at Pegg, or I might have gone further. As it was, I had to walk from Pegg, by the footpath, and unfortunately fell into the stream in the wood——."

"Bless my soul!" exclaimed Mr. Quelch, his face very serious. "That stream is very much swollen by rains, at this time of the year, Pawson—you must have been in considerable danger——."

"So much so, Quelch, that I should certainly have been swept away and drowned, had I not caught hold of the extreme tip of a branch that projected over the middle of the stream, and held on—till help came."

"I am thankful that help came, my dear fellow," exclaimed Mr. Quelch, quite forgetting interrupted lessons in his concern for the Professor. "How very fortunate that someone was at hand——."

"Very, very!" agreed the Professor, "and I am sorry to say that I do not even know who my brave rescuer was. I was upset and a little confused by what had happened, as you will easily understand—and never thought of asking him his name when I told him to run home quickly, and dry himself——."

Several Remove fellows jumped, as they heard this! It seemed to have a familiar sound, as if they had heard something of the kind before. Some of them glanced at Bunter.

Bunter sat with his eyes and spectacles glued on the Professor. He seemed hardly able to believe either his eyes or his spectacles.

"A mere boy!" went on the Professor. "A schoolboy, I think! This boy, Quelch, climbed out on the branch over the stream, at the risk of his life, for the branch might have snapped at any moment, especially as he seemed a very stout and heavy boy——."

"Oh, my hat!" murmured Bob Cherry.

"——and helped me to get into the tree, whence I reached, at last, the bank. I have wondered since, Quelch, whether possibly the boy may have belonged to this school, as it is so near the spot——."

"Indeed!" Quelch was very interested, at this. "Certainly it is quite possible, Pawson! I should be delighted to hear that it was a Greyfriars boy who rendered you such timely aid, and displayed such conspicuous courage. Did you notice the cap he was wearing?"

"He was bareheaded, Quelch, I remember—he had no cap——."

"Fan me!" murmured Peter Todd.

"Oh, suffering cats and crocodiles!" breathed Bob Cherry. "Did you hear that, you fellows? He hadn't a cap——."

"It couldn't have been Bunter——."

"It just couldn't!"

"It sounds like his yarn, but——."

"But the butfulness is terrific."

"It couldn't—Oh, listen!" breathed Johnny Bull.

"Possibly, you could give me some description of the boy, Pawson!" Mr. Quelch was saying.

"Very easily, Quelch! A junior boy, very stout in person, and wearing spectacles. Do you recognise anyone by that description?"

Mr. Quelch's eyes opened wide. Certainly he recognised someone by that description! Also he remembered that a person answering to that description—Billy Bunter to wit—had come in drenched the previous afternoon!

"Goodness gracious!" ejaculated Mr. Quelch. "Impossible! I—I mean, is it possible? There is a boy in my own form such as you have described, Pawson—pray glance over the form, and ascertain whether the boy who helped you is present here!"

"I should be very glad to find him, Quelch, to thank him for his courage, in endangering his own life to help a person who was a complete stranger to him——."

"Quite! Pray glance over this form——."

The Professor turned round to the breathless Remove. The gold-rimmed glasses glimmered over the form. They fixed upon a fat face adorned with a big pair of spectacles.

"Why, there he sits!" exclaimed the Professor, beaming at Billy Bunter. "That is the boy—I do not know his name—that is the brave lad——."

"Bunter!" said Mr. Quelch, dazedly.

"Bunter!" breathed the Bounder. "Wake me up, Reddy, will you? Of course we're dreaming this!"

"Bunter!" gasped Harry Wharton.

"The esteemed and ridiculous Bunter!"

"Then—then he was telling the truth——!"

"Who'd have thought it?"

"Well, nobody could guess that——."

"Bunter all the time——."

"Great pip! Bunter!"

"Wonders will never cease!"

"Bunter—my hat!"

"Bunter!" Mr. Quelch's deep voice cut through the excited buzz in the Remove. "Bunter! Please stand out before the form!"

"Oh! Yes, sir!" gasped Bunter.

Ten minutes ago, Bunter had expected to be called out before the form, for Mr. Quelch's cane to be given a little exercise. But that item had quite disappeared from the programme now! For once, Billy Bunter showed alacrity in stepping out before the Form! Even yet he could hardly believe in his good luck: and that it really was the old gentleman he had saved from Friardale Water who had walked into the Remove form-room. But he rolled out before the form with a happy grin irradiating his fat face.

"My dear boy!" Professor Pawson grasped a fat and
184

slightly sticky hand. "My dear Hunter—did you say the name was Hunter, Quelch——?"

"Bunter—— -!"

"Oh! Yes! Bunter! My dear Bunter, I am glad, very glad, to find you here. I could not thank you yesterday as I should have wished to do—I am extremely glad to meet you here, my dear boy, and to find you in the form of my old friend Mr. Quelch!—a credit to his form, I am assured——. I trust you are not feeling ill effects from your immersion, Punter——."

"Oh! Yes! No!" gasped Bunter. "I—I—I—oh, crikey!"

"I am proud to shake you by the hand, Hunter. I should like a few words with you, my brave lad, if you were not in class——."

"Bunter, you are excused from this lesson," said Mr. Quelch hastily—no doubt seeing a chance of getting on with Virgil. "You appear to have acted admirably, Bunter. Pray go with Professor Pawson—I shall be disengaged in half-an-hour, Pawson——."

Billy Bunter rolled out of the form-room with the Professor. He gave the Remove a blink as he went—a vaunting blink! Then the door closed on him, and the Remove were left to Latin and Quelch.

But if Quelch fancied that his form were going to give much attention to P. Vergilius Maro after that, he had another guess coming. The Remove fellows simply couldn't! Even the gimlet eye could not subdue the excited buzz in the form: and Quelch was probably as glad as the juniors when the bell rang for dismissal.

CHAPTER 37

SAME OLD BUNTER

"WHERE'S Bunter?"

"Anybody seen Bunter?"

"Seen Bunter, Coker?"

"Seen Bunter, Hobby?"

"Where is he——?"

"The wherefulness is terrific."

Everyone, or almost everyone, was anxious to see Bunter, when the Remove came out. Nobody would have guessed that Billy Bunter was in "Coventry", just then! In fact, the Removites had forgotten it themselves.

Bunter, for once, was wanted. But he was not in evidence. Generally he was not wanted, and only too much in evidence. Now he was not to be seen.

He was not still with the Professor. The Professor could be seen walking and talking with Quelch in the quad. Where was Bunter?

Harry Wharton and Co. looked in the Rag. But no fat figure was frowsting in the armchair before the fire there.

"Where the dickens has he got to?" asked Bob Cherry.

"Look somewhere where there's grub!" suggested Skinner.

"Oh, shut up, Skinner!" said the Famous Five, with one voice. Nobody wanted to be reminded of Bunter's little weaknesses, after what they had heard in the form-room. Skinner laughed.

"You had a parcel this morning, Wharton," he said. "You were unpacking a cake——."

"What about it?"

"Look in your study for Bunter! You're more likely to find him there, than the cake!"

"Shut UP!" roared Bob Cherry.

However, the Famous Five decided to go up to the studies and look for Bunter. Billy Bunter had done a plucky thing—a very plucky thing!—he had, as it were, redeemed himself in the eyes of the Remove. Nevertheless, he was Bunter—and only too likely to make good use of his time while he was out of form, and the other fellows still in the form-room. For though he was, at the moment, a fellow whom the Famous Five delighted to honour, it had to be admitted that his long and weary sojourn in "Coventry" had made little or no difference to his manners and customs. It was, in fact, probable that Bunter would be found where there was a cake—though perhaps improbable that the cake would be found.

"Hallo, hallo, hallo!" exclaimed Bob Cherry, as he arrived at the door of No. 1 Study, with the Co. and six or seven other fellows, at his heels. "Here he is."

The study door was open. Within, in the study arm-chair, a fat figure was visible. William George Bunter was sitting there, at happy ease: occupied, at the moment, in wiping his mouth with his sleeve!

He gave a jump as the juniors crowded in to the door-way, and a startled blink.

"I—I say, you fellows, it wasn't me——!" stammered Bunter.

"Wasn't you?" said Harry Wharton, staring. "You fat ass, we all know now that it was you—we all heard what the old johnny said in the form-room——."

"Oh! I—I—I mean——."

"We know all about it now, old bean," grinned Bob Cherry. "Sorry we didn't believe a word of it—but—but —but——."

"The sorrowfulness is terrific, my esteemed Bunter, but the butfulness is also great," said Hurree Jamset Ram Singh.

"We couldn't guess that you were telling the truth, you know," said Johnny Bull. "We're not magicians."

"Oh, really, Bull——."

"Blessed if I know how he did it at all," said Frank Nugent, "but he did! No doubt about that now! It was topping, Bunter."

"Top-hole!" said Lord Mauleverer.

"Ripping, old chap!" said Peter Todd.

"Some ass said the age of miracles was past," said Vernon-Smith, "but Bunter's done a plucky thing, and told the truth about it——."

"Ha, ha, ha!"

"Oh, really, Smithy——!"

"And we never knew——!" said Squiff.

"Didn't I jolly well tell you?" demanded Bunter.

"Oh! Yes! But——."

Bunter sat up, in the armchair. He had had an unmistakably guilty look when the juniors arrived. Now he was grinning with satisfaction as he realised that this was an ovation. He gave the Remove fellows a complacent blink through his big spectacles.

"Well, I did it!" he said. "It was plucky! You know that! Lots of fellows wouldn't have risked it! I did! Pluck's my long suit!"

"Oh!"

"It was frightfully dangerous," continued Bunter. "Some fellows would have thought twice about it, I can jolly well tell you. Did I? No fear! Without a single moment's hesitation, I plunged into the raging waters——."

"You whatted?"

"I—I—I mean, I—I climbed out on that branch——," amended Bunter: moderating his transports, as it were. "I did it! I'm not the fellow to brag, as you fellows know——."

"Oh!"

"But I did it! Pluck, you know! That's me, all over!"

"Oh!"

"That old johnny said I was a credit to the form!" said Bunter. "You heard him. Well, so I am."

"Oh!"

"And all you fellows can do is to send the pluckiest chap at Greyfriars to Coventry!" added Bunter witheringly.

Harry Wharton laughed.

"Coventry's washed out now, old fat man," he said.

"Hear, hear!"

"Yaas," said Lord Mauleverer. "We were goin' to keep Bunter in Coventry till he learned to behave, but that looks like a life sentence——."

"Ha, ha, ha!"

"Oh, really, Mauly——."

"No more Coventry, old fat frump," said Bob Cherry. "That's washed right out after what you've done——."

"Especially as you're so shy and modest about it," added the Bounder.

188

"Ha, ha, ha!"

"Well, that's all right," said Bunter, "and after this, I hope you fellows won't make out that I snoop tuck in the studies——."

"Oh!"

"What about a reward for valour?" grinned Bob Cherry. "You've got a cake in the study cupboard, Wharton."

"Good-egg! Like a cake, Bunter?" Harry Wharton crossed over to the study cupboard.

"Oh! No, thanks!" gasped Bunter. "Thanks all the same, old chap, but—but I—I shouldn't care for it."

"Wha—a—a—t?"

"I—I really shouldn't care for it, you know. I—I——."

"Rot!" said Harry Wharton. "It's a jolly good cake——."

"I know! I—I mean—I——."

"And you're going to have it," said the captain of the Remove, and he opened the door of the study cupboard. "Why—what—where's that cake?"

"Ha, ha, ha!" roared Bob Cherry. It was not difficult to guess where the cake was!

"I—I say, you fellows, I—I never had it!" gasped Bunter, in alarm. "I never knew there was a cake—I never saw you unpack it this morning, old chap—and that's not why I came up to this study! I—I haven't been eating cake, and—and I hadn't just finished it when you fellows came up——."

"Same old Bunter!" chuckled Bob Cherry.

"The samefulness is terrific."

"Ha, ha, ha!"

"I—I say, you fellows, it wasn't me—I—I never—I—I didn't—I—I wasn't—look here, you ain't going to send me to Coventry again because Wharton doesn't know what he did with that cake——," gasped Bunter. "I never had it! Besides, I'll pay for it if you like—I'm expecting a postal order——!"

"Ha, ha, ha!"

Evidently, it was the same old Bunter!

"You fat villain——!" said Harry Wharton.

"Oh, really, Wharton——."

"Never mind! We're going down to the tuck-shop!"

189

Like to come?—if you've got any more room after that cake——?"

Billy Bunter made one bound out of the armchair! Evidently he had room! It was a happy Owl that rolled down to the tuck-shop with the Famous Five. The clouds had rolled by: Coventry was a thing of the past: and Billy Bunter was no longer faced with the task—so far beyond his powers!—of learning to behave!

THE END

ARMADA BOOKS

They are wonderful, with their gay spines adding colour to your bookshelf. Are you collecting your own library of Armada Books? A book a week . . . or a month . . . and in no time you would have a marvellous collection! *Start today!* Always ask your bookseller or newsagent for Armada Books, but if you have difficulty in getting the titles you want write to Armada Books, 14 St. James's Place, London S.W.1. Overseas readers should write to the same address for information about their nearest stockists, etc.

BOOKS AVAILABLE INCLUDE:

School stories by—
> Angela Brazil
> Elinor M. Brent-Dyer
> Anthony Buckeridge
> Frank Richards
> Noel Streatfeild
> Geoffrey Willans and Ronald Searle
> P. G. Wodehouse

Mystery and Adventure stories by—
> Christine Bernard
> Enid Blyton
> Dorothy Clewes
> John Gunn
> Captain W. E. Johns
> Ralph Hammond
> Alfred Hitchcock
> Malcolm Saville

Pony and Animal stories by—
> Judith Berrisford
> Monica Edwards
> Ruby Ferguson
> Mary Gervaise
> Marguerite Henry
> Walt Morey
> The Pullein Thompson sisters
> Martha Robinson
> Pat Smythe

AND MANY OTHERS, including some Classics.

For current stock list please send a stamped self-addressed envelope to Armada Books, 14 St. James's Place, London S.W.1.